Their eyes held and compressed.

It was too much. Amber's body melted and her breath jammed in her chest. It was all she could do to keep from giving everything away. All those feelings she'd tried to hold at bay came rushing through her, sending a fountain of need surging up inside her. The tension that had seemed present from the moment they met tightened. The only sound was the crackle of snow in the air and the sound of the helo.

"We have to rendezvous."

As if trapped by his gaze, she stared back at him, unable to break away—not really wanting to. She was so lost in his eyes, in the pulse-racing weakness. "Oh, Master Sergeant," she whispered. "I think we're about as rendezvoused as two people can get."

He huffed a laugh. "What you do to me," he voiced in a puff of air. He brought up his gloved hand and bit down on the tip and removed it. Very gently, he caressed her cheek.

**Be sure to check out the next books
in this exciting miniseries:**

**To Protect and Serve—A team of navy miltary
operatives and civilians are called to investigate...**

* * *

**If you're on Twitter, tell us what you
think of Harlequin Romantic Suspense!
#harlequinromsuspense**

Dear Reader,

My To Protect and Serve series has brought you a murder investigation on an aircraft carrier, a kidnapped navy scientist and a drifting Coast Guard cutter with six dead men aboard. My next offering, *Her Master Defender*, dishes up suspense with a little bit of thriller on the side. When NCIS special agent Amber Dalton is waylaid just as she's about to head to the white sandy beaches of Aruba, she finds herself handling what is supposed to be an open-and-shut case of friendly fire at the Mountain Warfare Training Center.

But as Amber and her grumpy and gorgeous USMC liaison Master Sergeant Tristan Michaels delve into the mystery of what happened to one of his scout sniper students, it becomes clear it was no accident. As the two of them work together, the sparks fly and they find themselves struggling to remain professionally detached. The deeper they investigate, the closer they get as danger stalks them—until they are running for their lives in the cold, unforgiving Sierra Nevada Mountains.

Best,

Karen

HER MASTER DEFENDER

Karen Anders

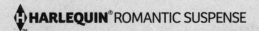
HARLEQUIN® ROMANTIC SUSPENSE

Recycling programs
for this product may
not exist in your area.

ISBN-13: 978-0-373-27939-5

Her Master Defender

Copyright © 2015 by Karen Alarie

This edition published by arrangement with Harlequin Books S.A.

For questions and comments about the quality of this book, please contact us at CustomerService@Harlequin.com.

Printed in U.S.A.

Karen Anders is a three-time National Readers' Choice Award finalist and an RT Reviewers' Choice Award finalist, and she has won a prestigious Holt Medallion. Two of her novels made the Waldenbooks bestseller list in 2003. Published since 1997, she currently writes romantic suspense for Harlequin. To contact the author, please write to her in care of Harlequin, 233 Broadway, Suite 1001, New York, NY 10279, or visit karenanders.com.

Books by Karen Anders

Harlequin Romantic Suspense

Five-Alarm Encounter

To Protect and Serve Series

At His Command
Designated Target
Joint Engagement
Her Master Defender

The Adair Legacy

Special Ops Rendezvous

Visit the Author Profile page at Harlequin.com.

To white, hot sandy beaches of Aruba, pool bars and mai tais.

Chapter 1

The Sierra Nevada, California

"One point six degrees is all that stands between us and death."

There was complete silence from the nine snipers USMC Master Sergeant Tristan Michaels was training on a mountaintop in the Sierra Nevada. They knew all this information, but there was nothing like driving it home.

"At 97.0 degrees there's mental impairment, poor judgment. One degree is all it takes to lead you to death's door. At 86.0 degrees, there's no more shivering—there's coma and lights out."

The frigid air and this trek into the clear, cold mountains drove home the truth of Tristan's lesson today. He exhaled, the heat from his breath fogging the air, and there it was again…that feeling, a heaviness in the pit of his belly and in his head, too, the backs of his eyes hot, a weight across the nape of his neck. As a member of Force Reconnaissance—known as both Force Recon and FORECON—Tristan heeded his gut feelings.

He'd felt this off-balance sense right before a battle, right before an explosion, as if the molecules of air were bracing themselves for conflict. With the snow-covered trees and the heavy snowfall, these training grounds were far from a winter wonderland.

All of those millions of lace-patterned water drops piling up on top of each other… The sound of it had a way of impeding hearing, just a bit, with a tone that came from everywhere and nowhere while creating a strange sense of urgency.

It felt like a pent-up breath.

It felt as if something was about to happen.

The only worry on his mind right now wasn't that these guys wouldn't hit their targets. It was about survival, as they were going to be out in these conditions for the next three days with no tents in the middle of January.

Crouching in the snow, Tristan said, "You all face a unique situation when you're sniping in this environment. The cold weather acts as an adversary that can be as deadly as an enemy soldier."

The intent young faces hung on his every word and he emphasized enough the first day of class how he would be their savior, his words were gold and he was the god of winter. Freaking Jack Frost had nothing on him and Old Man Winter was just blowing smoke.

"Every time. *Every time* you pit yourself against the elements, it's about survival. Regardless of the job you do, staying alive is all that matters. When we started out, it was clear and sunny—"

"Yeah, sir, it was downright balmy," one marine said down at the end of the line, and everyone chuckled.

"We can go skinny-dipping later," Tristan said, deadpan. "As I was saying, clear when we arrived, but always prepare yourself for blizzard conditions."

Jerking down his bark-colored cap covering his dark hair, he went to one knee and sighted his own scope across the tree-lined terrain. "Tell me why cold is a greater threat to survival," he said, his breath fogging the air.

"It decreases your ability to think," one marine replied.

"It weakens your will to do anything except to get warm."

"It sucks moisture, and dehydration is a threat."

"Good answers," he said. "But remember this, if you forget everything else. Cold makes it very easy to forget your ultimate goal—to survive."

Tristan didn't have to instruct these men on how to shoot a target. They were all seasoned snipers, but there was still a 10 percent washout rate for this class. *One shot, one kill* was their motto. His job was to teach them how to shoot in this terrain and at steep angles and how to survive against the insidious cold. He'd done both numerous times.

"Your target is the normal one-thousand-yard distance. I want you to work out the coordinates and take your shot."

As five successive shots cracked across the white noise of the falling snow, Tristan put his binoculars to his eyes and scanned the targets below him. As he went to lower the field glasses, something out of the corner of his eye caught his attention.

His breath backed up in his lungs as he stared and adjusted the clarity. It looked… Ah, damn! "Stay here," he ordered, and he took off at a run through the snow. Navigating the decline with the skill and ease of a pro, he slid slightly on the loose snow but got the traction he needed in his snowshoes. The cold air hurt his lungs as he loped, his muscles loose and pumping.

As he got closer, his heart slammed hard against his ribs and his mind froze in shock.

Memories assaulted him of another freezing-cold day, the snow splashed with blood.

He stopped at the foot of the slope, unmoving in surprise. He looked down to the ground, his mind clear as a bell, sure of what he was seeing.

So many shots and so many kills and he recognized it in an instant, as if he had been in slow motion and everything just went into real time. *Real freaking time.*

It hit him like it always did. As if a conscious thought was needed to drive it home every time. He was breathing his way into it like he'd done whenever he'd sniped. Settling his cheek against the stock, quieting his muscles, quieting his heartbeat and lining up his shot.

He was going to get only one shot, and like every shot he took, it had to be perfect, a cold zero.

It was the only truth he knew. It was the only one that mattered, and 2.5 pounds of pressure on the trigger later, a man's life would leave him in a vapor trail of pink blood and disintegrated flesh. Another millisecond, the shot would sound in the air.

A hand on his shoulder startled him out of his trance. "Sarge…what the hell…damn," one of his students said on a choking whisper. Then they all crowded around and that terrible heaviness he'd been feeling only moments ago deepened.

As his students all shuffled around, looking at each other, their faces contorting in compassion—shock, pain, anxiety—he crouched and brushed at the snow-covered face, revealing the fixed open eyes, the lashes thick with snowflakes.

Lance Corporal James Connelly, his missing marine student, who stared up at a frosty white sky from a face blue and stiff with cold, frozen in death. The kid had been at the top of his game, highly decorated in his tours in Afghanistan and the Middle East, dedicated to the corps with a recent reenlistment, and had been a complete jarhead through and through. One of his best students ever.

He liked this kid.

The body had been almost invisible, dressed in camo and deeply covered in snow. If it hadn't been for the flap of his jacket caught by the wind, Tristan might have glanced right over him.

He turned the body and saw it. A bullet hole, blood tingeing the snow beneath him.

His conscience kicked him hard and his throat burned from the deep breaths he took to mitigate the guilt that slammed heavy into him like a wrecking ball.

Lance Corporal James Connelly.

One shot, one kill—a cold zero.

Chapter 2

Naval Criminal Investigative Service (NCIS) Office, Navy Yard, Washington, DC

"Hey, you okay?"

NCIS Special Agent Amber Dalton cringed at the sound of Beau Jerrott's voice behind her. Part of the NCIS team, Beau had recently found his true love and was getting married. She loved the guy like a brother, but he'd told her she shouldn't let Peter—Lieutenant Peter Savich, USN—make her his second priority. A woman should always be number one, and if she wasn't, said woman should move on. There wasn't anything that Amber hated more than coming in second. But in this case, she hadn't even been in the race.

She turned around and one look at her face had Beau taking her arm and dragging her to the conference room.

"What happened?"

Her shoulders drooped and she squeezed her eyes closed. "He dumped me right before this Aruba trip. My first vacation in a year."

"That slime. Why did he dump you?"

"He's...engaged." It should have been a little more painful to say it, but it wasn't. She just hated the idea of spending her vacation alone and was mortified that she hadn't seen the signs.

"Oh, damn," he murmured and pulled her into his arms, rubbing at her back. "I'm sorry. If it's any consolation, I never liked that guy for you. He was too...bossy."

"Oh, really," she sniffed. "Nothing like you."

"No, nothing like me," he said, squeezing her tight and letting her go.

"It's not the end of the world. There's—"

"If you say 'there's plenty of fish in the sea,' I'll slug you," she said.

"There's a silver lining."

"Nice save." She punched his arm lightly. "What exactly would this silver lining be?"

"You can go to Aruba and have wild, crazy sex." He waggled his brows.

She rolled her eyes. Because he was trying to cheer her up, she laughed. "All settled down and that is what you still think about?"

"Guar-an-teed. I have Kinley at home."

"I don't jump in the sack with just anyone. So I would rule out wild, crazy or any other kind of sex on a seven-day vacation."

"Ah, right, you're one of those. Well, buck up. This is a vacation. There will be no pining or moping over your jerk of an ex-boyfriend."

Hours later, after she'd filed her last report and shut

down her computer, she was trying to dredge up some pain or even regret about the breakup and she couldn't. She just felt stupid for getting blindsided, for holding on to something that wasn't fulfilling or going anywhere. It was her competitive edge. She so hated losing.

Amber had spent most of her childhood playing second fiddle to her sister, Samantha, or as everyone called her, Sammy. Her older sister was outgoing and beautiful and took the lion's share of attention from their parents and relatives. Amber had to work twice as hard to get out of her sister's shadow. She excelled at sports and her studies, garnering scholarships. But no matter what she did, she got the sense her parents thought her second-best.

Sammy had married a very wealthy man while Amber went into the navy, then became part of the Judge Advocate General's Corps, or JAG, then finally left to become an NCIS agent.

She'd passed all her tests with flying colors, especially her PT tests. Because she was considered an athletic girl, Amber often found herself in the pal role with boys at school and was frequently used as a stepping-stone to her sister.

When Amber rose and grabbed her purse from the bottom of her desk drawer, Vincent Fitzgerald said, "Hey, why don't you come out for a drink with us?"

Damn Beau—he must have told Vin. "Us? Like you and Sky and Beau and Kinley?"

"Yeah, I'll buy you a drink."

"No, thanks. I've got more packing to do. Another time." There was no way she was going to be a fifth wheel to her happily engaged colleagues. It would make her feel ten times worse.

"Ah, come on," Beau said, stopping by her desk. "I'll let you win at darts."

Vin chuckled and turned off his desk lamp. "Right, Jerrott."

Amber brushed past Beau and laughed as she headed to the elevator. "Ha! First off, you won't *let* me win at anything. I would kick your ass!"

"Sounds like a challenge to me," Vin said, getting into the elevator after Beau.

"Another time," she said again firmly, and both men gave her sympathetic looks, which she hated. "Don't feel sorry for me," she said.

At the parking lot they both hugged her and wished her a safe and enjoyable trip. In her car, her cell rang. She looked to see who the caller was and her lips tightened. Pete. *Really?* What could he possibly say that she would have any interest in hearing? He probably just wanted to assuage his conscience.

She pulled into her driveway and entered the house.

It wasn't long before she was immersed in a hot bath up to her neck, her long blond hair piled on top of her head, sipping on a glass of wine and enjoying the time to indulge herself. It had been a week of ten-hour days and two difficult cases. She was officially off the clock.

Her phone buzzed again, but she ignored it. Tomorrow she would be arriving in Aruba and baking in the glorious sun on a beautiful beach.

She sighed. It would be wonderful.

After getting out of the tub and crawling into bed, she tossed and turned, waking up before her alarm clock went off. She got out of bed and assembled her luggage. Just as she was about to leave for the airport, her phone buzzed and this time she answered. "Pete, stop calling me, you complete jerk! I have nothing to say to you."

"Amber?"

Oh, damn. She recognized Supervisory Agent in Charge Christophe Vargas's voice. Her dismay at being an idiot to her boss dissipated when she realized there had been contrition in his voice. Oh, damn, he was calling her in. "Chris…no."

"Amber, I need your help on this."

She dropped her head back with a long, drawn-out sigh. "I haven't had a vacation in a year."

"I know. It's a potential friendly-fire incident. You'll be in and out. Done and on that beach in no time. I need you on this one. You've got the law-degree background."

"A year, Chris."

"In and out. I promise."

"Why can't someone else do it?" she whined. She wasn't proud of it, but she'd so been looking forward to this vacation, and not only was she going alone, but she had to postpone it for work. That just plain sucked.

"The only other qualified person——" he cleared his throat "——is on vacation with his spouse."

"What? That is not fair."

"I know, but he's already gone and he's a senior agent. It's the way it works, so that leaves you."

"You really are in a bind? That's the only reason you're assigning me?"

"The only reason."

Okay, that hurt. It was the only reason he was sending her. It wasn't because he trusted her or thought she was competent. It was because she was a junior agent and available. Well, then she would do as good a job as she could. This was a sensitive situation. Ruling a death as friendly fire wasn't a popular job and she would handle the family with care and compassion. Her heart already went out to the serviceman who had lost his life. Compared to a stupid vacation, there was no comparison. "I want the same number of days."

"Done."

"Where am I going?"

"California. I'll send the details to your phone. I'll pay for your flight to Aruba."

"And any fees that I am going to incur because of this detour."

"Yes, any fees."

"All right," she grumbled. "I'll do it, but you'll owe me."

"Thank you, Amber. You are a team player."

Twelve hours later, Amber wasn't feeling like a team player. In fact, her bitch ratio was way above the 50 percent mark. She was cursing her boss a blue streak. Who knew it would be snowing. *Snowing* in California! After landing in Reno, she rented a car and started driving. It wasn't until she was in the middle of nowhere that the heavy winds and blowing snow came with no warning. The conditions were terrible, and by the time she got close to the Marine Corps Mountain Warfare Training Center, or MWTC, in godforsaken Pickel Meadows, her grip on the wheel made her hands hurt.

Leaning forward so she could see the road better, her shoulders tense from the lack of visibility, she was momentarily distracted by her phone buzzing. Pete, again! When was that guy going to get the message, and what could he possibly want? When she returned her eyes to the road, she squealed and slammed on the brakes. A huge brown moose the size of an SUV was smack-dab in the way.

She swerved and just missed his tail. But her car spun on the slick asphalt, and with no traction, she careened right onto the shoulder. Coming to a jarring stop, she leaned her forehead against the steering wheel, her heart cartwheeling. There was no way she would have survived a collision with the big bull. A deer, maybe, but not a moose. "Thanks a bunch, Bullwinkle," she groused as he took off and ran down the road, then disappeared into the snow-covered trees.

"Great, *now* you run."

Taking a deep breath, she pressed on the gas, her gut twisting when the tires only spun. She tried again, but it was no use. The car was stuck. She slammed the palm of her hand against the wheel.

"Dammit!"

She was supposed to be on vacation! Damn Chris.

She closed her eyes and opened the door. She was within walking distance of the base, according to her GPS. She grabbed her phone and locked the door.

Cold smacked her in the face and took her breath, sheering right through the lightweight coat she'd brought with her, biting the skin of her legs through her slacks. She slipped in the snow, even with her flat-heeled, sensible shoes, and she grabbed on to the hood of the car to steady herself.

Once she had her balance, she started to walk very carefully against the blowing snow. Icy whiteness surrounded her in a cocoon of cold. Her teeth chattered and she started to lose her sense of time. Had she been out here for minutes or hours?

The frigid wind whipped and tore through her again, turning her blood to icy sludge.

She gasped at another gust and peered through the falling flakes. There. A light. She increased her speed and reached the gate. The guard ran out and helped her inside.

"Ma'am, what are you doing out in this on foot?" The name on his uniform was Caldwell.

"M-my c-car broke down. Special A-Agent Amber D-Dalton, NCIS. Does i-it snow like th-this often?"

"We're six thousand five hundred feet above sea level, ma'am. The unpredictability of the weather is the only constant here." He reached for the phone. Minutes later a jeep showed up. "I'll get someone to retrieve your vehicle. Colonel Jacobs is expecting you."

"Thank you," she said around her chattering, handing him the keys.

The jeep took her to a tan-and-red-roofed building and, after thanking her driver, she rushed inside. The man behind the desk rose. "Special Agent Dalton?"

"Yes." It was clear from his uniform that he was a corporal. His last name was Morgan.

"Please follow me."

He led her to an office, as she soaked up the warmth of the building.

Colonel Jacobs rose as his aide ushered her into his office. "Special Agent Dalton," he said, looking surprised. *Guess they didn't expect a woman.* "Please have a seat. You must be frozen to the bone. We had expected you sooner. Sorry about your mishap, but we'll sort it out for you."

"Thank you, sir."

"Morgan, alert Master Sergeant Michaels that Special Agent Dalton has arrived."

"Yes, sir."

"I had no idea that there was going to be a blizzard. I was sent here at the last minute."

"We do our best to keep on top of it, but this high up it's a crapshoot. It can be sunny one minute and a blizzard the next. Even we sometimes get caught off guard. You can visit the Base Exchange after our meeting to pick up a few things." He gave her an appreciative glance. It went a long way to assuaging her pride at her recent dumping.

"Colonel Jacobs, Master Sergeant Michaels reporting for duty, sir." The deep, raspy voice sounded from the doorway, sending ripples through her.

"Ah, Michaels, come in."

Amber turned and caught her breath.

He stood at attention, his eyes on Colonel Jacobs until she rose. Then they flicked her way but were soon back to the colonel. He was tall, taller than her. She was five foot eleven, but he had at least five inches on her.

The guy was *built*. He had a powerful chest that tapered down to a lean waist, and his muscles were so pronounced his fatigues molded over the thickness, tightening the shirt across his broad shoulders. Beneath the thick shirt was a brown T-shirt that covered the hollow of his throat. The sleeves of his white-and-gray camo were rolled up and stretched over his bulging biceps with a glorious curve of muscle that literally made her mouth water. Shocked at her reaction, she could only stare.

Then there was his face. Her eyes traveled up the strong column of his throat with a day's worth of dark stubble. Thick, midnight-black hair was spiked up into a flattop, the sides shaved. His broad forehead spanned above deep-set, startling blue eyes with an intense gaze, a firm chin and a hard jawline, a prominent but narrow nose and sharply defined cheekbones. He was drop-dead gorgeous.

His eyes kept drifting back to her as she moved forward. "At ease," Colonel Jacobs said. His posture relaxed as he set his hands behind his back at waist level in a resting stance Amber couldn't help thinking was way too sexy.

Colonel Jacobs turned to her and said, "This is Master Sergeant Tristan Michaels. Sarge, this is Special Agent Amber Dalton."

He nodded curtly as Amber tried to catch her breath and rein in her reaction to the impressive marine.

"Master Sergeant Michaels was Lance Corporal Connelly's instructor. He was the one who found the body, along with his class. We've already cleared him to work with you on this case."

"You found no negligence on his part."

Master Sergeant Michaels stiffened and scowled at her. "With all due respect, Agent Dalton, I can assure you that I take every precaution in making sure that none of my men are in the line of fire."

"Then how did Lance Corporal Connelly die?"

He clamped his lips closed and looked at Colonel Jacobs. The colonel nodded. "Full cooperation," he said.

"Truthfully, I don't know." *He's upset*, she thought immediately. She could hear it in his voice and the fact that he didn't know was gnawing at him. "I thought he'd gone AWOL."

"When?"

"He didn't show up for class yesterday. I went to the barracks and checked for him in case he was ill. He wasn't there, but his bunk was made and all his belongings were in his locker."

"Yesterday? You didn't report him?"

He glanced at the colonel again. "No," he said softly, looking her straight in the eyes. He was a bold man, obviously a warrior who took responsibility for his actions. She couldn't help but admire that.

"Why?"

He sighed. "He had an exemplary record and was the best student I have ever had. He was always on time, eager, and he excelled. I wanted to give him time to reconsider."

He was more than a student to this marine. She would bet her next paycheck on it. Michaels had a soft spot for him. "I'm sorry for your loss, Sergeant."

His jaw worked and he looked away. "He was my responsibility. I will do everything in my power to find out what happened here. His parents deserve at least that."

"They do. I have read his record and it was as you say. Remarkable." She stepped closer to him and breathed in the scent of his aftershave. "Tell me about finding him."

"I had taken my sniper class back up the mountain for a three-day training session. The class was coming to a close, and after they had taken their shots, I caught a glimpse of his jacket in the wind in the distance. He was lying on his back. He was frozen, so I believe he must have died last night."

"Were you shooting last night?"

"Yes, night training."

"So it was dark with no lights at all?"

"Yes, it's part of the training."

"He could have been killed then?"

"Not by my men."

"How's that?"

"Nine men, five shots. I acted as spotter for Lance Corporal Sheppard, who had partnered with Lance Corporal Connelly. When I checked the targets, there were five bullet holes. All accounted for. It was the only time there was active fire."

That explained why he'd been cleared.

"We confiscated all handguns, including mine. None of them had been fired. The crime-scene guys collected the shell casings they could find."

"What do you think he was doing up there?"

"Again, I don't know. He didn't have his pack with him. I know he was accounted for when we came down to break and refuel before the three-day session." Now he sounded frustrated, his voice filled with grief.

Colonel Jacobs said, "Our police department removed the body and sent him off to the Mono County Sheriff's Department and he's now being autopsied at Trevor Mortuary in Bishop. Dr. Carl Thompson out of Northern Inyo Hospital will be performing the autopsy. Sarge has his contact info."

Colonel Jacobs picked up a file folder off his desk and handed it to her. She opened it to find James, his skin and lips blue tinged and his body buried in snow. The grisly pictures moved her because he was so young. He had a strong face, his eyes a deep brown, his expression one of surprise.

Chris had already alerted her that his parents were being notified by the Marines. After surviving two tours, it was so tragic that the kid was killed at home, presumably by his own platoon. She glanced at his service record, which was included. Twenty-five, decorated, and he'd just reenlisted.

"May I take this to look at it more closely?"

"Yes, that is a copy for you. There are also pictures of the scene after we removed the body. I'd appreciate any insights you have on this."

She nodded.

"It's getting late and you must be exhausted." The colonel looked at Master Sergeant Michaels. "Michaels will accompany you. I'm sorry, but our billet is completely full at the moment and the only room we have right now is with the Sarge. He is in a two-room town house on base. Obviously, we can't put you in the barracks and I'm not going to subject you to tenting it with the enlisted."

Amber chuckled at the twinkle in the colonel's eyes. "Bless you," she said, her stomach jumping at the thought of having to bunk with the hunky marine. "It should be sufficient. If this is friendly fire, it shouldn't take long to determine that. Then I'll be on my way to Aruba."

"Aruba?" Jacobs said, envy in his voice.

"Yes, delayed vacation."

She shook the colonel's hand and left his office, following the master sergeant's broad back. He paused to pick up a coat. Slipping into it, he zipped it up to his neck, where he wrapped a scarf. He pulled a fleecy brown cap over his dark cropped hair, then pulled on a pair of tan gloves.

Colonel Jacobs's aide, Corporal Morgan, stopped them at the entrance to the outside. He said, "They dropped off your suitcase, ma'am. I took the liberty of putting it in the master sergeant's jeep."

Without a word, he led her back out into the weather.

"Sergeant, I need to go to the BX if you don't mind."

"The colonel mentioned that to me. I don't mind." He smiled, "Here it's MCX for Marine Corps Exchange. The army calls it the BX for Base Exchange."

"We both know that the only other organization that has more acronyms than the US government is the US military."

He nodded, eyeing her. "You're not prepared for this weather? We are in the mountains."

She sniffed. "I wasn't aware it snowed in California." His censorious tone got Amber's back up.

He snorted, staring at her over the hood of the jeep.

She narrowed her eyes, but he didn't seem affected. She ducked into his jeep and was soon at the MCX picking up some boots, pants, shirts and a heavier jacket.

"Anywhere else you need to go?" he asked once they were back in his jeep.

"No, the billet is fine."

"Where did you come from?"

"The Navy Yard in DC."

"Don't they have agents in the Southwest to handle this?"

She shrugged. "I don't ask questions. I go where they tell me to go."

"It's apparent you don't ask questions, since you weren't prepared for the snow. How long you been an NCIS agent?"

"Eleven months."

"You're still a probie?" His mouth tightened at her inexperience.

Amber tried not to take it personally, but he was beginning to tread on her last nerve. "Yes, *technically* I'm still on probation. But I'm a fully trained NCIS agent and have plenty of investigations under my belt," she said through gritted teeth.

"You want me to cut you some slack?"

"Yes, but you're not going to."

"You should have made it your mission to know everything about where you were going. It's the uninformed that walk into danger."

"Thank you, Sergeant, for that pearl of wisdom. I was supposed to be getting on a plane to fly to the warm sands of Aruba. My bag is packed with bikinis, shorts and skimpy tops." When his eyebrow rose at her snippy tone, she bit her lip. Jeez, he pushed her buttons so that she was getting defensive. She went on more calmly. "I knew all about Aruba with its warm ocean water and heated pool. You know that hotel I'm going to? There's a bar that serves drinks right in the pool."

"Does it? Convenient. Then your suitcase full of bikinis will fit right in."

She huffed. "Why don't you educate me, then, Sergeant Michaels?"

"About what?"

"About the base. About the mountains."

Looking as if he'd rather be chewing glass than being her liaison, he said, "Yes, ma'am. MWTC is a part of Marine Air Ground Task Force Training Command and conducts unit and individual training courses to prepare not only the USMC, but all branches of the US military and foreign allies for maneuvers in mountainous, high-altitude and cold-weather environments. MWTC supports other commands, as well as DOD agencies involved in waging war with specialized equipment for use in mountain and cold-weather operations."

"What do you teach?"

"Along with cold-weather sniping, I teach mountain recon."

"What is your background?"

"Classified."

That was a convenient answer to keep her in the dark about him. Well, she wasn't an agent without means. The colonel might have cleared him, but Amber was going to make her own decisions about who was innocent and guilty. She raised her chin. "Go on. The area?"

"MWTC is at the base of the Sierra Nevada, a range of mountains that encompasses four hundred miles bordering the eastern edge of the state—fifty miles across with eighty miles being the widest. Peaks here can rise up to nine thousand feet. The highest part of the range is between Tahoe and Yosemite. The range is largely made up of volcanic rock and not so good for climbing, but great for scrambles, hikes and taking in the spectacular beauty because the Sierra Nevada are all about the scenic view. Most of it is protected and heavily forested. The northern boundary has some of the highest peaks, known for their rock climbing and some of the most stirring sights on the planet. It's inspiring, and once you climb to the top, the solitude is tangible."

"Rock climbing? I think I'd like to try that." She sounded wistful.

"Maybe you'll get a chance. Be a shame to come here and not give it a try."

"You know a lot about this range."

"It's imperative that I do. These boys are in my hands, and I take that seriously."

"Lance Corporal Connelly is a personal loss to you."

His gloved hands gripped the wheel. "He was a fine kid and he didn't deserve to die that way."

He'd sidestepped the question with a noncommittal answer. Amber was sure it had affected him.

He pulled up in front of a small house with a garage that was connected to a row of houses. The walk had been recently shoveled and she had a relatively clear path to the door.

"Here we are."

"As long as this place has some heat, I'll be happy."

"Yes, ma'am. We have heat here," he said with a mock smile, getting out of the jeep. "Do you need some help?"

"Could you grab the MCX bags? Thank you."

"You're welcome, ma'am. Morgan will dig your car out and get it to you."

She nodded and got out. She pulled up the handle of her suitcase and headed up the still-slick walk.

He fit the key into the lock and turned it, just as she hit a patch of ice. His reflexes were lightning quick as he grabbed her around the waist and held her suspended against him. He was warm, and their breaths mingled as she tried to get her footing under her.

His eyes were so blue as they stared down at her and, for a moment, she lost focus. Then he swore softly under his breath and set her back on her feet. With another curse, he grabbed her case and carried it into the house, all the while holding on to her arm.

He set the case down and closed the door with the heel of his boot.

"Upstairs to the left is your room." He gestured to a

set of stairs straight ahead. The aroma of a just-cooked meal wafted to her and her stomach grumbled.

She huffed and took the MCX bags out of his hand and dragged her suitcase up and into the room he'd indicated. She wasn't sure what to make of him. Dropping the bags on the bed, she hefted the suitcase up. It was obvious that he wasn't too keen about her at all. But he was quite stuck with her until this case was over and solved.

She changed into a pair of warm gray sweatpants, socks and slippers, along with a thermal shirt and sweatshirt. She was feeling marginally better and beginning to warm up. Going back out into the short hall and down the stairs, she headed toward the living room. The delicious scent of food lingered in the air as she stopped near the table. He was working on a laptop as he ate.

"There's grub on the stove. Plate in the cupboard to the right. Coffee brewed."

He was a man of few words. But when he talked, the way he moved his mouth mesmerized her. His upper lip was as full as the bottom, and it looked yummy and oh-so-kissable.

But she wasn't falling into the military-man trap again. Competing with the Marine Corps or, as in Pete's case, the Navy wasn't going to work for her. Her relationship with Pete might have been fine if they had been in the same place, but the distance had caused indifference between them. At least, that was what it felt like to her. She better get her mind off the delectable quality of the master sergeant's mouth.

She went into the kitchen and found a pan of meat loaf, green beans and buttermilk biscuits. She helped herself and poured a cup of steaming coffee, sighing at the first sip. Walking back to the table, she set her plate down and dug in.

"Thank you for the food," she said.

He nodded without looking at her.

She sighed. Thank God she was going to be here for only a few days.

Chapter 3

*G*reat. Just *great*, Tristan fumed, totally annoyed to have a woman like Amber in his space. Well, this was a kick in the balls. He wasn't too happy about having tempting Agent Dalton in his quarters, but he couldn't very likely throw her out into the snow. The fact she was an NCIS agent only made matters worse. He was well aware he had to work with her, but he didn't want anything to do with a damn civilian cop. He wasn't too enamored with the agency when they investigated the incident at the consulate in Banyan. Those navy cops had treated him like crap.

When he was exonerated, they didn't even so much as apologize. He was sure she was cut from the same cloth. Damn cops were all alike in his book. Even stunning ones. What he didn't want to admit was that Amber was not only a distraction, but her presence reminded him of James's recent death. Doubts assailed him on whether he could have somehow prevented the tragedy, and he resented her for that.

Something caused you to break protocol and go off the grid.

I fulfilled the mission. It's a win.

That may be, but that mission was aborted. You're in bad shape, dehydrated, malnourished and strung out. You didn't check in. The corps doesn't want to lose even one man.

Price of battle.

Is it because Corporal Levis was killed? Is that bringing back any memories?

No.

I think it is. I see that you often take the solitary, dangerous missions. You were a scout sniper before you went into Force Recon.

So.

Another solitary duty. You not a team player?

It reinforced to Tristan exactly what a shrink knew. Dr. David Cross, lieutenant, army. Dweeb. Tristan called him Doc Cross. He'd lost it then and he was escorted back to the ward, made to relax. It was exactly how he found himself here at MWTC and had been for eighteen months. Forced duty-change to recover from battle fatigue. Tristan found it ridiculous. There was nothing wrong with him. He was a marine and he was born combat-ready. All this bullcrap about needing rest wasn't necessary. Why that conversation came back to him puzzled him. Banyan didn't have anything to do with why he'd chosen solitary assignments. Nothing at all.

The scent of Amber's perfume brought him back to the present. He resented the fact that she was so goddamned gorgeous. Pure California-girl looks: sun-streaked hair that fell to the middle of her back, the front cut in layers, and almond-shaped mossy-green eyes. It was obvious that she'd got caught unaware in the snowstorm. All she had been wearing was a flimsy coat. He'd noticed her legs in those formfitting slacks, the tight curve of her hip and backside. She wasn't delicate-looking, but more sturdy, as if she could actually climb a mountain. Her refined nose and her cheekbones went way beyond classic to exotic. She stirred something in him he hadn't felt in a long time. And it had been a very long time that he had put the corps first, vowing not to get distracted or sidetracked. Getting involved was for when he got out of the military. It was no life for a family.

Her delicate brows bunched into a frown. "I got a feeling you're not thrilled about me being here and it doesn't really have to do with the death of your student."

He wasn't intimidated. "I'm not a big fan of navy cops." Amber gave off all the signs of being a smart, competent woman—well, unless it came to snowstorms. There was something different about her…something he didn't want to examine too closely. She piqued his interest immediately and set to blipping on his radar. Attraction. It was just there, heating his body and making his heart pound.

She moved to butter her biscuit, and the scent of her… Jeez! Lovely and warm, female. It filled him up and arrowed right down to his groin. He didn't want to have any interest in her. It would be less complicated that way.

He had plenty of options. Even though his reenlistment was coming up to coincide with the end of his forced rest, he was going back to Force Recon and back into combat. With that decision firmly entrenched, it was stupid to get involved with a woman who had happily-

ever-after written all over her. At this point he could retire from the Marines if he wanted to, but it was all he'd
known for most of his life. He didn't like that he was
second-guessing his loyalty to the corps.

All during the Banyan incident, the corps had had
his back.

"Why is that? Do you have something to hide?" she
said in a matter-of-fact voice that was most likely generated from his unfriendly attitude.

Anger came from a well of unresolved torment. That
was exactly what the agent had asked him after the Banyan consulate massacre. He'd had to make sure to keep the
consulate secure so that all the sensitive documents could
be shredded and destroyed. It was what he'd done. The
moment he was free from that, he'd gone to help protect
personnel. He'd been wounded, gutted by the deaths, including the ambassador's. All of them had perished while
he was focused on documents. His mission had been accomplished, but the cost was high.

He shut his laptop and picked up his plate, pushing
away from the table. After walking into the kitchen,
he deposited his plate and silverware into the sink with
a noisy clatter. Tucking the laptop under his arm, he
strode across the room and climbed the stairs to his
bedroom, slamming the door.

He set his laptop onto the bed and stripped off his
camo shirt, ripping off his T-shirt, pacing with the pent-
up memories and the regret that he hadn't tried harder.
He should have tried *harder*. Of course, she would say
that. Cops were a suspicious bunch by nature and, in
his experience, had a tendency to jump to conclusions.

There was a banging on his door, and when he opened
it, Amber said, "Listen, I'm sorry. This must have been

a terrible day for you and now I'm invading your space. But the job has to be done and they've sent me to do it. I've been traveling all day and was totally blindsided by this storm. I've had my car run off the road by Bullwinkle, walked all the way to the middle of nowhere in freezing temperatures, and I'm still chilled to the bone and totally exhausted. I'm supposed to be on vacation! Hot beaches, cool drinks, relaxation. I wish it were different. I really do."

"I wish you weren't here and James was alive," he said, his voice subdued.

She nodded. "I really am sorry."

She turned and headed to her room. He had a clear view of her fine, tight ass, her thick, gorgeous blond hair flying around her shoulders and upper back. She paused for a moment, giving him a sympathetic look, and his chest tightened up. He didn't want to be moved by this woman. He scowled at her and closed the door, not wanting to give an inch. It was a good thing that beautiful, distracting Amber was going to be here for only a short time. And he got the feeling she wasn't going to take any of his crap.

He went to unsnap his jeans, but swore and rubbed his hand over his face. He had been rude, but he hadn't wanted those reminders of his failures. Feeling he'd let James down somehow made all that consulate stuff and other failures from his past surface. What had James been doing up on that ridge? Had he lost his way? That seemed so completely unlike him. The sniper was very competent and had already been to that part of the mountain. He wouldn't have forgotten or got lost.

His thoughts went back to Amber. He had to give her points for standing up to him.

With a curse he walked to his door and opened it. He knocked on hers, and it was a moment before she pulled it open, and every delectable inch of her was on guard. He met her green eyes and his chest expanded, and for a moment he was caught up in just looking at her. He certainly didn't miss the way her eyes traveled over his bare chest.

"Still not keen on NCIS, but thank you for caring about James on more than just a case level," he said, then spun on his heel and went back into his bedroom.

Morning came all too swiftly, regardless of whether he'd slept or not. He'd got some sleep, but his thoughts about James's death had raced and tormented him, and when he wasn't feeling god-awful guilty about that, he was thinking about Amber and all her smooth skin, soft silky hair and firm, tight ass. How it would be so nice to sink into oblivion with her, into the comfort of a woman's arms.

It had been way too long since he'd been laid. That was all. He was lonely and horny. The trick was remaining professionally detached around her. He could do that. He wasn't the most diplomatic guy, but he could be adept at being courteous if he put his mind to it. He got up and went out into the living room and stopped dead. He had to take several breaths.

Courteous and professional went out the window. Trouble. God, he was in trouble here.

Tristan had an unobstructed view of Amber's firm, shapely ass as she stretched out on a mat in front of the couch and the picture window. Her ass was currently in the air in some yoga pose. She was wearing a pair of very tight black shorts and a sports bra, leaving her creamy shoulders and midriff bare. Everything male in him responded to her, immediately. It was good that he was wearing a T-shirt over his groin, where his dick was loose in his pajama pants. Make that *was* loose. Now he was just painfully erect.

Which was so damned professional.

She looked at him through her legs as she did some other kind of pretzel move that was limber and mesmerizing. "Good morning."

He grunted and headed across the living area to the kitchen to start a pot of coffee. He needed the pick-me-up after the night he'd had.

"Someone isn't a morning person," she said with a chuckle as she continued to torment him with more impossibly pliant moves.

Fifteen minutes later, he poured himself strong black coffee in a mug that had a bulldog on it and *USMC* in red beneath it.

He turned and she was now sitting cross-legged on the floor, stretching and thankfully looking as if she was almost finished.

She groaned softly as she folded down over her knees, and he gritted his teeth against the sensuous sound. He'd never bunked with a gorgeous woman before, had never cohabitated. He went into the Marines at eighteen and had spent most of his years with a bunch of sweaty guys. The woman who had promised to wait for him didn't last long, and he'd avoided any type of long-term commitment. So this was a revelation to him. He'd had no idea how…stimulating it could be to watch a woman work out.

He took a sip of his coffee and closed his eyes against the sight of her. The coffee was hot, damn hot, and so was she. She stretched out full-length on the floor and he looked down the length of her body. A damp sheen of sweat covered her skin, especially right in her mouth-watering cleavage.

Beat sweaty guys every time.

His breath caught when she went over her knees again and he noticed ink just beneath the waistband of the sinful shorts. They should be called "come get me shorts" instead of "workout shorts."

She rose, stretched one last time, walked toward the kitchen and unabashedly started going through his cabinets. When she found what she was looking for, she pulled it out and set it on the counter.

"You want some pancakes?" she said. She stood close to him and her scent wasn't at all as though she'd been exercising. It was just warm, delicious woman.

He took another sip of his coffee and grunted again. Brushing past her, he reached down and snagged his skillet, handing it to her. "Knock yourself out."

"Bowl?"

He walked over to a cupboard and grabbed a mixing bowl, then handed it to her.

"You're pretty well stocked for a bachelor."

He shrugged. "My mom wanted to make sure I had the essentials. I cook sometimes. When the mood strikes me."

"You make that meat loaf yesterday?"

"Yeah, it's my mom's recipe."

"Not bad, marine." He tried not to be pleased at the compliment. He certainly wasn't going to acknowledge it.

He leaned back against the counter, realizing that he should get on with his morning routine, but his routine was now tied with this woman. They were going to be working together for at least the day. The colonel had canceled class for today to give his students time to deal with their loss and grief. There were only two classes left and he wasn't scheduled to teach again for two weeks. One more six-week stint and he would be back to Force Recon.

Tristan's cell phone rang and he picked it up off the counter.

"Hey, jarhead! What's shaking?"

"Rock. How the hell are you?" Tristan stepped away from Amber and went to the wide picture window.

"Full of piss and vinegar, as usual. I heard through the grapevine that you've had a bad spot out there. You doing okay, buddy?"

Russell "Rock" Kaczewski had been his longest-running scout partner. Tristan's partners turned over frequently because he was a control freak and most guys didn't want to work with him. But Rock put up with all his crap and was an exemplary marine on top of it. Rock had retired from the corps five years ago when Tristan went into Force Recon. They had kept in touch that whole time—well, mostly Rock had.

He now owned a chain of sporting-goods stores in the San Diego area.

"I lost a man, Rock."

"Damn tough. Any confirmation that it's friendly fire?"

"Not yet."

Rock's gruff voice was full of sympathy. "Well, hang in there."

"I will."

"I called for another reason. I know your tour's up,

and with the early retirement and bonus they're offering right now, I wanted to make you an offer."

"Offer?"

"Yeah, get out. Come work with me. You've done your time."

"Get out? I don't know, Rock. I'd have to think about it."

"Sure, sure. I know you're gung ho. My business is growing and you'd be a great asset. You buy in, own half. Partners again."

"Thanks for the offer. I will consider it," Tristan said, flattered that Rock would offer him part of something he'd worked so hard to make a success.

Rock's voice dropped an octave. "Really think about it, buddy."

But his loyalty to the corps weighed on him. The corps was all he knew, and they had supported him and stood by him through that ordeal in Banyan.

He disconnected the call and wandered back into the kitchen.

Knowing that he was just asking for trouble, but wanting to know about her, he said, "Where you from that you don't know it snows in California?" He was quite aware of his tone but didn't moderate it to a friendlier one.

She gave him a sidelong glance and a sheepish grin. "Vermont. Stowe."

He laughed and it felt rusty. He hadn't laughed in a long time. "That's good."

She simply stared at him and, for a second, dropped her guard. It unsettled him the way she looked at him. It could be something totally different than that she was attracted to him. Could be his wishful thinking, but he amended that. It would be better if her guard was up. It would make it easier on him. He was a grumpy bastard on a good day.

Finally she said, "I didn't say I didn't know about snow. Just never realized it snowed here. But to be honest, I was pretty pissed when I left DC and my focus wasn't on the assignment. You're right. I should have done my homework."

"What were you pissed about?"

She looked tired, as if she hadn't slept, but if he wasn't mistaken, she was also more than a little unsettled. Whether that was by what was going on here or by something else entirely, he had no idea. He didn't know Amber or what was going on in her personal life. A salient point—he made a personal note.

Her cell rang. She looked at it and then angrily pushed the ignore button. She dumped flour into the bowl and added milk, egg and other dry ingredients "I'm pissed about being...ah...detoured." She rubbed her nose and left flour there. She started stirring. "It seems I was convenient to send."

Yup. There was something she wasn't telling him, all right, but since he kept his own counsel, he wasn't going to push her. He shouldn't even be doing this... casual conversation or getting to know her. He didn't want to like her. She was an NCIS agent. Lust was a different thing altogether. He was too confused about where he was going and had too much emotion tied up in the corps to deal with any type of attraction. "I go where the Marines send me. I don't talk back." Jeez, she looked good in his kitchen. He'd been in lust before, had even come close to falling a few times in his life, but he'd never really much thought about domestication. His focus had been wholly on his military life. His liaisons were just that. Meager and spaced apart, usually opportunistic. He'd always had the need to get back to his own personal space more strongly than the desire to live under one roof with anyone.

She snorted. "Really? I bet you do when you have something to say."

"You got me there." He smiled again. She definitely had an effect on him. "Okay, so I don't *usually* talk back."

"You been in for some time?"

He shifted, the need to wipe that flour off her nose a compulsion, but he took a sip of his coffee instead. "Fifteen. Went in at eighteen. Have only known the corps," he said, keeping his face expressionless, his tone of voice flat and professional. "It's always come first."

She scowled at that. Not that she had any dibs on him. He was potent. That was all. She was reacting to him with his tough-guy stance, tousled hair and beard-shadowed jaw, and the obvious required reality check she needed.

He was closed. Buttoned up tight. Rude. Well, mostly rude. It was clear he was reacting to her as an NCIS cop. Of course he was. He certainly couldn't be reacting to her as a woman. Gorgeous men like him went after women like her sister, Sammy.

It was true she dealt with alpha men all the time. First during her tour with JAG, then working with Chris, Beau and Vin at her current job. She'd had her share of challenging men.

It was also hard to believe that Tristan Michaels was thirty-three. He looked younger than that.

She set the skillet on the stove and checked the batter while he watched her intently. It was unnerving to have so much power focused on her.

While the skillet was heating, she poured herself some coffee. It smelled good. "Cream?" she asked.

He gestured to the milk on the counter. "All I got. I drink mine black."

Grabbing up the container, she poured some into her coffee. "Used to it, I suppose?"

"Yeah, not many amenities in the field."

She watched him over the top of her mug of coffee. He was beautiful, yes, in that rough-edged way that she was getting used to, but he looked tired, too, as though he hadn't got any more sleep than she had got.

James Connelly had kept her up long past bedtime as she pored over the report of his death. She wondered if the kid had kept him up, too.

Looking out the window, she groaned. "There were supposed to be palm trees outside my window today. I wish I was in Aruba."

He rinsed his cup out in the sink. Without warning, he grabbed her chin and brushed his thumb over her nose. "Flour." His mouth tightened and he whispered, "I wish you were in Aruba, too." For a few seconds he stared down into her eyes, his fingers tightening on her chin. Then he let her go. He turned and left the kitchen. Minutes later she heard the shower start up.

She glowered at the snow. *I'm such a man magnet.* He wished her away from here. That was no surprise.

She squeezed her eyes shut, thinking about the trip she would have to spend alone. Suddenly it didn't seem as appealing. She dreaded the rest of the day. Meeting with James's parents and delving into his death was going to be tough, but she couldn't imagine how hard it was going to be for the master sergeant—Tristan. Turning toward the skillet that was now sufficiently warm, she dropped in the batter. At least the pancakes would be good.

After her shower and getting dressed in a heavy sweater, jeans and her new snow boots, she came back down to the living area. Tristan was sitting at the table in his camo, scarfing down a stack of her pancakes.

That gave her some satisfaction at least.

"You ready?" he said, getting up and setting his plate into the sink.

"Yes."

"What's the drill?"

"I'd like to consult with the MWTC Police Department. According to the report, they were called in on the scene and sent the body off for autopsy. Looks like both the MWTC Police Department and the Mono County Sheriff's Department were and are involved."

"Yes, ma'am," he said and led the way out of the town house and back to his jeep. "The PD handles all law enforcement for the base, and the sheriff's department handles suspicious deaths."

"I saw the PD at the gate. I want to go to the scene, as well. I could go alone if that's—"

"I'll come with you," he said flatly. "It's quite a ways up the mountain, but we can go by helo. That will be faster. Hopefully the weather holds. I'll clear it with the colonel."

"Thanks." They backtracked out of the neighborhood and passed plows clearing the snow to the building that housed the police station. Once inside they met Officer Craig Mendez and he ushered them into the police chief's office. Scott Werner rose as they entered.

"Special Agent Dalton, we've been expecting you." He nodded to Tristan. "Sergeant."

He was small, thin and balding, and when she went to clasp his hand it was soft as a grandmother's. They settled into seats in front of the desk. "Sorry we had to meet under such circumstances, Chief Werner," Amber said.

"Agreed. We sent Connelly's body to the Mono County Sheriff's Department for autopsy with a rush request. We should have it within a day or two at the latest."

"I'd like that report as soon as it's available."

"Of course."

"I want to see the scene."

"We protected it as much as we could, and I'd like to head up there with you." The voice was a warm, well-modulated baritone.

Amber turned to find a man standing in the doorway. He was tall and long limbed, the personification of authority in his well-fitting brown-and-tan sheriff deputy's uniform. His hair was black and short, not quite as short as Tristan's.

"Deputy Garza," the chief said as he rose, suddenly looking very small in the man's presence. "This is—"

"Special Agent Amber Dalton, NCIS," she said, rising and walking up to him. He was as imposing as Tristan, but unlike Tristan, there wasn't an ounce of attraction even though his features were more smoothly handsome. She was almost nose to nose with him, as he was shorter than the master sergeant, coming in at just about six feet tall. She reached out her hand and he squeezed it just a bit too hard.

"Sean," he replied with a soft smile, his gaze capturing hers the way an eagle captured a small mouse, his eyes an odd, striking shade of pale blue and set deep above a strong, straight nose. "I can see why you've got 'special' in your title, Amber."

But Amber wasn't a small mouse, and the tingle of wariness buzzed at the base of her neck. Just like Tristan, she'd dealt with these kind of alphas all of her working life. She kept her face implacable, ignoring his patronizing and intimate tone. He still held her hand and, with a concerted tug, she pulled it free. "Your assessment would be valuable," she murmured, moving away from him and turning in time to see Tristan's eyes narrow. So he didn't like Garza, either. She wondered why and what his assessment was of the man who would have conducted this investigation if NCIS hadn't been involved.

Tristan's gaze held hers, steady, unblinking, calm. Flat calm, like the sea on a windless day. He would be a formidable adversary if he wasn't on their side. She knew it instinctively, could feel the power of his personality in his gaze even while he kept his thoughts shuttered behind his unusual eyes.

Her attention returned to Garza as he said, "I'm sure my input would be valuable." He smiled. "There are plenty of accidents that happen on that mountain with the weekend warriors and skilled hunters roaming around. As I told Colonel Jacobs, though, we could have handled this. Looks pretty clear-cut to me."

She brought her chin up a notch and looked at Garza hard in the eye. There were issues with this case already that were telling. It was anything but clear-cut to her. "NCIS has jurisdiction over any navy and Marine Corps personnel anywhere on the planet," she said flatly, far from under what he thought was his charming spell. "Thanks for your help, but I'll make my own judgments and come to my own conclusions."

Her tone didn't faze the man a bit. His smile curled a little deeper at the corners of his mouth. "I'm just a deputy in a small town, so we'll defer to you, Amber."

Damn right he would.

"Officer Mendez can accompany you up there, as well. He was also on the scene. He is the one who is working with Deputy Garza on the death. We are ready to fully cooperate with NCIS," the chief said.

Tristan's phone rang and he answered it and talked for a few minutes. "The helo is secured, Special Agent Dalton," he said. "I would suggest that we go now while the weather is good."

She nodded, following Tristan out of the office. Deputy Garza and Officer Mendez followed behind her and they got into Tristan's jeep and drove over to the airfield.

A medium-sized gray helicopter with its single rotor blade whirring waited for them.

When she went to step into the aircraft, Tristan clasped her arm to help her inside. She settled into one of the seats and he sat beside her, buckling himself in.

As soon as everyone was seated, the helicopter lifted off and powered toward the mountains. As they flew, Amber looked down into the snowy meadow that gradually gave rise to tree-covered inclines and craggy, jutting rocks. The helo passed over a slew of marines digging out snow and setting up camp.

Tristan leaned over to be heard above the rotor, his mouth close to her ear, his breath feathering her skin and sending tingles downward. "Let me know if you get a headache or feel nauseous. Some people can get altitude sickness. We're not giving you enough time to ascend, but we should only be up here for less than half an hour. The site is about 8K up. Some people don't experience any symptoms below 10K."

His face was close, so close to hers that she suspected her shortness of breath had nothing to do with the altitude. His cheek brushed hers as the helicopter banked and started to descend.

He pulled away immediately, but the place where his skin had touched hers tingled. The scent of him lingered in the air.

He pulled on his cap again and she followed suit. As she got out of the helo, she saw that the snow was deeper up here but had been packed down by a lot of feet. The whirling blades of the helicopter slowed, the engines making a whining noise as the blades stopped spinning and the engines shut down.

She followed Tristan, who moved steadily through the snow. They followed a trail to the sight where a tent cover had been set over the spot where Tristan had found Connelly's body. Garza and Mendez stood away from the site as Tristan lifted the tent flaps and exposed the scene. Amber walked closer. There was displaced snow on either side of his resting place, discolored with Connelly's blood. She pulled a small camera out of her pocket and started to snap some pictures.

"There's not a whole lot of blood," she murmured.

"Most likely due to the cold. Doc said it would be difficult to determine the time of death. It was twenty below, and that kind of cold would constrict his veins and he would bleed very little," Mendez said.

"Which way was his head positioned?"

"Horizontal to the mountain."

"Parallel?" she asked, looking over her shoulder at Tristan. Something wasn't sitting right with her, and when she had that feeling, she rarely ignored it. "He was on his back?"

"Yes."

She stood and stared at the spot.

"Looks like the kid got caught in the path of sniper fire from one of his fellow classmates," Garza said.

"Unlikely," Amber said.

"How's that?"

"No exit wound, Deputy." She looked at him and he still had the placid calmness around him that grated on her nerves. "Sergeant, sniper rifles use a full metal jacket, correct?"

"Yes, ma'am."

"The bullet at that velocity would most likely penetrate and exit the body, correct?"

"Yes, ma'am.

"Look at you," Garza said, his brows lifted. "You know your sniper rounds."

"I was in the navy, JAG Corps. Learned a lot from my trials." Dread filtered through her. This was looking even less like friendly fire to her and more like something…else.

"JAG, huh? A lawyer, too. You're a versatile woman. Hopefully the autopsy will shed some light."

The wind came whipping up, and her breath blew hot, steaming the air. She rubbed at her forehead and Tristan stepped up to her. "Do you have a headache?"

She looked at him blankly.

"Amber, do you have a headache?"

The sound of her name in his deep voice sent a spiral of reaction all the way to the pit of her stomach, and it released a slew of butterflies. With the cap on his head, it hit her how really handsome he was. His eyes so darn blue and…full of concern. He might act like a tough guy, but there was a soft center in there.

"No. I was just thinking."

He looked up at the sky and took her arm. "There's another storm coming. We need to go. Getting caught on this mountain in a blizzard is not a good idea. The temperature is already starting to fall."

She nodded and waited while they secured the scene.

Tristan rolled down the flaps of the tent and staked them into the ground. "That's about all we can do. Time to go."

The whole trip back she was quiet, her brain going a mile a minute. After they landed and Tristan dropped Garza and Mendez back to the PD, it was late afternoon.

"I'm starving," she said.

"We can grab a bite at the mess."

She nodded.

Inside the busy and crowded mess hall, after they got their food, Tristan said, "Something is bothering you."

"There are a couple things that aren't adding up for me."

"Okay, what are they?"

"If snipers only use full metal jackets—"

"That bullet should have gone right through Connelly with about the same size hole as it went in," Tristan said grimly.

"But no exit wound."

"I said as much to Jacobs, and that's why he wanted

NCIS involved instead of leaving it up to the PD and sheriff's department."

"Exactly." His response only confirmed her worry that Connelly wasn't killed by someone in the sniper classes. "The other thing is he was shot in the back. Was there any evidence that he rolled?"

"I didn't see any, but it snowed pretty heavily during the day and into the night."

"So it's possible?"

"Yes, it is."

"Where was he for forty-eight hours and how did he end up on that mountain if he intended to go AWOL?"

"Again, I don't have an answer. It's been bothering me, too."

"I know. It's something we'll have to figure out."

"We'll wait for the autopsy."

"I'd like to interview the men in your class."

He bristled. "Why? We just established that it wasn't my class that killed him."

"I have to interview them and I should also formally interview you. I understand your protective instincts—"

"No, you don't. Don't use that bullshit with me." He picked up his plate and cup and deposited them noisily on his way out the door. Amber sighed and picked up her own stuff.

As she set her dirty dishes into the bin and watched Tristan stride angrily from the building to his jeep, Amber took a deep breath. This case was turning out to be much more than she'd expected.

It was time to get tough, whether Master Sergeant Tristan Michaels liked it or not.

She was betting he wouldn't.

Chapter 4

The man's phone vibrated softly and he answered.

"What's the situation?" the voice said on the other end of the line.

"The woman—that NCIS woman. She's going to be a problem and Michaels is suspicious. It's clear to me."

"Mayer screwed up, bad." He heard the clink of a cup. The man did like his tea.

He felt calm. He never panicked like the others when something went marginally wrong. He figured he was hardwired that way. In a hushed voice he said, "Hypothermia is a strange thing with victims removing all their clothes. Mayer froze to death without a scratch on him. I'll accidentally find his body when all this crap is over."

"You're a scary son of a bitch. Well, do what you need to do to protect our operation or I'll have your ass. Talk to Carl," the man on the phone said.

"He's not going to like it."

"Persuade him. You're good at that."

He chuckled. "I enjoy it."

The man chuckled back. "That's why I keep you around. We get what we want and we make good money, so status quo. Squash this or we're all going down, hard." His words weren't sharply spoken, but he felt their bite.

His eyes tracked an Apache helicopter as it took off from the field. The Marine Corps thought that he wasn't soldier material. He hadn't passed the psych test. Every branch of the service he'd applied for gave him the same answer. "I've got an idea. Don't worry. I'll make sure this doesn't blow back at us."

Who was smarter now?

"I want a name," Tristan said as Amber opened the door and settled into his jeep.

Amber looked at him, her expression registering the lethal sound of his voice, the promise of violence in every syllable.

"I want a goddamned name!"

He gripped the wheel, his hands curling into fists. His gut churning, thinking that it was possible that someone could have deliberately ended James's life. Someone could had pulled the trigger on that kid and taken him from the corps, from the service of his country, from his family and his girl, from the world he should still be living and breathing in.

"We'll find out who did this. I'm not leaving until we do." She pushed her hair back and said, "One look at that kid's face and I was resolved to find out what caused his death. If he's been murdered, someone will have to pay for that."

James's face so cold and still in death. Tristan braced his back against the leather seat, and the memory came at him like a demon, painfully sharp and so bright. He squeezed his eyes closed against it. He held himself rigid until every muscle quivered with the effort, but nothing stopped the memory from coming. It broke over him like a wave, washing away the present and dropping him back in time.

His breathing was harsh as he looked down at the row of dead lined up on the floor in the lobby of the bombed-out and bullet-riddled consulate in Banyan. He dropped down to one knee and removed the sheet from the face of the man beneath it.

He might not have failed his duty, but it felt as if he goddamned had. The ambassador was dead.

"Looking at your handiwork, marine?" *A man loomed over him in an NCIS vest, his eyes cold and calculating. It was the beginning of the accusation that would haunt him for a year until the corps had conducted their investigation and exonerated him. Given him back his stripes, his dignity and his sense of duty.*

The hand on his arm jarred him back to the present. "Tristan," Amber said softly.

He didn't want to be placated. He turned to her and bit out, "I won't have them railroaded into anything. They're all good boys and they have nothing to be ashamed of or to be blamed for. They were serving their country, learning new abilities to keep the US safe from harm. All those shots are accounted for. I have also been cleared."

"I'm just going to question them."

"Sure you are. I've heard that before."

"Would you like to elaborate on that?"

"No, I wouldn't. I'm sure you'll read something into that, too!"

"Tristan, don't make me go over your head. I want a good working relationship with you, but if you don't cooperate, you'll force my hand."

That tough-girl tone made him look at her, at her hard, heartbreaking green eyes, her just-as-heartbreaking, soft-looking lips.

He swung his gaze away from her, realizing that looking at her would only weaken his resolve. "Negotiating with me now. I bet you're really good at interrogation."

"I'm not negotiating. So don't make me say words like *obstruction* and *uncooperative*."

He laughed without mirth. "Nice. That's going to help."

"What is going to help? You don't even know me, yet you don't trust me. How do I warrant that when I've given you no reason not to trust me?"

"I have my own reasons."

"Put them aside for James. I'm here to make sure he gets justice, and I won't give up when it gets tough. Don't give up on me already."

There was something quite…naked in the expression that crossed her face. But the way he'd been treated was hard to forget. He'd reserve his judgment, then. But trusting her wasn't on the table just yet.

That open look hit him and stuck. He had to wonder what was going on in her head, but he'd be damned if he'd ask. No. Keeping her strictly in the adversary club was what he was going to do as long as she didn't disarm him any further. He wasn't sure if she used manipulation in her job, but with his past NCIS experience, he couldn't rule it out.

Now he had to figure out a way to do all that and not want to take her up against the nearest wall. He might actually survive this.

He started breathing evenly to alleviate some of the tension, remembering the counselor he'd seen after the Banyan screwup had told him that would help with his anger. It did, marginally, stemmed the avalanche of memories that threatened to bury him every time he let his guard down for half a second.

"I want to be present when you question them. I'll answer your questions to the best of my ability. It's important to me that we find out what happened to James."

When she moved her hand again, he realized she was still holding on to his arm. He looked down. Her hand was delicate-looking, but he had no doubt that she knew how to use that weapon she carried in the small of her back.

As if she'd just noticed that she was touching him, she drew her hand back, rubbing her palm against her jeans-clad thigh.

He didn't say a word as he started the jeep and put it in Drive.

Dammit, why couldn't NCIS have sent a big, burly male agent? Not that he'd be more inclined to trust him, but he wouldn't have this uncontrollable attraction to someone he wasn't sure he could trust. With a male agent, he would be firmly in the no-trust camp, but with Amber, it was difficult not to succumb to her... what seemed like her sincerity. He realized if he had met Amber all those years ago and she'd treated him as if he was a person, he might have a totally different view of NCIS.

He drove toward the center of the sprawling base and parked in front of the bachelor enlisted quarters, the same sandy color as HQ, with the same red slate roofs in a slope to better control the heavy snowfall.

He got out, and as soon as he walked into the area where his men were housed, he said, "At ease."

The men came around their bunks and stood at ease, eyes forward. The marine who recognized him first was James's partner, Lance Corporal Mark Sheppard. When Amber entered the room, there were some small sounds of appreciation. He let it pass, as these men hadn't seen a beautiful woman in six long weeks.

"Listen up. This is Special Agent Amber Dalton from NCIS. She is going to ask you questions about Lance Corporal James Connelly. Answer these questions to the best of your ability. Rest," he shouted, and the men relaxed their stances and collectively fixed their eyes on Amber.

Beside him she whispered, "Where should I talk to them?"

"In the locker room, there's a bench you can use." He turned toward the room again. "Fall in."

They complied, and he motioned to the next guy in line and said, "As soon as Sorenson comes back, you're up, Hackett."

"Yes, sir," he replied.

He led the way to the locker room and Amber settled on a bench. "Sit, Sorenson," Tristan said.

"Yes, sir," he replied, his Adam's apple bobbing.

Amber said, "There's no need to be nervous."

"Yes, ma'am."

For the next thirty minutes, she went through her questions that basically consisted of when was the last time they had seen Connelly, did they notice anything out of the ordinary on the mountain that night, and did they know why Connelly was alone on the mountain and not with the class?

All the answers were pretty much the same until they got to Sheppard. Even before he sat down, he looked pensive and Tristan got the feeling the kid knew more than he was saying. But he responded the same as the others. Tristan met Amber's eyes and she gave him the same look. *He's lying.*

When Sheppard left, Tristan put his hand out to Amber. "Let him go."

"Tristan…he knows something."

"I know, but browbeating him won't get him to talk."

The look on her face said she wasn't going to listen, and it was important that he make her. When she made her move, he took her elbow and gently swung her back around to face him.

"I'm not going to—"

His gaze locked with hers. "Yes, you are." He looked into her worried, determined eyes, and something turned over in his chest. He wanted to take that all away, but he was sure about this course of action. "Trust me on this and let it go for now." He said it fiercely enough that her eyes widened.

She made a move to go around him, and he grasped her other elbow. "I know that kid." He closed his eyes and let out a breath. He then opened them to look deeply in her eyes. "Just…trust me."

"I guess that does go both ways." She looked pointedly at his hands, and he lifted them, palms up.

"Thank you," he said.

"I'll give him some time, but not a lot."

He nodded. "It'll work better when he's ready to talk. Keeping information to himself regarding the death of a fellow marine will eat at him."

"Never leave a man behind?"

"You are very astute."

"Be careful, Sergeant. That sounded like a compliment."

He grunted and led the way out of the barracks.

"You tried to find him, didn't you?" Her voice was soft and he didn't want her to affect him this way. He didn't want to talk about James, about how he'd felt like a big brother to him, how worried he'd been when he hadn't shown up. That was too much emotion to cop to.

"So, Stowe," he said. "You ski, then?"

She paused at the jeep, giving him a knowing look before she pulled open the door. "Like a boss."

"Downhill?" he asked, settling into the seat next to her and starting up the jeep.

"Downhill, cross-country and snowboarding, baby."

"Don't tell me. You competed?"

"Yes, moguls. But I wasn't really good enough to take it further than that."

"You were a jock? In high school?"

"Yes, and in college. Played volleyball. You?"

"Track," he replied.

"Marine Corps Marathon?" she asked.

"Three times. You?"

"Five."

"That's impressive. You run in addition to bending yourself into impossible positions."

"It's really good for the body, helps you to relax. You could use that."

"I'm not uptight," he deadpanned.

"Okay, sure," she scoffed. "I could give you a few lessons if you're interested."

He grunted, then laughed. Once again it felt rusty to him. He wondered if he was in her presence for longer than a day or two whether it would come more naturally. "No. I don't do pretzel."

"You could learn to bend. It'll be painful at first, but then you'll start to loosen up. Believe me. You need to loosen up."

"Why do I get the feeling we're not talking about yoga anymore."

"I can't imagine," she said as they pulled up to the town house. "I'm going to check on the autopsy."

"In a hurry to get out of here to those white sandy beaches."

She shivered. "I am, but not at the expense of James." She got out of the jeep, then looked at him sharply as he closed his door and rounded the hood. "Are you in some way insinuating that I want to hurry through this investigation because I've got someplace better to go?"

"You're dealing with an unknown and tragic situation. It's freaking cold here. You have to put up with a grumpy bastard who challenges you every time you turn around. Yeah, I think you'd rather be somewhere else."

She strode up to him and said, "You are mistaken if you think that I'm immune to this tragic situation. I looked at his face and I read about his life, about his service. He has parents who lost their only son to the service of his country. Just because I work in a civilian capacity, don't presume to know what military service means to me. It is my intention to dig until I get to the truth. Until James gets his justice, no matter the cost. I grew up in one of the coldest states in the US, so it's nothing new to me. Is a warm sandy beach appealing? You bet your ass it is. So don't presume to know me or narrow me down into this little box you want to put me in because you don't like NCIS agents. There is way more than just a badge and a gun here. There's a passionate, hardworking, caring woman here." Her chest was heaving. She grabbed the keys out of his hand and stormed up the walk. Unlocking the door, she threw it open, then came storming back.

"There is only one thing you got right!"

"What is that?"

"*You* are a *grumpy* bastard."

The wariness was back in full force, and something inside him rejoiced at that because he was struggling with his distracting and disarming attraction to her. He hadn't wanted to like James. See that James wanted and openly competed for his approval and attention. He hadn't wanted to see the young man in the uniform so open and gung ho, so downright optimistic, mostly because it reminded him of himself. Before he'd lost his innocence in a blood-soaked day that had transformed him from a boy into a man.

Cynicism had its merits.

So, good. She was wary again. Why did that also piss him off?

When he had no answer, she poked him in the chest. "You asked me to give Corporal Sheppard the benefit of the doubt. Why don't you try that with me?"

"My experience dictates otherwise."

She threw her hands in the air and turned to go back into the house. "I'm going for a run."

That suited him fine. Some more distance was good. He was the triggerman, used to setting off fear, confusion and uncertainty in all his targets. He'd been in the field most of his military career. There had been sleep and food deprivation, stress, danger, and one time his partner had been spotted and killed. Tristan had been wounded. It was a harrowing experience to get back to base with not only his weapon and himself intact, but his spotter across his shoulders. Leave no man behind. He was certain the same principles had been instilled in Corporal Sheppard and he would do the USMC proud by relaying that information to them. It was a matter of time.

The chill permeated his jacket and propelled him into the warm town house. Amber was in her assigned room, cursing and mumbling to herself. She was some kind of spitfire. An NCIS agent, one who was on her own here, up against a tough investigation. He hadn't been out there with a squad or platoon or with someone else in charge of telling him what to do. He got his mission statement from his supporting commander and accomplished the mission by his own wits and his own know-how. Same deal with Force Recon. He had to admire the same grit in Amber. She had the same traits and was NCIS's trigger woman, and she'd solidly put him in his place.

And damned if he didn't admire her for that, too.

She came out of her room dressed in a formfitting blue top that accentuated every damn thing about her that was female, from her beautifully formed breasts to her strong, shapely thighs to her slender calves. She was completely covered up, her hair in a ponytail, her face devoid of makeup, nothing really sexy about any of it. And yet he had a hard time keeping his eyes off her.

She went to the hall closet and opened it, grabbing his USMC windbreaker, shrugging into it even though it was too big for her.

She walked past him and out the door, evidently reining in her temper, because it only closed sharply instead of being slammed.

He stood there, his own sense of fairness warring with his fear of letting go of the control he'd used to keep himself severely in check, to survive his combat missions, cope after the Banyan incident.

But no matter how he tried to stay neutral, detached, that woman got to him.

"Dammit!"

He'd asked her to trust him and she had. She'd given Sheppard a chance to handle his own thoughts, his own loss and grief over Connelly. They had been tight. It was something that Tristan recognized and had shunned with his partners. He hadn't wanted to ever get into a situation again where he would be betrayed by anyone. A guard that had stood heavy against any entanglements.

All except for Russell "Rock" Kaczewski.

Rock and his personality punched through Tristan's armor, and he'd been a steadfast and supportive teammate for a good solid five years until Rock had retired five years ago. Tristan was convinced that Rock would move on, but he hadn't. He'd remained just as solid as he had when they worked as a pair to complete sniping missions all over Afghanistan.

Rock had asked for his trust, too, but Tristan wasn't sure if he'd given it. Still wasn't sure.

He stalked into his room.

Stripping out of his clothes and donning his own running gear, he went out the door and looked both ways. He could see her retreating form some ways off in the distance. The girl was fast.

The afternoon was turning to dusk, and the sky above the jutting, snow-covered peaks of the mountain range spread out before him had turned a colorful red, orange and purple, tingeing the uppermost peaks in a colorful hue. The wind had picked up and the cold slapped his face. He loped after Amber, marveling at the progress she'd already made in the snowy footing.

He heard a car come up behind him but kept his eyes on that blue vision in front of him. It wasn't until he saw the car was way too close to the side of the road that he focused on it. The idiot! Was he drunk? His heart climbed into his throat when it continued to barrel toward Amber without swerving away from a dangerous trajectory that would lead to directly hitting her.

"Amber! Look out!" he shouted at the top of his lungs. She jerked her head up, but the car was almost on her. For a minute he lost them in the long shadows of the mountain, but then he saw her body sail into a snowbank as the car roared past.

"Amber!" he shouted as he increased his speed, his lungs burning, thighs pumping, feet slipping on the snow-covered road. He raced toward her still body, his mind frozen in fear.

When he got closer, his heart racing, he heard her groan, and relief rushed through him. As soon as he reached her prone body, he knelt down. "Amber, geezus, are you all right? That stupid nut job!"

He reached out as she opened her eyes and their gazes collided. She took in his face and blinked a couple of times. He wasn't sure what she saw, but the fear in him was still stinging, thrumming through him with adrenaline and panic. And he fell into the deep green pools of her eyes, fell like a meteor, a stone into warm, seductive liquid. The silence between them stretched out, expanded in a way that lent texture to the very air between them. The sun was disappearing behind the mountains, smudging her beauty with purple shadow. He swore he stopped breathing, her gaze still locked on his face. Her body was so close to his as he bent over her, aware of how much bigger he was, responding to her in ways that were instinctive and fundamentally male—warming, hardening.

He got hard. It happened in the field, in combat mostly from the surge of adrenaline. But he wasn't sure he could pretend in this situation his erection had anything to do with his adrenal glands.

"Can you sit up?" he said, his voice rough.

"In just a minute. I thought while I was down here, I'd make snow angels." He closed his eyes against the way his chest filled at her attempt at humor. But he couldn't laugh, not this time. His fear had been so acute; he swallowed hard against the thought of this bright and beautiful woman no longer here.

"Did the car hit you, for Pete's sake?" he growled.

"No. I threw myself out of its path, just hit my shoulder in the fall. I'm fine."

"Jackass didn't even stop."

"Did you get a look at the car?"

"Yes, silver sedan, late-model Honda. Got a partial plate. Most of it was covered up with mud. I'm turning that madman in."

He slipped his hands under her, not asking permission. He deadlifted her up out of the snow, holding her securely around her lower back and under her knees, pressing her to his chest. She felt good in his arms and he realized the barrier that he needed to protect himself against her just wasn't there. She'd disarmed him and charmed him from the moment he walked into Jacobs's office. Yet, he was stubborn.

He didn't look at her as he carried her back to the town house. Ignored her protests that she could walk. She was fine. Well, he wasn't fine and he needed to hold her in his arms, carry her against his body to prove to himself that she was okay.

When he got to the door, he let her feet drop to the ground, kept her close as she slid down the length of him. Steadied her with his hand on the small of her back as he retrieved the key from his pocket and unlocked the door, pushing it open.

She stepped inside and she moved easily, just rubbed at her shoulder.

He closed the door behind him. "You're sure you're all right?"

"Yes, thank you, but I'm fine."

"You don't need medical assistance?"

"No, just a bump and a close call. Scary."

He couldn't stop himself. He reached up and ran the backs of his fingers against her cheek. She closed her eyes and melted into his touch, and he stood there, frozen by his need and his desire to touch her more, kiss her. As if she read his mind, her mouth parted and a little gasp escaped.

Without another word, he walked to his room and carefully closed the door behind him before he did something he'd live to regret. This was the right thing to do. He knew it and he bet she knew it, even if she was pissed off at him. Inside he leaned his back against the door and closed his eyes. Caught his breath and shored up his badly damaged defenses. He rubbed at his forehead, running his hand over his thick flattop, and discovered a whole new shade of meaning for the word *yearn*.

She was something more. Something special. Not a carnal opportunity, not a quick lay. This was a woman he could talk to, get lost in. This was a woman to savor, to sink into, to go slow with, to promise things to. Those were the best reasons for him to keep himself in check.

Because he was damaged, had scars and pain that he'd buried, still hadn't dealt with, and he wasn't going to dump his baggage on her. His life was so entwined with the corps that he couldn't see clearly. His duty and honor were twisted up inside him, tied to a common ground and a common fight. Something that filled him up. He wasn't sure what would happen if he put anything else in his life first. If who he was would drain away and leave him nothing but a hollow husk.

It was the corps. First and foremost. He still owed his fealty, his duty and honor to them.

Semper Fi.

Chapter 5

Tristan nursed the third glass of Scotch and, even though his body was reacting to Amber's warmth, his head was going around and around about James. However he was killed, it wasn't a fitting death for a kid... man like him. He still felt sick about it and he wondered if it would have been easier to take if it had been a warrior's death.

Yeah, he was a marine through and through. It would have been easier to take.

He did the same thing he'd done when the ambassador had been killed. Went over everything he said or did the days leading up to the attack in Banyan, looking for a weakness, a missed opportunity, insight.

But in James's case, it was more about how the kid had got under Tristan's defense, just as Rock had.

Just as Amber was doing, and she was sleeping, all warm and sweet-smelling in her room, the door closed.

He swore he could smell that sweetness in the room. He took a deep breath and decided that getting drunk alone in the middle of the night was completely irresponsible, especially when he needed every wit he possessed sharp enough to keep from doing what he'd been thinking about doing yesterday.

He closed his eyes, remembering the scent of her hair, how silky it had been against his rough chin. How perfectly her body had felt against him, how much he wanted to sink into her softness and stay there for a long time.

She was a reminder that he might have missed something with James. Her very presence at the base called into question his ability to do this job and it reminded him too much of Banyan. He took a swallow of the Scotch and it burned in his mouth and in his throat, going down smooth as the amber liquid appeared in the heavy cut of the glass.

Unbidden, Doc Cross's words penetrated his inebriated brain. *I think you're harboring pain about that consulate incident and you've closed yourself off, so you never have to feel it again. The corps has become your crutch and you use it like a goad to punish yourself. It's not just your relationships in the corps. It's all relationships.*

He closed his eyes again. Damn him. It wasn't true. He'd spent fifteen years with the corps. It just wasn't true!

He'd dedicated his life to the corps, but he couldn't help wondering what it would be like to be free of the strict rules and regulations and come home to a woman like Amber every day. He distracted himself with her. Desperately needed something to erase Doc Cross's words. He thought about this morning and the way she'd bent herself into those provocative poses, limber and slender. He clamped his jaw.

Even with the alcohol, he hardened in his pajama pants at the thought of that sweet, smiling mouth beneath his. And the minute he thought about kissing her was when it was all over. Time for lights-out. He went to rise and his hand slipped on the edge of the table where some of the Scotch had spilled. His out-of-control hand then clipped the glass and it careened off the table, hitting the floor with a loud popping sound.

He groaned when Amber's door slammed open and she pelted down the stairs. She arrived in something too skimpy for his libido at this moment. Then it registered— she had a gun.

"Tristan?" she whispered. "Are you all right?"

"It's in the middle of the night and you're locked and loaded?"

She dropped the gun. "It sounds like you're just loaded."

"Yeah, I've been drinking. Mind your own business. You're not my mother or my commanding officer."

"I didn't… I wasn't reprimanding you, just mad because you didn't offer me one."

Goddamn, he didn't want to like her.

He swore at his clumsiness, bent down to pick up the visible shards and hissed, dropping the broken pieces in a tinkling storm as pain sliced into his palm and blood welled.

She took a few more steps closer and he lunged at her, catching her around the waist and lifting her off her feet. "Stop! There's glass on the floor. You'll get cut."

And just like that he found himself in the one position he didn't want to be in—anywhere close to her soft skin. It was customary for him to sleep without a T-shirt, but he wasn't even sure the cotton between them would have helped. He hefted her easily and took a few steps away from the possibility of glass and set her down.

Her eyes narrowed in on his hand and she set her gun down on the coffee table. "You're bleeding."

"Be careful. You'll cut your feet." He was trying to ignore how soft and creamy her skin looked.

"My God, you are so bad tempered. I'm just trying to help."

"It's not helping."

She made an exasperated noise and grabbed his wrist and dragged all six feet four inches, two hundred and sixty pounds of his reluctant ass into the small downstairs bathroom, talking the whole time.

"I swear, Tristan. I have never seen a man who is so damn contrary all the time."

She opened the door to the medicine cabinet, still talking. "All I'm trying to do is help, but you have this chip on your shoulder about NCIS agents. Don't even give me the benefit of the doubt, just jump to all kinds of conclusions…"

"Amber," he said, desperately trying to get her to stop, using up his last ounce of willpower to ignore the roar of chemistry between them, which was as difficult as hitting the tail end of a flea from a thousand yards. But she just kept talking, her soft lips dragging him closer to her. He thought about begging her.

"…and getting your *Semper Fi* skivvies all in a twist when this is my job—"

"*Amber*, for Christ's sake." He grabbed her wrist, trying to hustle her out of the bathroom and back to bed. Ah, damn, why did he have to go and do that? Think about a bed? He swore under his breath as he tried to propel her backward from the small room and away from him, but the opposite occurred. Instead of him pushing against her, he pulled, as if Newton's law of universal gravitation had taken over and he was powerless. He now had her undivided attention as she turned right into him, her breasts pressing flush against his bare chest.

Tangling themselves up any further than they already had was just begging for trouble. He couldn't stay focused on the job if he was focused on getting her naked. And he would be. Hell, he already was. And the little tugs he was experiencing inside his chest whenever he looked at her were downright terrifying. He'd only just met her and there wasn't any way she should have this effect on him. But there was no denying she was affecting the hell out of him. And it was more than sexual need fanning those flames.

And that was bad. And good. All at the same damn time.

He almost...almost had it under control. Was almost able to step back, but she did the damnedest thing. She met his eyes and he'd never been so...*looked at*, connected as if she saw him behind his eyes right into his mind and knew what he needed. Her huffiness faded, melted away, and her features softened. His stomach tightened hard, his gut telling him what his heart didn't want to hear. There was a reason he was grumpy around her, a reason he didn't want to show any interest in her, and something must have changed in his face because she opened even more. But he was stubbornly ready to pull back until—his breath caught—either by accident or design, she shifted her hips and brushed against his aching erection.

Passion came to life inside him like a fire that had been smoldering beneath cold ash. And it was a different kind of passion, something he'd never experienced before. It wasn't about getting off or taking her because she was a woman and he needed the feel of her or physical release.

He wanted *her*. Amber. *Her* body, *her* mouth, *her* hands all over him.

Something that had been held so tightly inside snapped, snapped and whipped back at him, lashed him with his own needs and desires as if all of it had been trapped behind a dam of his own making and with these realizations that dam burst and flooded him with more than he could handle. The sensory goads of her smooth, soft skin, the scent of her an intoxicating mix of floral and heat and just plain Amber, disarmed him completely.

The combination of tough-cookie, give-as-good-as-she-got attitude, smart mouth and even smarter mind took him down without mercy.

He crowded her back a little, until her backside was against the sink and everything about her melted. And he caved in. The surrender felt so good, giving in to this…whatever it was…wrapped around him in a soft, aching vise.

Tristan growled low in his throat as his lips brushed against hers, feeling weak in the knees when she made a soft gasp and her mouth toyed with his, retreating just enough to make him go after her, on the offensive until he captured hers, dropping down to her lips like a man in need of salvation.

Her mouth relaxed beneath his, and her hand slid up his chest wall, over his collarbone, to wrap around his nape, her hot palm sending rippling pleasure down his spine, over his skin. Her other hand wrapped around his waist, her thumb stroking, dipping in and caressing the skin just below the waistband of his sweats.

His mouth got more demanding and she matched his intensity and need. Her hunger was apparent with the way she moved over his mouth, frantic and fierce. Her reaction stripped him, demolished his defenses like a fluffy, pink bulldozer.

He wanted her, had wanted her from the first moment, this angel with her alluring combination of grace and take-no-prisoners attitude. He wanted her in a way he hadn't wanted a woman in a long time—possessively, obsessively. He wanted her to be his in a way she had never been any other man's. He would have seen it as dangerous thinking if he had been able to think at all.

Without breaking the kiss, he guided her hands to his chest and down to his waist and abandoned them there. Heat poured through him, molten, liquid heat, searing his veins, pooling in his already-hard dick. He gasped a little at the feel of her hands, so cool and soft, gliding back up his chest.

His breath hitched and he sent his hands down her back, caressing, exploring, interpreting every graceful curve, every plane and hollow. Lifting her into him, he pressed her hips to his, pressed her into his arousal, letting her know how badly, how urgently, he wanted her. She wrapped her arms around him and hung on, mirroring his actions as he kissed her throat, her shoulder. He felt her tongue dip into the hollow at the base of his throat, and the flames of desire leaped, licking at his sanity.

How had she got to him so fast? He wasn't sure. He wasn't sure of anything and that made him remember, and making him remember brought back the confusion and the fact that if he let this happen now, he would regret it. Not because he didn't want it to happen. Damn, he was crazy for her to do everything she was doing and more.

It was about her in a deep, more fundamental way than he could ever have imagined, and if it had been any other woman, he'd already be inside her. Doing her. Taking her.

But that was not what he wanted with Amber. He wanted something more, and that was what made him bury his face in her neck and why the soft sound of despair came out of him so involuntarily.

"Tristan."

He stilled, hearing his name whispered so intimately. It threatened to pull him back in, but he resisted, clenched his hands in the silky garment she was wearing.

"What's wrong?"

"I can't. I'm screwed up and I can't do something with you until I get my head straight about it. I would regret it and I so don't want to do that."

"What is it?"

"I devoted my life to the corps. I'm entangled and entwined with it and I can't seem to separate—" He stopped again, shook his head. "I don't do long-term commitments. I have casual sex."

"What are you saying? The corps comes first, even in this?"

He looked her in the eyes. "It always has and I…"

"You don't have to say anything else." Her face fell and the wonderful openness that had been there evaporated and disappeared. She closed down, and where there had once been desire, now showed only hurt.

She pushed on his chest and he saw the blood from his cut on her clothes. She opened and reached into the medicine cabinet, pulling out bandages. He felt like a fool and didn't know what the hell was wrong with him. She pushed him again until he was sitting on the commode.

He was going to say that this was more already and that he'd better stop it now before he got in too deep, got them in too deep.

And right there was the raw, stunning truth of it. Shocking, really, since he'd never come up against that particular problem before. And he sure as hell hadn't expected to here, now.

"Amber."

"Please, don't talk. I don't want to know that I'm a secondary thought."

"That's not it," he said adamantly.

"Okay," she said. "The corps comes first. I get it. Excuse me if I'm sensitive about being an afterthought. I *hate* it. I've had a similar situation just recently where I came in second best and I'm just not up to that again."

He rose and grabbed her upper arms, his cut stinging now, dragging her against him. "What? Damn, Amber. You should have mentioned that," he said testily.

"I'm not interested in spilling my guts to someone who's been nothing but disagreeable since I met him, especially about getting dumped." Her face registered her surprise and then she looked downright embarrassed. "I can't believe I just said that. Jeez, Michaels, you bring out the very best in me."

"Look, I'm not happy about this, either. It's complicated."

"Right, and you hate that. You just want your sex easy and uncomplicated. Well, I'm easy. Wait, that didn't come out right. I mean I can be casual about it and uncomplicated. I'm only here for a few days and then I'm off to the beach…alone."

"I wish this was easier," he said through clenched teeth. "I can't even unravel it myself, and until I do, I'm not going to do something that I would regret."

"Oh, for the love of Pete! Why couldn't you have just…been…more of a…an…insensitive jerk?" she said and tried to get out of his grip.

For some reason that made him laugh and she wasn't amused at all. Damn if he didn't want this woman, now. Right damn now. He couldn't let her go, but he put his forehead against hers and ran his hands up her arms.

"We've got to work together on this case…one that's messing with my head."

"And you think dancing around this and pretending we don't want to drag each other's clothes off is preferable to just giving in to it, enjoying ourselves, then going on with life as it happens? I'm a big girl. I can handle disappointment. If that's what happens. Who knows, we might go to bed once and find out it's not all that we thought it was cracked up to be."

He gave her a fierce look. "That's a load of bull and you know it. It will be good. Damned good."

She took a breath and looked at his face, her eyes going over him in a way that felt more intimate than touching him. She settled on his mouth and he groaned.

"I want you. I can't deny that and I don't know what it is about you that makes me crazy just to look at you, so I concede that, yes, it would probably be out-of-the-world amazing. But us working together is going to be a juggling act anyway. Why can't we just recognize all the bullcrap and still just do what we both want."

He took her hands from his waist and held on to them. "It's not as if I don't want to." He cupped her jaw and cradled her delicate face in his hand. "But I won't do something that may hurt you in the end, not until I'm sure about my own feelings in this. I'm going back into combat and there are other things you don't know. I can't muddle myself up more or be dishonest with you." He stepped back, his body resisting the action with every beat of his heart, but he did it, nonetheless. "With any other woman, maybe, but not with you."

She lifted her hands in disbelief, then let them drop to her sides. "You're really something else, Tristan."

"I'm sorry." And he was. Sorrier than he'd ever been. But what he felt at the moment was relief, not fear that he'd just made a big mistake. Which told him it was the right thing to do. He stepped farther back before he changed his mind.

"Have you ever thought about getting out?" she said, as his eyes drifted over her face, her lips.

"Of the service?"

"Yes, doing something else with your life."

He sounded so…spooked, he cleared his throat then responded. "I have thought about it. Even have a partnership offer from my former teammate Rock… Russell Kaczewski. But I'm not sure about leaving the corps. It's all I've known."

"Of course. I get that. So…now what? We pretend that

there's no screaming sexual tension between us and just go about our business?"

He clenched his teeth and then a smile worked at his mouth. She was direct. He liked that about her. "We try. At least until we find out what happened to James and get his death figured out. Until we know more about what's really at stake here."

And he wasn't talking about the case. The idea that he was worried about getting emotionally involved should have been the douse of cold reality her raging hormones needed.

Not so much, as it turned out.

"I already know all I need to know." She turned away and went to the bathroom door, then stopped abruptly, her back still to him. Even in the dim lighting, he watched as her shoulders slumped a little and finally felt the twinge of the regret he'd hoped not to feel.

"I believe there's a cold shower with your name on it," she said at length, quietly, but with no overt recrimination in her voice, either. Weary resignation was more like it.

He took a step toward her, couldn't stop his eyes from sliding over her. "It's not because I don't want you. But because we'll want too much."

Or I will.

Amber woke to the scrape of a snow shovel and the sound of the rough motor of the snowplow as it trundled past the house. Even though she'd grown up in Vermont, she had never wanted to live there. It was too cold, too much snow, too…not cosmopolitan. She'd got out as soon as she could. Now she only liked snow to ski on. That was it.

Groggy, she sat up and pushed her hair out of her face. Damn, what time was it? She grabbed her phone and woke it up. Six thirty. That was what she got for being in the company of a military man.

Then the fog cleared and she remembered. She flopped back onto her pillow and stared unseeing at the ceiling. It had driven her crazy because she'd been truthful. He made her crazy and had been driving her to the edge since he'd walked through the colonel's office door, looking both hot and cool in his uniform, his features drawing her eyes. In her mind's eye, she pictured him, standing there in the bathroom, all gorgeous muscle and that pain in his eyes. The way he had sounded and tasted as he pinned her to the sink. The feel of him, strong, hard, sure, moving between her legs. All but dragging each other into whatever bedroom was the closest.

She squeezed her eyes shut. Rejected twice in one week. The rawness of Tristan's rejection hurt the worst. Which was really strange because she'd known him for a lot less time. And maybe she was trying to compensate for her feelings of inadequacy when it came to not only Pete's rejection but to Chris's blatant response that she was just the next-best thing.

She sighed and decided to be an adult about it instead of a whiny bitch. Push her percentage back up and over, into more sweetheart. She wasn't really mad at Tristan, not really. He hadn't been playing games. He'd been sincerely confused, trying to do what he thought was right. Odd that he thought he'd disappoint her in some way, when he seemed to have a stronger sense of himself and their usual dynamic than she did. Maybe that was part of his problem, too.

She heaved one last self-indulgent sigh and got up. He was probably right anyway. It probably was better, or at least smarter, for them to leave well enough alone. She talked a good game about them being consenting adults who could do what they wanted, when they wanted, but he might have had a teensy point there about risking wanting more. Wanting too much.

What was important was finishing out this investigation into Connelly's death and getting herself to Aruba. For just a moment she thought about how exciting it would be to go with Tristan, explore every inch of his damn fine body, but that was a fantasy. The reality bite of going to a tropical island with more time to kill than she knew what to do with was probably going to be torture.

He was a corps guy and she wasn't going to play second fiddle to the damn military. No damn way. She had more pride than that. He would reenlist, get back to making war, and she would go back to DC and… She squeezed her eyes closed. Be Chris's second choice.

Dammit. She would just have to work harder. The residual from growing up in the shadow of her sister needed to be jettisoned. She would have to make that her number one priority in the coming year. There. She was thinking about a future apart, which meant that somewhere in her subconscious she'd at least contemplated the idea of a future together. Which was completely impossible. *Grumpy bastard meets optimistic albeit neurotic NCIS agent—whom he hates.* Yeah, like that was ever going to work.

Her cell rang and she answered it. "Dalton."

"Agent Dalton, this is Corporal Sheppard. I'm sorry to bother you, but I didn't want to tell this to the Sarge when you interviewed us because he was so broken up over James."

"What is it?"

"James worshipped the Sarge. He told me that he wanted to go up into the mountains and pit himself against the elements and prove to the Sarge that he was tough and capable. I told him the Sarge already knew. I'm afraid he might have done that. Gone up there. I don't know for certain. I didn't say anything because I didn't want to ruin his…challenge. I also didn't want him to get into trouble. But now, now that he's dead…" His voice clogged with emotion. "I'm sorry I didn't say anything. They might have… I don't know."

"Corporal Sheppard. Thank you for telling me this. If you want my opinion, I don't believe he would have done that and gone against Sergeant Michaels's orders."

"You're probably right. That's why I didn't say anything to him. Could we keep this between us? It will kill the Sarge if he hears it. He's got enough to deal with."

"Absolutely, Corporal Sheppard."

"Goodbye, ma'am."

"You take care."

She disconnected the call and squeezed her eyes closed. She decided to keep this information to herself. Tristan didn't need to know and the investigation wasn't complete. If it had to come out, she would divulge it. But she knew it would devastate him to think that James had gone alone into the mountains to prove himself to Tristan.

The man was so damned honorable.

As honorable as he'd been last night. Damn him. She glanced at the bed anyway. He could be sprawled there right now, sheets draped over a body she might have pressed against so intimately last night, her hands molding over every hot, muscled part of him…the power of his body taking hers, moving against her, driving her crazy… Yeah. She might find herself wanting a bit too much.

She stripped out of her jammies and slipped on a pair of yoga pants and racerback bra, both in a hot pink.

She pulled her hair back and took a deep breath. Slipping out of the room, she grabbed her mat and rolled it out on the floor. Tristan was outside. She could still hear him shoveling. She tapped her phone and started up her soothing music, a beautiful blend that she'd got from Vin's fiancée, Sky. She let the cares and worries drift away.

She made the mistake of looking outside. Tristan was clearing the walk and she unabashedly watched him. He had on only a sweatshirt and a pair of tight, sinful jeans. That sexy spiked flattop and his unshaven face. Damn, he sorely tested her sense of balance. Their chance bond was as unexpected as it had been unwanted. She didn't mind him being more approachable, but she could ill afford to let herself become any more attracted to him. For one thing, she hadn't yet determined if he was friend or foe with his grouchy attitude. Although, there was something surprisingly sexy about his grumpiness. But even if it was the former, she didn't want to risk being rejected again…well…unless he made the next move. And that was unlikely after his reluctance…ah…no, his out-and-out resistance. She shouldn't have given in to temptation. Very potent temptation. Besides, what was the point? Her time here was limited.

He reached the edge of the path and she watched him walk, just move. Man, he was…gorgeous.

He turned abruptly and she jumped back. She wasn't sure if he'd caught her staring or—*ogling* was probably a better word. She dropped to the floor and immediately started stretching. The door opened, bringing him in along with the chill air. He stamped the snow off his boots and unlaced them.

She could feel his gaze on her. "Good morning," she said, looking up at him.

He grunted and leaned back against the closed door. She tried not to stare at the way his folded arms pulled the fabric of his sweatshirt tight over his biceps. Or the way it made his shoulders look wider. She forced her gaze up to his.

"I reported the car that almost hit you to the police department."

Now that she was more in tune with him, she saw that he was working hard not to notice her. "Thank you. He was driving pretty erratically."

He nodded and turned to go into the kitchen.

"Why don't you come over here and try this. You really could use…"

"No," he said flatly. "I don't bend into a pretzel."

"Oh, come on, Tristan. It doesn't hurt and you'll feel great."

He looked away and murmured, "I doubt that."

"I'll show you one position."

He closed his eyes and swore softly under his breath. "Is it your plan to torture me now?"

She jerked up and said, "No, jeez, I was just trying to help."

He came over to her and said, "And you think that watching you—" he swung his hand around, indicating her elongated body "—is going to help me? The word *position* also should be struck from your vocabulary while you are here, or whenever I'm within earshot."

"Oh," she said.

"Yeah, 'oh.' Now she has it," he mocked.

"I get it," she grumbled. "But it would still do you some good."

He walked away just as her cell phone rang.

"Special Agent Dalton," she said, picking it up and activating the call.

"Agent Dalton, this is Officer Mendez calling from MWTC PD."

"Yes."

"We tracked down the owner of the vehicle that Master Sergeant Michaels reported almost hit you. The car belongs to a man named Randall Mayer. He works at HQ as a clerk. We're in the process of tracking down both him and his car. We'll let you know when we find him so that you can come in and lodge a complaint."

"Thank you."

She walked into the kitchen and Tristan was getting the coffee ready to brew. She understood why he wasn't willing to jump into bed with her, and she was sure that if he'd continued kissing her as if he was going to inhale her last night, that was exactly where they were headed. She had no doubt. She shocked herself. She never did that kind of thing. Ever.

It also stuck in her craw that he was putting the military first. First she got dumped by a guy long-distance, one who had got engaged without telling her. Then she ended up in the middle of nowhere when she was supposed to be on vacation and a really sexy, albeit screwed-up guy rejected her.

Yeah, she was batting a thousand.

"You want coffee or you just going to stare at me?"

"I could do both. I have multitasking skills. And, since you've already rejected me once, I think I'm safe."

He leaned back into the counter and very slowly let his gaze go over her from the top of her head to her toes. "You're not safe, Amber."

Suddenly she wanted to stick her head into a snow-bank. Hoo boy.

"That was the police. The car belonged to Randall Mayer. Officer Mendez said he works at HQ as a clerk."

"I know that guy. I'll be happy to set him straight about driving around the base intoxicated." He shifted and leaned back. "What's on the agenda today?"

"I want to go back up the mountain."

"Amber, I've got to tell you that it's unlikely we'll—"

"I know what you're going to say, but it's a chance to gather more information. Until the autopsy report comes back we're kinda dead in the water."

"If James was shot somewhere other than where he was found, there's very little hope of discovering it. There's been at least eight to ten inches of snow since we were last up there."

She just stood there with her NCIS face on. Vin and Beau had taught her to use it when someone was reluctant to do what she asked.

He sighed. "Amber."

The NCIS face got fiercer.

He sent his hand over that tantalizing mop of flattop hair she wanted to get her hands on.

He really needed to shave because he looked so damn good with stubble, and she really should stop staring at his mouth. Like now. *Really, stop.*

He shifted his lean, sexy hips, looked away, then back

at her, struggling with his knowledge against pleasing her. "I must be a twisted son of a bitch, but that face does something to me. The weather should hold and I can clear us for a helicopter ride. How are you on snowshoes?"

"Damn good."

He smiled and her heart nearly stopped. He should do that more often— Wait, no, he shouldn't do that at all. She would have to jump him, rejection or not. "But I would prefer cross-country skis."

His brows shot up. "Would you?"

"Vermont girl. Some days that's how I got to school. It's fun."

She was rewarded with another one of those smiles. *Hot damn.* She'd have to get him to do that more often.

Her cell rang and she looked down. Pete again. She pushed Ignore.

Chapter 6

The helicopter set down in the same spot, and without the threat of weather Amber was able to take her time. She went back to the tented area and brushed off the snow. Tristan, laden with skis and poles, set everything beside her as the helo took off, blowing stinging snow in their faces.

She started to unroll the tent flaps. God, she needed this cold, bracing air slapping her skin to keep her focused. She needed a return to some semblance of rational thought. Maybe she had been responding to being dumped. Maybe she had fallen into that kiss because she needed the validation that she was still desirable. But then he'd had to explain that the corps came first and she'd been hurt all over again. Why couldn't she for once in her life be someone's number one? Maybe she wanted that too bad, and she recognized that quite easily as her weakness. She craved a man who understood her, found her just as attractive when she was being a bitch as when she was being a sweetheart.

She wanted to be priority number one.

Pete's rejection had hurt her, but not her heart, mostly her pride.

Tristan hadn't said a word since they got out of the helicopter.

She cut him a look. He continued to ready the equipment. She was really good at reading people. She got vibes off them. When she'd been at Quantico, she was sure one of the trainees was off. She couldn't put her finger on it, but it was as if she got an itch under her skin whenever the trainee was around. She was getting that same itch here, now. Something was off about Connelly's death—she just hadn't figured it out yet.

As a JAG it was her job to assess situations, people, and either set up the best defense or go hard on the offense. Those skills had been baked in

Tristan wasn't happy, that was clear by the set of his face and his methodical movements, but she wasn't here to please him. She was here to investigate a suspicious death. "I know you think this is a waste of time, but if I can get any clue from going over everything more than once, it will be worth it."

He speared the ski poles into the ground with more force than was necessary. "I was out of line, Amber. I'm not an investigator. I'm a marine and I teach these boys how to shoot at an angle and survive in the cold." Bemused, all those words delivered with a tightly clenched jaw, she stared at him for a moment, shocked at his answer. Damn, he was cute when he was grumpy, and she was beginning to believe there was a lot more to his belligerence than just being grumpy. Trouble was she wanted to know why, but she was completely sure he had no intentions of telling her.

For the first time in an adult situation with a man whom she really wanted to sleep with, she craved more. Okay, she wasn't one to indulge in many one-night stands, but it had happened.

It didn't feel like this.

Nothing felt like this and she'd just met the man.

She smiled in the face of his grouch. "Ah, don't beat yourself up too much, Michaels. I'm sure you're good at what you do or you wouldn't be here." She crouched down. Pulling out her phone, she brought up the crime-scene photos. She studied them for a moment, then knelt in the snow, the cold permeating her winter pants and chilling her skin.

She sent her eyes over the area, and this time she didn't have Garza and Mendez breathing down her neck and trying to feed her information about this being a friendly-fire incident. She wasn't going to come at it from any angle other than the facts.

She held up the camera, then pulled off her glove, digging into the snow with her finger until she'd inserted it all the way down to her knuckle.

Pulling it out, she got on her side and looked at the layering of blood in the snow. It hadn't taken long for the biting cold to numb her finger. She slipped the glove back on. There was no pooling, no volume. No indication that copious amounts of blood had saturated this area. She got up, climbed around the tent and hiked up a few feet. She peered down at the resting place, then looked back up the hill.

"Tristan, could you please go stand where you were before you found his body?"

He nodded and took off, climbing a fair ways up the hill.

She looked up the hill, standing forward and then turning and standing with her back to Tristan. She looked down the hill and took a breath. It frosted the air. James Connelly would have seen the targets from here with the naked eye. He would have known where he was and he would have realized he was in the line of fire. No doubt remained.

James wasn't shot here.

She looked right and left and thought about in what direction someone would have approached to deposit his body. This person would also have to have known these mountains.

She cupped her hands around her mouth and shouted for Tristan to come back.

As he loped down to her, the snow crunching beneath his boots, she said, "Are there signs posted that this is an area of live rounds?"

"Yes. We always post so that anyone approaching would be aware we're conducting training exercises here."

"That's what I thought." She shaded her eyes against the sun, the glare even more punishing off the blinding white snow. "If James had been standing here with his back to you, he would have seen the targets. He would have known where he was, and if he was facing you, he would also have seen you."

"And I would have seen him."

She nodded. "I'm convinced that James didn't die from friendly fire but was placed here. The 'why' I don't know and the 'when' we'll have to hope the doctor examining him can determine as close to an accurate estimate as possible."

She trudged through the snow to the tent and let down the flaps securing them to the poles. Setting her boot into the binding of one ski, then the second, she looked up at Tristan. He donned his skis and shouldered the backpack that carried water and his radio to communicate with the helo at the rendezvous time.

"Which direction?" he asked.

"Let's go west first. I studied a map of this area last night. The terrain is less steep and would be easier to maneuver." She planted her poles and slid her skis along the snow. He took good care of his equipment. The resin on the bottom moved as if it was oiled.

He set a hand on her arm before she could jog off. "When I say we go back, we go back."

"Tristan…"

"No arguments." Breaths rolled from him in short frosted puffs. "One point six degrees from death," he said. "At 97 degrees, you lose cognitive functioning. That's all it takes and it spirals fast from there. Any shivering, I want to know."

"You make me shiver," she said, and he cocked his head to the side and gave her an even grouchier look.

"Amber…this is serious."

"Yes," she said softly. "Very serious."

His lips tightened, his eyes going to her mouth. "At 97 degrees you'll start to shiver. That's very bad. At 95 it'll get violent. With every one degree drop in body temperature below 95, your cerebral metabolic rate falls off by 3 to 5 percent. When your core temperature reaches 93, amnesia competes for consciousness.

Apathy at 91 degrees. Stupor at 90. Then it's lights out, sweetheart," he growled.

"Okay, I hear you. If I have any of those symptoms, I will let you know."

He held her gaze. Then finally he let her go.

"Hypothermia is a very real threat here. It's why I insisted you wear clothing that wicks the sweat away and why I brought the water along. You will do as I say when it comes to your safety in the cold. Not to mention, if at any time you start to experience a headache, tell me. Altitude sickness is another worry."

An hour of fun later, Amber, who did yoga, ran, played basketball with Vin and Beau, and sparred with the best at NCIS, was winded. Tristan, on the other hand, wasn't even breathing hard.

She followed him through the snow and he was right. This was futile. They hadn't found squat. She was irritated, frustrated, and felt completely out of shape.

He slowed and stopped. Pushing up the goggles covering his eyes, he said, "Are you doing okay?"

She bristled. "I can keep up with you any day."

"I have no doubt of that, but this isn't any altitude. You're feeling winded because there's less oxygen up here. I'm used to it and my lungs have compensated. Yours haven't."

She looked around. They were currently in a thick stand of trees, and everything was white, completely blanketed in snow.

"I know you're disappointed. I am, too. I really want to know what happened to James... Corporal Connelly."

Her gaze returned to his. She heard the emotion catch in his voice, and the way he looked made her think of a whipped dog. He was feeling responsible for his death.

That was pretty clear. "Tristan, this isn't your fault. You've been cleared of any neglect. I think—"

"It doesn't matter what you think! I was responsible for him. I was his instructor. I can't shake the feeling that..."

"What?"

"That this is my fault, somehow."

"Why would you think that? You couldn't stop him from going AWOL or for breaking protocol."

He flipped around to face her. "I was his lifeline. His guardian."

"He was a seasoned soldier with two tours under his belt. A scout sniper, one who was adept at finding a target, taking the killing shot and evading his enemy. Are you going to tell me that you think you needed to babysit him?"

He dug his poles into the ground, hanging his head. "No. James didn't need babysitting, but I wished I had gone that extra mile."

"What? And done what, not go to the barracks and not chased down his whereabouts, not reached out to him by calling his cell?"

"How do you know I did all that?"

"You might be a grouch and testy and contrary, but I could tell right away that you handled James differently. You had a special relationship with him. He got to you somehow. I don't know much about you and I don't expect you to be forthcoming, because, well, I'm leaving soon and we are just two ships passing in the night, but that's what I think."

"Were you a shrink in another life or something?"

She smiled at the half teasing, half serious tone. The kind of tone that said he was surprised at the depth of her insight. "Something like that. I was in the JAG Corps."

"Don't remind me you're a lawyer, too."

"Oh, you don't like lawyers, either?"

"Not especially. In my experience they speak out of both sides of their mouths."

"Is there anyone you do like besides James?"

He smiled. "I have a healthy respect for Colonel Jacobs. I love my family. I'm stuck with my former teammate Rock, and…despite your professions and me losing tough-guy points…ah… I like you. Against my will."

"Oh, no. Losing tough-guy points? Those are hard to get back, right? Shoot, you'd have to go out and earn another medal or something."

His voice was subdued. "How do you know that I earned any medals?" He pulled off the backpack and unzipped it.

She accepted the water bottle he offered. "You've got it written all over you, sir."

When she went to take it out of his hand, he held on to it and, startled, she met his eyes. "Drink it all. Every drop. You feeling cold?"

"No. Not at the moment," she said. How could she when he was generating so much damn heat.

"So, family? How many brothers and sisters?"

"Is this an interrogation?" he said, bringing a bottle of water to his lips and drinking half down in a few huge swallows.

"No, Tristan, this is called dialogue between two adults. It can happen spontaneously or it can be like pulling teeth. You can guess which one I'm experiencing right now. I will really begin my torture when

I start asking you where you went to school, et cetera. Do I need a court order and search warrant for that?"

He had just brought the bottle to his mouth again and was in the process of gulping the rest of the water, but he choked, sputtered and spit out the liquid. Coughing, he wiped his mouth on the back of his spiffy wick-sweat-away sleeve of his tight-fitting jacket that did nothing but remind her what kind of chest and shoulders he had beneath his clothes. She could only wish she had his personal search warrant signed, sealed and delivered. Her hands itched to mold over all that stunning muscle.

"Cute." He shook his head and sighed. "Brother and twin sisters." He took out another bottle, zipped the backpack and shrugged back into the straps. After unscrewing the top, he guzzled over half the contents, his strong throat working. "Nova will graduate soon from Coast Guard flight school and Neve is a Coast Guard rescue swimmer. She's also a mixed-martial-arts instructor. They really take after my mom and it's easy to see our heritage in them. They were a surprise pregnancy, but my dad was over the moon to have daughters. They're twenty-five. My brother, Thane, is two years older than me and is an instructor at the Naval Academy in Annapolis and he looks a lot like me. We got more of the white genes." He said it softly, as if there was more of a story regarding his brother. And, good God, there was another man that looked like him running around?

"That instructor thing runs in the family, huh?"

"I guess it does."

"And your parents?"

"My dad is a fisherman, no military background, and my mom is a schoolteacher. She also kicks asses for a living."

Amber laughed and he smiled, looking away again. "She must teach high school."

"All the more power to her. I couldn't handle it. I'd have the whole damn pissant class down on the deck doing push-ups. They would be too tired for snotty teenage comebacks."

She giggled again at the way he delivered those words with his grumpy attitude. "So, that's where you get it. From your mom?"

"My ass-kicking attitude?"

"No, the teaching thing, but I'm sure she taught you a thing or two."

"I guess. I never really thought about it too much."

So, he could be charming, which wasn't exactly helping. When Tristan Michaels let down his guard, he certainly made for one handsome, distracting package. She shivered and it had nothing whatsoever to do with the cold.

"What about you?" he asked.

"I've been known to kick a few asses."

His bark of laughter lit up his face and made his eyes all twinkly blue. Major shivers, or maybe she should say master-sergeant shivers. He brought that smile to bear on her. Lethal.

"C'mon, Dalton, give."

"A sister named Sammy, but she only knows how to be a pain in the ass."

"Oh," he said, giving her a wry look. "Seems like that might run in the family."

"Ha!"

"I've honed my skills."

That word sank in.

"Honed."

"What?" Tristan said, frowning, confused by her change in conversation.

"James. He was honed. Would he have broken protocol and come looking for you on this mountain alone?"

"No."

"If he had gone AWOL and changed his mind, he wouldn't have come looking for you without his weapon."

Tristan bit his bottom lip, his midnight-blue eyes unfocused. Then he looked at her. "No, he wouldn't have."

"So then that begs the question. What was he doing up here without his weapon?"

"I don't know."

"I intend to find out."

"I have no doubt, Amber." His sure response did something really mushy to her heart, bolstered her ego and made her feel that at least one person on this planet didn't treat her as if she was incompetent. "You ready to head back?"

"Not really. I was hoping to get answers and now I have more questions."

"You just don't have all the facts yet."

This time she shivered. Her body was cooling from the hour-long trek here. She'd seen no sign of churned-up snow, blood…or…anything. Just snow, snow and more snow. She was at a complete dead end in this case. She would have to wait for the autopsy to see if she could get any leads there, though she didn't expect they'd find any DNA.

"Come on. I'll race you back," she said, after handing him the empty bottle to put into the backpack.

He tucked it inside and said, "You'll lose, sweetheart."

"We'll see about that."

"Amber, it's not a good idea to fool around…" But

she turned and took off. She heard him swearing behind her as her long strides slashed through the powder, only the *swish* of her skis audible in the pristine white.

Then she heard him coming up on her. She twisted around to determine where he was and saw him close. Exhilarated at the chase, she laughed and surged ahead, her lungs pumping. She was only slightly winded, thinking she would show him who couldn't keep up.

She skied around a tight bend, the beginnings of a switchback that led straight down with a tricky turn at the end. She started confidently down, but as she hit the bottom of the slope, her ski tip caught on something and sent her flying and sprawling into the snow, getting a face full of freezing flakes.

"Dammit," he cursed, and she turned in time to see him navigate the hill with expert skill. As he hit the bottom of the slope, he slipped out of his bindings and pelted for her.

"Amber?" he said as he knelt down. With a little bubble of glee she was ready. As he touched her shoulder, she twisted and threw a wad of snow right in his face, laughing and scrambling away.

Tristan sputtered and then pinned her with a lethal, oh-it's-so-on look. She reached for more snow, but Tristan was fast. He was up and already scooping and chucking a snowball her way. It hit her hard in the center of her chest and drove her a few steps back. She let her own snowball fly, but he ducked it and came up with more snow. He looked predatory and so sexy as he crouched. The hat covering his head and framing his roughly stubbled face, his blue eyes looking all the more vibrant from the brightness of the sun, the lashes thick and dark. He was cut, powerfully male, and as dangerous in a snow battle as he was up close and personal.

He feigned a toss and she raised her arms to counter, but he charged her instead, catching her totally off guard, and that was no easy feat.

He slammed into her and took her down into the snow, his laughter the most carefree she'd ever heard it. That underused, rusty sound gone.

She made an *umph* sound as her back hit, but then she recovered, her training and her own honed instincts taking over. Before he could bring his full weight to bear on her, she twisted, used her knees against his chest to keep him off her and shoved backward. Clearing him, she pressed to her feet just as he snagged her around the waist and had her beneath him so fast she didn't have a chance to counter.

He pressed her down into the snow, some of it slipping into the back of her collar. But she barely noticed its icy trail as it melted and slid down her spine to soak into the fabric of her thermal shirt.

She could hear the chopping blades of the helicopter coming back for them.

She smiled. "You know that I'm going to make you show me that move sometime."

He still wasn't breathing hard after their tussle. There was no returning smile, not even in his eyes. Instead, he was watching her with an intent, steady look, as if assessing the situation. His voice was quiet and low when he spoke. "I don't give away my secrets," he rasped, staring down into her eyes. "You should really run. I mean it, Amber."

Amber could handle a man with secrets, but the concern in his voice got to her. "I bet you don't," she countered, "but I'll use my womanly wiles on you, as meager as they are."

"What are you talking about? There is nothing meager about you, Amber. At all."

Their eyes held and Amber's lungs compressed. It was too much. Amber's body melted and her breath jammed up in her chest. It was all she could do to keep from giving everything away. All those feelings she'd tried to hold at bay came rushing through her, sending a fountain of need surging up inside her. The tension that had seemed present from the moment they met tightened, and the only sounds were the crackle of snow in the air and the helo.

"We have to rendezvous."

As if trapped by his gaze, she stared back at him, unable to break away—not really wanting to. She was lost in his eyes, in the pulse-racing weakness. "Oh, Master Sergeant," she whispered. "I think we're about as rendezvoused as two people can get."

He huffed a laugh. "What you do to me," he said, his voice a puff of air. He brought up his gloved hand, bit down on the tip and removed it. Very gently, he caressed her cheek. "You're so warm."

"Yeah, that's what happens when you have a two-hundred-sixty-pound heated blanket right exactly where you want it."

"Twenty-one Bravo to Michaels. Over."

He reached down and pulled the radio off his belt. He didn't break eye contact. "Michaels, copy. Over."

"Wheels down. Over"

"Roger. ETA five mikes."

"Roger that. Angel transport at the ready, over."

Amber smiled and Tristan laughed. "Solid copy. Out."

"I think those flyboys are sweet on you," he said.

He got off her slowly, pushed to his knees, then to his feet. He reached his hand down. She could, of course, easily rise on her own, show him that she wasn't a damsel in distress. But something made her deliberately take his offer. She reached her hand up to his. The contact was every bit as electric even through her glove. His palm was wide and warm, his grip strong and steady as he tugged her easily to her feet. But rather than let her go as she'd expected, he kept tugging until she stumbled a step closer and came up flush against his body. His free arm was instantly around her back, steadying her, keeping her tucked up against him.

"I'm not playing games," he told her, the intensity of his gaze impossible to look away from at such close range. "Just so you know."

She opened her mouth to speak, but nothing came out. It had been a very long time since there was anyone in her life who was so darned direct. She thought Pete was good at communication, but boy, had she been wrong there. Tristan might say he wasn't into playing games, but she couldn't risk her heart again with a man who was much too dedicated to being where she wasn't. The corps was his life and that meant she had to come in second. She didn't want to *play* that game again. Not ever again. Was he warning her or preparing her? She wasn't sure. "I can handle myself and anything you can dish out, Michaels." Her voice, she was happy to say, was tempered steel, even though her knees were wobbly.

"I have no doubt. I'm a little rusty with the social skills. Been isolated way too long."

"You don't need to worry about me."

"I may not need to, but I do. Just do me a favor and follow my orders up here. This is my domain."

Rather than set her loose, his arm flexed against her back, drawing her even closer, making her gasp as she came up against the full, hard length of him. Harder in some places than others. "It's dangerous up here. Death stalks us."

She lifted her chin, giving him bravado. "I'm a survivor."

He pulled her hand up to his chest, pressed it there before letting go so he could slide his fingers beneath the hair at nape and tug her mouth closer to his. And she didn't do a damn thing to stop him. "You make me crazy, and all that sass and beauty takes away all my defenses."

"Tell me you're not making excuses."

"No excuses. Just the facts." He brushed a strand of hair off her forehead, and when he spoke, his tone was gentler, completely doing her in, unraveling her.

"Just…stick close. Do as I say. Okay?"

Her voice was nothing but a puff of air. "Okay."

And then—he tasted like the heat of a hot, scorching day, no chill at all. And all she could do was soften, give up any pretense of trying to control herself where he was concerned.

Everything was so tangled up in her head and her heart. She didn't even try to convince herself that she was making a mistake. It didn't feel like any mistake she'd made in the past. She was aware, knew the score, and, like she'd told him, she was a survivor and a big girl. She closed her eyes.

His lips retreated and she opened her eyes.

"The flyboys are going to get antsy."

"Too bad," she said hoarsely and made no move to strap back on her skis. Instead, she turned her mouth back to his. Only this time, as their lips met, they slowed down, gentled the onslaught, which made her feel liquid. She teased, he taunted, and they slipped their tongues more sinuously along the other, tasting, touching. Soft moans filled the cool air. His, hers, she wasn't keeping track. She was drowning, and she didn't want to be saved.

"Twenty-one Bravo to Michaels. We're burning fuel. ETA? Over."

He took a breath and they parted enough for him to grab his radio. As he pressed the mike switch, she pressed her mouth to his warm, musky skin, breathing him in.

His voice wobbled when he spoke. "Five mikes."

Amber raised her head and froze. She blinked. "Tristan," she said, her voice holding enough of her dismay and warning for him to turn his head.

His breath whooshed out as he saw, too. "Randy Mayer."

"The guy who tried to run me down?"

"Correct."

He brought the radio back to his mouth. "Twenty-one Bravo, negative on the previous ETA. Alert command. Alert PD. Alert Mono County Sheriff's Department. We have a body, over."

The airwaves crackled. Finally their response came back. "Roger that. Out."

She peered at the macabre sight. The wind picked up and blew snow over Randy's naked body, his skin blue and his face frozen in death.

Chapter 7

"That woman is a menace," the man growled into the phone.

"So, she found the body a little sooner than we thought. Just means her ass will be out of here that much sooner and it'll be business as usual."

"Is Carl on board?"

"Reluctantly."

"Are we going to have problems with him?"

"I think we might."

"Too bad."

"Don't worry. I'll take care of it."

"You'd better."

"Special Agent Dalton, what is your assessment of the situation as you see it?"

She was seated alongside Tristan in Colonel Jacobs's

office. The colonel's face was solemn. There was no doubt in her mind that this wasn't a simple open-and-shut case. Lance Corporal James Connelly had been killed in what she considered a suspicious way.

"Randy Mayer's death will be considered suspicious until we also receive an autopsy report. His cause of death isn't apparent, but the fact that he was naked may indicate he could have been murdered. Master Sergeant Michaels told me that when a victim is in a hypothermic state, that person will sometimes strip all their clothes off. When a body gets that cold, apparently it feels as if the person is burning up. Victims sometimes hallucinate that they are either in front of a roaring fire and too hot or are on fire. I believe that it's best to wait for the autopsy on Connelly and Mayer before I come to any conclusions."

"I see. James's parents are in the conference room waiting for you." Amber's stomach dropped. This part of the job was always the tough part.

"Colonel, could I get a copy of Mayer's personnel file and anything else you think might be helpful. I'd also like to speak with anyone who knew him or worked with him."

"I will compile a list for you and also get his records."

"Thank you, sir."

She started to rise and Tristan said, "Amber…"

She glanced at him and it was clear to her from the strained look on his face that he wanted to go with her. She put her hand on his arm.

"Do you want to speak to them?"

He nodded. "Yes. I would."

"All right. If that's okay with the colonel, let me interview them before you speak to them. This is going to be hard enough on them, and I'm sure what you have to say is going to be emotional."

He rose as she did and held his eyes, which were a deep well of meaning.

She walked out of the colonel's office and entered the conference room. A middle-aged man was sitting at the table, looking as if he'd been through his own minefield. He eyes were moist and his face showed the devastation of losing a son.

James's mother sat with her hands in her lap. She appeared dry-eyed but by no means unaffected by the loss of her son. She looked up when Amber came in.

Amber already had her badge in her hand, reaching out with the other one. Mrs. Connelly rose and glanced at the badge and clasped Amber's hand strongly.

"Special Agent Amber Dalton, NCIS. I am investigating your son's death. Could I please have a few words with you about James?"

Mrs. Connelly said, "Yes, of course." She turned to her husband and reached out her hand to set it against his shoulder.

He lifted his devastated eyes to Amber's and she tried to muster all the compassion that was now clogging her chest.

"I'm sorry we had to meet under these circumstances." Tucking her badge into her back pocket, Amber sat down in one of the chairs. "Did James mention anything to you that was out of the ordinary here on base? In his personal life?"

"No, he said it was awesome. His instructor. Sergeant Tristan..."

"Michaels."

"Yes, him. James said he was the best instructor he'd ever had. He was learning a ton and he would be able to take so many practical things that he'd learned back into the field. James didn't mention anything to us about any problems either on base or in his personal life. He was very popular with everyone."

"If you think of anything that could help, please contact me."

They both nodded.

"Speaking of Sergeant Michaels, he is outside waiting in the colonel's office. He would like to have a word with you before you leave."

"That would be fine."

"Mr. and Mrs. Connelly, did James ever mention that he was unhappy with the service?"

Mr. Connelly startled and his eyes focused then narrowed. He frowned. "What are you saying?" he growled.

"Was there a chance that James could have gone AWOL?"

Mr. Connelly stood. The chair hit the back wall. He clenched his fists and shouted, "No! James would never desert! He was dedicated to the corps! He was… he was…"

He covered his face and sat down heavily in the chair. His wife leaned over and wrapped her arms around him, pulling him close. She looked at Amber and there were tears in her eyes.

"Agent Dalton," she said, her voice thick, "I…we understand that you are asking us hard questions. But the answer to this one is easy. James loved the service. He was going to make it his career. Both my husband and my brother Rick served, and James was very proud of them. He would never have gone AWOL. Never. He would have died before he would even think that."

Amber had to tamp down the sympathy and emotion she was feeling right now. This was about getting information about James so she could solve the mystery of his death. Give these people closure. "I know this is difficult, but I have to ask these questions. The more information I have, the more I can understand about what happened to James."

"James was…oh, God…maybe about six when my husband came back from his tour of service. We were there when he got off the plane, and as soon as he saw him, James stood to attention and saluted. He said, 'Welcome home, sir.'" The soft sound of Mr. Connelly's grief tied Amber's stomach up in knots. "He said, 'Daddy, I want to be just like you.' And my husband said, 'A soldier?'"

Mr. Connelly raised his head, his feelings of grief over the loss of his son streaming down his face, and his voice caught when he said, "'No, a hero.'"

Amber nodded. "I understand completely. Did James get along with everyone as far as you know?"

"Yes. He was very outgoing. Well liked."

Amber knew it was time to go. "I really appreciate you talking to me. I am so sorry for your loss."

"When can we take him home?" Mrs. Connelly asked, her husband clasping her hand.

"Soon. I will let you know."

"Find out what happened to our boy," Mr. Connelly said.

"I will do everything in my power to get you those answers. Here is my card." She slid the card across the conference-room table and rose.

She opened the door, then closed it behind her and leaned against the wall for just a minute. She looked up to find Tristan standing in front of her. His eyes said everything. The door opened and Mr. and Mrs. Connelly came out. Tristan turned to them and she went to walk away, but he put his hand on her arm.

"Hello, I'm Tristan Michaels."

"It's so good to meet you. James really enjoyed your instruction. Thank you for all that you did for him."

"Mr. and Mrs. Connelly. I wanted to let you know that James was the best student I've ever had in my class. I love everything about teaching what I know to men like your son. He gave more to me than I gave to him. I will always be thankful for that. You should be very proud of him. He was an exemplary student, a fine soldier and an even better man. Thank you for your sacrifice."

Mrs. Connelly wiped at the tears on her cheeks and squeezed Tristan's forearm. "Thank you for taking the time to meet us, Sergeant Michaels."

"Tristan, please."

She nodded. Mr. Connelly shook Tristan's hand and then, supporting each other, the Connellys walked down the hall and disappeared around the corner.

Amber didn't say anything for a moment, caught somewhere between respect and surprise that Tristan had opened himself up to the Connellys. It had been brewing since yesterday when he'd been drinking all alone at the table, broken that glass and then kissed her so... passionately, as if he'd been saving it up his whole life. She wanted to know more about him. Wanted to explore everything there was to know about Tristan Michaels.

But that wasn't why she was here. She was here to solve this incident, find out what happened to James and give those brave, grieving people some measure of peace.

"Now you want it even more than you did before," he said softly. His bent head made her want to smooth her hand over his enticing hair.

"Yes," she whispered. "I want it for them." She looked back down the hall. Of course they were gone, but her determination was solid. "What do you know about Randall Mayer?"

"Hardly interacted with the guy. He was always here. Rarely missed a day of work. Did a good job as far as I know."

"Why do you think he wanted to run me over?"

"Because he had something to hide. He wanted you to stop whatever investigation you were conducting."

"You think he shot James?"

"I don't know, but you have to admit that he must have tried to run you over to keep you from finding out about something."

"Maybe. What I don't get—and it's the same question I asked you about James—is why was he up in the mountains? Why didn't he run? Why did he go back up there?"

"That's a good question."

"We didn't find a weapon, either."

"No, we didn't. Maybe if we take a look at his house we can get more information."

"I thought you said you weren't an investigator, Tristan."

"I'm not."

"You're sounding like one."

"I care what happens with this investigation, Amber. I haven't cared about something in a long time."

She wished he could say that about getting involved with her. It was stupid to think that there could be anything long-term with Tristan. Hadn't she learned her lesson that long-distance relationships were a disaster? Maybe. She should have. But the problem was she hadn't felt the same way about Pete that she was feeling right now about Tristan.

It was so different. Pete was blond, shorter than Tristan and not as…big…or…broad. With Tristan's dark hair, aching blue eyes and his big, hard body, Amber was saying…Pete who?

Tristan was trying to resist her where Pete had jumped in with both feet. She had also gone to bed with him too fast. And she had to admit that it had probably been mostly physical with Pete.

No surprise there. He'd gone and got himself engaged. That said volumes to her now that she could think about it rationally and not react to the duplicity or the hurt his phone-call breakup had caused.

It was definitely more than physical with Tristan. She couldn't deny that she wanted to get her hands all over him, but there was something…more here.

Heat blossomed under her skin. Nope, no surprise at all.

"Let's go to his house and see what we can find."

Randall Mayer had an apartment in the nearby small town of Colesville. Amber wasted no time. They used Randall's key that was found in his pants discovered a few feet away from his body. As they walked inside, there was no visible gun cabinet. She disappeared into the back bedroom and Tristan looked around the living room and kitchen. Nothing out of the ordinary and nothing unusual. The guy had several hunting magazines on a long black leather ottoman coffee table. Tristan picked up one with a wolf on it gnawing on a bloody bone that was titled *Predator Xtreme* and another one, *Outdoor Life*. He threw the magazines back down as Amber came out of the bedroom.

"No gun cabinet in there."

One of the magazines slipped off the edge of the ottoman to the floor. Tristan bent down to pick it up and the toe of his boot hit the edge of the ottoman. It made a hollow sound. He froze with the magazine in his hand and gave Amber a sidelong glance. Straightening to full height, he threw the magazine in his hand onto the couch, then grabbed up the others that were there and chucked them onto the couch, too. Sure enough, the ottoman had hinges. He lifted the lid and encountered a throw and a couple of pillows. He removed them as Amber crowded him.

"What is it?"

"It could be a gun concealment bench. They're like decorative furniture that can hide guns away from small children or thieves."

As soon as the throw and pillows were removed, Tristan looked down into the obvious hidden door panel with a lock.

"Hand me his key ring," Tristan said, then searched for the appropriate key. Finding the right one, he inserted and twisted the key, pulling up the lid. The outer lid fit nicely into a groove specifically made to notch the lid and brace the cabinet open.

There was a handgun, a Ka-Bar knife and ammo in a small wooden tray suspended over four gun slots. One held a shotgun; the others were two rifles, one with a scope and one a .22. There was one more slot that must have held a gun because it was worn where the stock and muzzle would have sat.

"There's one missing," he said solemnly.

"Fuel for the fire that he was the one who shot James and then tried to run me over to derail the investigation. But what I don't understand is why try to run me over when I wasn't even close to discovering it could have been him who had maybe shot James."

"Yeah, but he did work in the colonel's office and he might have believed it was prudent to get rid of you. Something could have spooked him."

"Like what?"

"Like maybe the ammo, shells or something like that. Maybe he went back up there to cover his tracks better after he missed hitting you. Maybe he panicked and then got caught in a storm up there. It's happened before. People don't realize how fast they can freeze to death, even sportsmen."

"Speaking of that, I found this renewal notice for Sportsmen Unlimited in the other room. Looks like it might be a local chapter for the organization, but I can research that more when I get back to my laptop."

Amber and Tristan turned at the sound of the apartment door opening.

"It's customary to wait for local law enforcement before you go messing with evidence."

The sound of Garza's voice grated on Tristan. He looked over to where Garza was standing, one hand on his hip and the other propped casually on the butt of his gun. Another deputy stood just behind him. Tristan was well aware of the subtle threat men like Garza wanted to project. *I'm in charge. You are one step away from having my gun in your face if you do something I don't like. I'm the alpha dog here.*

Tristan had spent his whole life around control freaks, men who needed to exercise their authority over other men, which was exactly what made up the military. There were role models, leaders and then the guys who got off on lording it over others weaker than them. Tristan guessed that Garza had been a bully as a kid and it only escalated when he became a teenager. He was the kind of guy who also got others to do his dirty work.

Egomaniac was a mild description for the deputy. The other was that he thought Amber was his conquest and that made Tristan shift and suddenly feel proprietary and protective of Amber, who straightened away from the gun closet.

Garza caught her frown, and her eyes blazed. She turned and marched up to him, pulling out her badge. She shoved it into his face and said, low and strong, "You see this badge? This is an NCIS badge. I am a federal special agent in the Naval Criminal Investigative Service of the Department of the Navy and *any* navy or marine *anywhere* is under my jurisdiction. I don't need your permission or your sanction to investigate a crime against navy or marine personnel that I deem necessary. This badge gives me that right. Are we clear, Deputy Garza?"

"Whoa, you are feisty when you're in official capacity, Special Agent Dalton. But the sheriff's department would like to be kept abreast of the situation if that is agreeable with you."

"Just as long as you understand I don't answer to you or the sheriff."

"Got it, Special Agent Dalton," he bit out.

"Good. Now tell me what you know about Randall Mayer."

It took all of Tristan's control not to smirk, but damn. She was something else. This was a side of her he hadn't seen, and he realized that she could have dismantled him the first time they met. If there was one thing he'd learned about her it was that she could hold her own.

But she also could melt in a man's arms. He hadn't really wanted his mind to go that route, but he couldn't help it. She had made him laugh and actually participate in a snowball fight, something he hadn't done since he'd been a carefree kid with his brother, Thane, and his twin sisters when they'd been young children.

"We are looking for his car, but so far, no luck."

"Anything else you know about him?"

Garza shook his head.

"All right, pull all his licenses for any of the guns he owned. Confiscate these and have them cataloged as evidence in this investigation. And I want the autopsy results on James Connelly today, or I'll officially take possession of his body and ship it to my own medical examiner. I'm not waiting anymore for that report."

"Yes, ma'am. What is that in your hand?"

"Looks like he belonged to Sportsmen Unlimited and there's a local chapter here in town. I'm going to see what they know."

Garza nodded. Without another word, she watched them collect evidence. As soon as the door closed on the two deputies, Tristan hauled Amber against him and planted his mouth over hers. He had no idea he was going to do it. It just happened.

Her startled sound of pleasure only fueled his desire more. Ramped it up. He pushed her against the wall.

She pushed him right back against the opposite wall. They parted and she said, "Either you liked the way I chewed up and spit out Garza or you're trying to do some alpha, I'm-claiming-this-female caveman thing because he is so overtly sexual to me."

"How about both? Is that a problem?"

"No." She pressed her mouth to his again. He sent his hands through that thick head of blond, silky hair, over and over again, letting the strands trail through his fingers. He rubbed his fingers against her scalp and held her tantalizing, velvet mouth to his.

His perception clouded. He felt her tugging at his uniform shirt and then the T-shirt beneath until her palm was on his waist.

"Hmm," she murmured curiously as if she'd just encountered a puzzle.

Hmm, hell.

"Sweetheart," he cautioned, reaching around her with his free hand and gently disentangling her fingers from the material.

"What is this dang thing called?" she asked, obliging him by letting go of the T-shirt and smoothing her hand across the muscle curving over his hip and down to his groin.

"Dangerous," he replied with a grimace, catching her wayward hand before he lost it completely and let her do whatever she wanted to him.

"You are being a tease," she said.

"I'm being prudent and smart. I know my limits and, sweetheart, I'm already right there." He let go of her and quickly shoved the tail end of his T-shirt back in his pants, only to have her pull it back out.

He huffed out a laugh. "Amber, be reasonable."

"Nope. I don't want to be reasonable. You've been flaunting your great big beautiful body for days."

"I have not."

"Yes, you have. You were out shoveling snow with those amazing broad shoulders."

"I kinda needed them to…you know…heft the snow. My arms *are* attached."

"Flaunting."

"What about you with—"

"Oh, no, we're not talking about me."

He laughed again as he tried to grab her hands, but the woman was determined.

"And the first night I'm under the same roof with you, you were completely bare-chested *and* your pants were unbuttoned."

"They were? I didn't notice."

"Sure. Right. I'm a trained observer and I noticed. Oh, man, did I notice. So, admit it." She kissed over his face, down his throat, and he got totally distracted by the feel of her mouth on him. "When you broke the glass, you were also bare-chested."

"Is this a cross-examination?"

"Yes, and you'd better have a good defense. Men get to walk around half-naked and then don't think they're being teases. I'm calling you out."

"*Come* on, Amber." He tried to capture her hands again but this time failed. His T-shirt came free again, and he swore under his breath. "Well, I'm an enlightened male. I wouldn't have any problem with you being half-naked." His voice was compressed. "Equality and all that."

"Ooh, good defense."

Her hand slipped up around his back, her palm smooth, warm, intimate.

Her mouth was now in the hollow of his throat and she kissed him so gently. It had been such a long time since a woman had done that, he closed his eyes, getting lost in the sensation.

But his eyes popped open when her hand slipped lower and curved around the globe of his ass.

He grabbed for her hand and she licked him. It galvanized his balls and his dick leaped and tightened.

"Amber, the manhandling party is over."

"Tristan," she whispered. "Stop thinking all the time."

When had he ever ordered a woman to take her hand *out* of his pants? Ah, that would be this side of *freaking* never.

He captured both sides of her face in his hands. "I know I started this, but we're…somewhere…and…and I just needed to…damn…get my mouth on you."

"See, tease," she said, amusement sparkling in those deep green eyes.

She didn't wear makeup. He hadn't noticed that until right now. She didn't need it. Her lashes were thick and dark, her mouth soft and pink. Her hair was wild, absolutely wild, as if she'd been dragged across the pillows and rolled over on a mattress, the way a guy might, if he was…crazy or lucky or simply out of his ever-loving mind.

He knew better than to kiss her again. Knew it like he knew how to sight down a rifle and pull off a shot that most men couldn't make.

Knew it with all that was in him as a man.

He was losing his perspective. The one he'd had the

night he'd kissed her and sent her back to her room. The night when he'd sprawled on his bed and taken the edge off, thinking about her while he pumped his hand over his rigid dick.

He moved his hand up to cup her cheek and smooth his fingers over her skin.

Hell, he was sure that this was going to happen, even though he was trying to resist. Then she'd taken Garza apart limb by limb and set him firmly in his egomaniac place. It was worth the price of admission.

Yeah, he knew better than to do this and let her hand roam over his body like this, but he did it anyway— just let go of every freaking thing he'd believed in for fifteen years, tilted her face toward his and brought his mouth down to hers.

Heat, as pure and simple as anything he'd planned, washed through him. He groaned with the pleasure of it, gave himself over to it. Her skin was damp, and he was breaking out in a sweat, and he suddenly knew it didn't matter where they were. This ache in him for her went beyond mere walls.

She removed her hand from his backside. The other one slid through his hair, across the nape of his neck and up toward the top of his skull, holding him for her kiss. His brain was fogging. Her mouth was wet. He reached for her leg and drew it up around his waist, settling in the hollow of her pelvis, getting her closer, reveling in the tease of the silken softness he'd encounter between her legs.

Then that tantalizing, wayward hand was back against his waistband, heading south, driving him wild, and he knew—he knew she was going to take him in her hand, stroke him, get him even harder than he already was, and he was going to let her. Oh, man, was he going to let her.

"Tris," she moaned, her hand sliding the last few inches home. Oh, damn, her palm was so soft, her fingers so delicate, her leg wrapping around his waist, her hand doing the same to his cock—and he was dying... dying. But it was the sound of her voice that turned him on. Her shortening his name like that. As though they had already been lovers. He knew he was in trouble the moment he laid eyes on this woman. He couldn't breathe and he thrust into her hand, trying to find his brains in the right head.

She wanted him, and deep, deep down inside, in a dark place where he'd locked, bolted and chained the door, and thrown away the key, his emotions stirred. They stirred hard and fast, like the faster-than-the-speed-of-sound bullet that issued from the muzzle of his rifle.

He never heard her coming.

One shot to his heart, one kill. A perfect hot zero. *Ooh-rah.*

Chapter 8

Amber opened her mouth wider, took him deeper, and it still wasn't enough—not even close.

She was doomed. Nothing should be this hot, this fast, and nothing ever had been, not in her whole life, except Tristan Michaels. She'd come to MWTC for a mission—an expected short mission.

She needed to check all these loose ends, like Randall Mayer and why James Connelly was up on that mountain, where he had been for two whole days.

She hadn't come here to kiss him.

She had not come for this. But ever since she'd met the man, her heart hadn't stopped racing. It was crazy. She knew it—but God, she was a professional, and everything should have been kept at that level. Except Tristan had taken it to a different place.

The way he felt, the way he smelled, the angle of

his jaw, the nape of his neck, the way he held her in his arms, his strength—with his mouth on hers and his arms around, she never wanted to let him go.

And, damn, it wasn't supposed to be this way. She had her hand down his pants and that was not at all professional!

But she couldn't help it. What she said was true: the man was a tease, a sensual tease. All six feet plus of warm, smooth skin and ironbound muscle. He was so beautiful, a warrior with black hair and blue eyes and a face stripped of all pretense. He was what he was, and he was the first man she'd been unable to resist.

A need was building in her, totally irresistible, damnably inevitable.

Doomed.

She held his face in her hands, covering him with kisses, and he slid his hand over her buttocks and pulled her against the erection she'd just had her hand wrapped around. *Yes* was all she could think. It was too easy with him and hard all at the same time. She wished she could understand him better.

"Damn, Amber." His voice caught on a gasp as she bit his lip.

He pressed her back against the wall. It was so incredible, the sensations so intensely sweet, the rush of emotion overwhelming.

He swore softly as she ran her hands up the length of his arms. He felt so good, hard and male beneath her hands. He threaded his fingers through her hair again. The whole thing was amazing—the heat, the scent of him, the hardness of his body. It seemed like forever since she'd been with a man like this.

All he had to do was breathe to turn her on.

He sealed his mouth over hers and sucked on her tongue and just flat-out filled her whole body with the sensation of sex, from the top of her head down. Everything. Consuming her.

He moved one arm down around under her bottom, holding her tight, lifting her hips into his…

Her cell phone rang and she broke away from him, looking up at him for a startled moment. He groaned and rested his head into the hollow of her throat while she dug and fumbled for her cell phone.

"Dalton," she answered, her voice breathless.

"Agent Dalton, this is Corporal Morgan. I'm calling because I know Randall Mayer. He and I had a loose friendship since we worked together in this office. The colonel instructed me to speak with you about him."

"Yes, that would be very beneficial. Tris…" She cleared her throat. "Sergeant Michaels and I are at his apartment right now, and I want to check out the local hunting chapter for Sportsmen Unlimited, where he was a member. Ken Marshall is listed on the renewal notice as the local chapter president. We could be back to base in about an hour. Would that work?"

"Absolutely, ma'am. I will be expecting you."

She said goodbye and tucked the phone back in her pocket. Tristan had retreated, setting his clothes right, and she remembered pulling his shirt out of his pants numerous times.

He was looking out of the window, but as she'd hung up the phone, he turned back to her.

"Amber…"

She held up her hand. "What happens between us happens. You can say it was a mistake or that we shouldn't be indulging ourselves during our investigation or that we are completely out of our minds, but the bottom line is we're attracted to each other. Stuff's going to happen. You are much more uptight about it than I am. And if anyone should be uptight about it, I think that would be me. After all, I was dumped only days…ago."

"Dumped?" He stepped forward. "What the hell? You're kidding me." His face showed his disbelief and he shook his head. "Who would be such an idiot?"

Okay. What was she supposed to do with that? It was clear he was interested in her, but she didn't want to push him into something he wasn't ready for or didn't want to pursue. The fact that she wanted him was clear and she wasn't going to analyze that. Not a bit. It was embarrassing that she'd blurted it out. But she couldn't get that cat back in the bag.

"What happened?"

"Tristan…"

He took another step closer. "Amber, what happened?"

"Really none of your business."

"I'm aware of that and I don't give a damn. If we give in to this…craziness between us, I'd like to know who hurt you and why."

She didn't back down. She might not be the most experienced person in the world when it came to relationships, but what Pete had done to her was definitely rotten. Tristan wouldn't judge her—that wasn't what held her back. It was that he would have a piece of her if she spilled about it. Not that she necessarily worried about power in a relationship, because she knew she could hold her own. It was…almost…too intimate for him to hold this information about her and she knew virtually nothing about him. Well, except for the fact that he wasn't attached.

"I get it. You don't really trust me."

"It's not that. It's just that I hardly know anything about you."

"I told you, Amber. I don't do long-term relationships... Wait, do you think *I* might be involved with someone?"

She shrugged. "Men lie about that all the time."

"I'm not lying." He stepped closer still and her breath got trapped in her lungs.

Pete's duplicity had hurt her pride more than anything else, but she realized all of a sudden she was wary about getting into the same emotional situation she'd just experienced. She wanted to make it about the physical because that was easier. She would hate to think that she could come in second again. God, that would kill her. It was already the corps with him. A hidden girlfriend, fiancée or wife added to the mix just didn't sound like fun.

"I sleep around, but I'm choosy, Amber. I don't do commitment and I don't have anyone on the side. I don't think I could handle juggling two women. I have enough just handling one."

She smirked at that and the corners of his mouth curled. "So, tell me what happened now that you know a bit about me."

"That's not enough," she said, tipping her chin up slightly as he shifted closer. "How about where you're from and favorite color?"

He stepped closer still. It was a small apartment to begin with. He was definitely invading her personal space. Again. "Alaska and green, exactly the shade of your eyes."

His eyes were so intent, so deep she swore she could fall right into them and never find her way out. "Alaska... I've never been there. Your coloring might indicate you are a native Alaskan. Are you?"

"My mom is Inuit, my dad white. I really take after my dad more."

He was launching a full-out assault on her senses and it was working. "You're stalling."

"Lieutenant Peter Savich, US Navy Intelligence. He and I were in what I thought was a committed relationship, but he was in Germany and I was in DC. He was supposed to come with me to Aruba, but I found out only hours beforehand that not only wasn't he coming, a trip we planned three months ago, but he's engaged and had been for six months out of the eighteen that we were together."

"Sounds like he oughta find another line of work. Intelligent, he ain't. Is he the guy that keeps calling you and you press Ignore?"

"Yes. I can't imagine what he wants." She laughed and it felt good, leaving Pete in the past because that was where he really belonged. "You seem to think that you would somehow be taking advantage of me. You wouldn't be. Just chill about it."

"My head tells me we should cool it." But when he lifted his hand, barely brushing the underside of her jaw with his fingertips, and tipped her head back a bit farther...she let him.

"Right. It would probably be smart."

"Trouble is, beautiful Amber, I think about you,"

he said, his voice nothing more than a rough whisper. "Much too often. In a wholly distracting way."

"Ditto," she whispered back. "So, let's give ourselves a break and go talk to this Ken Marshall and see what he has to say about Randall Mayer."

"Are you always so straightforward?" he said, letting her go and stepping back.

She started walking backward toward the door. "Yes. I find beating around the bush just so annoying. It's best to talk plain."

He followed her as she made her way back out to the cold afternoon. The sun was getting low in the sky and the temperature was still frigid. She thought fleetingly of the warm sands of Aruba.

"You really aren't what I expected for an NCIS agent."

"Maybe I'm growing on you."

He settled in the driver's seat. "Maybe you are."

She leaned back against her seat and took a deep, steadying breath as she replayed, truthfully, what had just happened here. It had been good fun between two consenting adults. Nothing more, nothing less. Certainly nothing to get all worked up over. Fortunately, she'd pushed the situation and it was solid as to where she stood. So it was crystal clear. She was back in control, if not of him, at least of herself. She was sure he knew she was no pushover he could do with whatever he pleased.

She clenched her jaw at that. Her body was already responding to even the merest thought of him doing what he pleased. *Right, you're in such control. Does a hand down his pants ring a bell?* She closed her eyes, willing herself, almost desperately, to take a quick moment to gather her wits. In his smile had been a sure promise that if he ever let loose, he was the man who knew how to keep those promises.

The drive to Ken Marshall's real-estate office took about ten minutes. Inside they found him behind a desk, his white shirt and red tie paired with a dark pair of jeans. His white hair was brushed back off his face. He had a hawk-like nose and pleasant features and was as tall as Tristan.

He rose and stuck out his hand. "Hello, folks—in the market for a house?"

"Not exactly." Amber flashed her badge instead of taking his hand. It dropped as Ken peered at it. "NCIS."

He mouthed the acronym for a moment, and then his face brightened. "Like the TV show?"

The office smelled like just-brewed coffee and mint gum. A printer was spitting out paper in a soft whirring, the only sound in the room. "Yes, just like that." She introduced Tristan. "I'm here to ask you about Randall Mayer."

The open look on his face never wavered. "What about Randy?"

"Were you friends with him? We're aware he is part of your local Sportsmen Unlimited chapter," she said.

"Yeah, he's been with the chapter since he moved here, oh, about two years ago now." He frowned. "Did he do something wrong?"

"He was found dead on the mountain this morning."

"Holy God," Ken said with what sounded like genuine shock in his voice. "What can I do to help?"

"What exactly is your chapter about?"

Now he looked more wary. "Everything sportsmen, but mostly about hunting and fishing. We share the best places to hunt and fish, about dogs, ammo, guns and scopes and bow hunting. Our members come from all around here."

"When was the last time you saw Randy?"

"Last week at our regular Thursday meeting."

"Anyone you know who might not have liked Randy very much? Would want to do him harm?"

"Not a one. He was an amicable guy, excellent skeet shooter and a seasoned hunter. How did he die?"

"Looks like hypothermia."

"Hypothermia. Hmm."

"Is that a surprise to you?" Tristan asked.

"Yeah, it is. Randy has been all over that mountain hunting and fishing. He is well aware of the dangers of hypothermia."

"It doesn't take much to muddle your thinking," Tristan responded. "Just one degree."

Ken nodded in compliance. "True, but I just find it hard to believe that Randy got caught up in that. But I guess it can happen to the best of us," he said, his voice more sad now. "I think I'll plan to talk about hypothermia for our next chapter meeting as a refresher."

"Tristan is an expert in it."

"Are you?"

He gave her a sidelong glance and said, "I teach cold-weather survival to all branches of the military, including international forces."

Ken's eyes brightened. "Would you mind presenting some of your tips to our group? We could pay you a modest speaking fee."

"No need for a fee. When is your next meeting?"

"This coming Thursday evening at seven."

"I can swing that."

As they walked out, Tristan looked pensive. "Should I have kept my big mouth shut about your skills in cold-weather survival?" she asked.

He glanced at her and smiled. "No, I don't mind speaking if it can save even one life. That's not what's bothering me."

"What is bothering you?"

"Ken's comment that he was surprised that Randy could have died from hypothermia."

"I thought the same thing. Randy lived here for two years, and according to Ken, he was a seasoned hunter. This case is puzzling because we have two dead bodies and don't know exactly why either of them was up in the mountains. James without his weapon after he'd been missing for two days and Randy after he almost ran me down. It was a risky move when the investigation was just beginning. Unless he just got spooked because he did shoot James in error."

"There doesn't seem to be a connection between James and Randy. At least not one we have found, anyway. So if we theorize that Randy did shoot James, there doesn't seem to be a reason why he would want him dead."

"Well, so far, no. There's no motive. But he did have means and it could have been an accident. I'm not sure that we will ever know since both Randy and James are dead."

"Strange we couldn't find the rifle."

They pulled up to headquarters almost to the minute that Amber had given to Corporal Morgan. He was at his desk outside the colonel's office.

He stood when they came in, and Tristan said, "At ease," indicating that Morgan should sit.

Morgan settled back in his chair, and Amber and Tristan sat down in front of his desk. Amber said, "When was the last time you saw Randall?"

"That would have been the day before yesterday."

"He wasn't scheduled to work yesterday?"

The corporal leaned forward. "No, he was. He called in sick, but it was late, like around nine or so. Randy was always punctual, and whenever he couldn't make it in, he'd call right at the duty time."

"How was he acting the day before yesterday?"

"He seemed stressed to me, like he had something on his mind."

"You don't know what, though?"

"No, ma'am."

"Anything out of the ordinary happen lately?"

"Yes, ma'am. He left early because he got a phone call."

"Did he say what the call was about?"

"No, ma'am, but the guy on the other side of the line was shouting as if he was very angry. I could hear him from my desk but couldn't make out what he was saying."

"What time did that call come in?"

"About three, maybe."

"On the office phone," Amber said hopefully.

"No, ma'am. On his cell phone."

"We didn't recover his cell," she said.

"I'm sorry I couldn't be more help, ma'am."

"No, that's a big help. Thanks for your time." She leaned forward. "Corporal Morgan, could you please pull together some stats for me?"

"Yes, ma'am," he replied, picking up a pen. "What are you looking for?"

"MWTC AWOLs in the last two years. Every branch of the service."

"Will do, ma'am."

As she rose, her cell phone rang. "Dalton."

"This is Garza. We found Mayer's vehicle at the base of the mountain. It's being towed to Impound right now. Thought I should tell you before you chewed my ass again."

"And the autopsy?"

"It'll be ready in an hour," he said.

"Send it to my email."

"Yes, ma'am."

"What about Mayer's?"

He huffed. "I asked the doc to rush it. He said he will have it for you tomorrow."

"We'll be right there."

Randy's car yielded no clues. They didn't find his rifle or his cell phone, and a previous search of his desk had also come up empty.

They were cooling their heels in the sheriff's department in Bridgeport, waiting for information from Garza on his permits.

A tall man ambled toward Amber. He was dressed in the requisite khaki uniform, with the distinctive star on his chest. "Special Agent Dalton?"

"Yes."

He reached out his big, meaty hand. "I'm Sheriff Doug Stafford."

She took his hand and he engulfed hers in a firm handshake. "This is Master Sergeant Tristan Michaels. He's my MWTC liaison."

The sheriff shook Tristan's hand, as well.

"We have those permits for you. Mayer was licensed for all the weapons you found in his apartment, including a rifle that seems to be missing."

"No leads there."

"If you'd like, the doc has finished with the body and could answer any questions you might have. He's in Bishop. I can get you directions."

"Thank you, Sheriff Stafford."

After following his directions they ended up in a lab with the autopsy tables on the left. Amber shivered, the temperature seeming as cold inside as out.

There was a balding man with a fringe of gray hair running around the side and back of his shiny pate. He was standing at a metal table with James Connelly's prone body stretched out. Soon, his parents would be able to take him home. Her heart contracted.

As they approached, the doc turned and she could see he had brown eyes with a pair of half-glasses perched on his nose. He was dressed in a white lab coat with a clipboard in his hand.

"Can I help you?"

Amber introduced herself and Tristan, and he nodded. "Yes, I've been expecting you. Dr. Carl Thompson," he said.

"The distinction of the wound is significant and answers one of your questions regarding the possibility of friendly fire. Rifle bullets fall into two general categories—hunting bullets and military bullets. Hunting bullets are designed to expand." He fanned out his fingers in demonstration. "In the process at least some fragmentation of the bullet occurs. Thus, with this type of bullet, wounding is more extensive with tissues ending up being a combination of crushed and shredded.

"Military bullets, by virtue of their full metal jackets, tend to pass through the body intact, thus producing less extensive injuries than hunting ammunition. Military bullets usually do not fragment in the body or shed fragments of lead in their paths, because of the high velocity of such military rounds as well as their tough construction. This is not the case for your victim. There is no exit wound and I found fragments that exhibited the characteristics of a hunting round. He had the requisite lead-snowstorm effect, which went in through the back but missed the heart. Your victim might have survived the gunshot wound if he had received immediate medical attention."

"What was the cause of death, then, Dr. Thompson?"

"Hypothermia." He took off his half-glasses. "I recovered enough of a fragment to run ballistics. I sent that to our expert."

"Thank you," Amber said as Tristan stared down into James's face. She could see the regret and pain there, and now it seemed as if there was also guilt. After they left the morgue, Tristan was quiet. The news that James might have lived if he'd been found sooner had shaken him. She could see it in his eyes and the solemn look on his face.

By this time, it was full dark and she was exhausted and had to come to the conclusion that this was an accidental death. She had found no evidence that Mayer had shot Connelly. With both of them dead and no witnesses, she would have to consider this case inconclusive, which meant that her work here was done.

Unless she found Mayer's gun.

She decided to stay until she received the autopsy report from Dr. Thompson regarding Mayer's death to wrap up any loose ends and thoroughly investigate his death.

When they walked into Tristan's town house, her phone buzzed and she accessed her email on her smartphone to discover that the autopsy report had been delivered.

"No friendly fire," Tristan said, reading the report over her shoulder. "Just a hunting accident. His life was ended by mistake."

"I know," she soothed, tenderness making her chest hurt. "It's a tragedy, but at least his parents will get closure."

Tristan nodded, looking exhausted and lost again. Alone.

"I can make—"

"I'm not hungry," he said.

"Tristan, this isn't your fault."

"I keep going over it in my head, over and over. I just don't know what I could have done differently. Do you know what it did to me when the coroner said he would have survived if he'd gotten medical attention? He lay out in the cold and froze to death, alone. Probably scared to death. He was just a kid!"

She reached out and touched his forearm, which was just as tense as the rest of him. He sat down heavily on the sofa. Amber lowered herself next to him and without hesitation wrapped her arms around him. He resisted at first, then made a soft sound and buried his face in her neck. She held him against her, his breathing ragged, wishing she could ease his pain.

He had to handle his grief the way he needed to handle it. No matter how much she wanted to soothe him, she could only offer the comfort of her words and her embrace.

Chapter 9

Amber stirred and opened her eyes, taking a moment to orient herself. She was still on the sofa. It was still dark in the house. No lights, but the warmth of Tristan's big body was gone. She blinked in the semidarkness, the ambient light from the cold full moon shining through the front window.

She was so in tune with Tristan's presence that she felt him before she saw him. Being in his dark house with him just standing at the window seemed so intimate. It was as if her skin was electrified, and her heart pounded hard. Struggling to hang on to her equilibrium, to maintain some balance, she swallowed hard, then rose.

Tristan didn't turn. "You should go to bed, Amber," he said, his voice very low and gruff.

Amber wanted to stay, go to him and offer whatever

comfort she could. Clenching her hands into fists, she eased in an unsteady breath. "Good night, Tristan."

She heard him follow, and he said, "Good night, Amber."

Unexpectedly close to tears, she headed for her upstairs room. Then she stood in the hall watching as he went into his room and closed the door.

She slipped into her room and shut the door behind her. Her expression taut, she toed off her socks, then stripped her clothes off, donning a pair of thermal underwear with hearts all over it and a pink tank top. She climbed blindly into bed. Draping her arm across her eyes, she tried to will away the ache, tried to collect a modicum of common sense. This was just chemistry, she tried to tell herself. Attraction and just two lonely people, she mentally argued. *You're kidding yourself* was all her conscience had to say.

She pulled up Tristan's file on her computer. Her finger hovered over the open button. She'd had the file for some time. Beau had sent it to her a while back, but she'd been reluctant to open it. She had initially requested it because she wanted to go over everyone and everything related to this case. But if she opened that file now, she would be doing it because it was personal. She'd be violating his privacy. Still, she had a deep-seated need to find out more about him.

She clicked Open and started reading. Fifteen minutes later, she was twisted up inside and her heart was breaking for him. She closed the file.

Feeling heavy compassion for Tristan, she wrestled with the fact that she was probably going to be gone by tomorrow night. There was no more time to explore any kind of situation with Tristan. He didn't want it and she was out of time.

Turning on her stomach, Amber pulled the pillow under her and groaned. She didn't think she could stand that awful unsatisfied ache throbbing through her whole body. Even the weight of the bedding was torture against her sensitized skin.

Feeling as if she was going slowly crazy, Amber got up and went to stand by the window, hoping the view and the cooler air would bring her some peace.

Trying to breathe around the thick emotion in her chest, she fought for some control, closing her eyes, willing whatever amount of calm she could muster into her body.

But the squeak of the door to Tristan's room snapped her eyes open, and her pulse began to hammer all over again. And she knew, as sure as she was standing there, that he was downstairs, also unable to sleep. Just like her. And she wondered if he was still beating himself up over James or if he, too, was wrestling with something else. Like that Banyan consulate incident she had just read about in his file. Could it still be tormenting him even fourteen years later?

As if that one thought connected her to him, Amber got nailed with another immobilizing rush. Her mind spinning, she rested her face against the cool glass.

God, he was so alone. She couldn't stand the thought of him down there, struggling with that aloneness laced with guilt. A terrible ache settled around her heart and she remembered how he'd tenderly carried her after Mayer almost succeeded in running her over. How he had fought his desire even then.

Experiencing another heavy rush, Amber clenched

her jaw, her whole body responding to that memory. She was losing it, really losing it. It was almost as if he'd reached out and touched her, caressing her in the most intimate way. She flattened both hands against the glass, her breathing coming in ragged puffs. She could not bear his aloneness. She just could not stand it anymore.

Never in her life had Amber acted on impulse, but she acted on impulse now. Her eyes burning with tears, she snatched up her robe and roughly tied the belt around her waist, a weird kind of anger setting her resolve. She just could not—could not—leave him down there alone. Not Tristan.

Fortified with a crazy kind of determination, she slipped down the stairs, her heart growing larger and more cumbersome with every step, her nerves vibrating so badly that she was shaking. She didn't have a clue what she was doing. But she didn't care. One thing she did know for sure—going to Tristan could never be a mistake.

She hit the bottom of the stairs, looking for him in the dim light. Clasping the front of her robe, she turned, the flooring cold against her bare feet.

The full moon cast long milky shadows in the yard, glinting off the snow, and far in the distance, one of the MWTC choppers broke the silence. Her pulse sounding like heavy surf in her ears, she rounded the corner to the kitchen, her insides turning over in a crazy roll when she spotted Tristan.

The kitchen had only curtains, no blinds, and the moonlight draped him like liquid silver. He was standing with his head bowed, both hands clamped on the counter, the coffee carafe filled with water. Dressed only in a pair of blue pajama bottoms, his bare back gleamed in the moonlight, and even in the faint light she could see the awful tension in him.

Her vision blurring with the enormity of her feelings, Amber spoke his name and started toward him.

Tristan abruptly straightened, his body going still. Amber could swear she could feel the tension leaping between them. She didn't have a plan, hadn't thought it out, but just when her nerve nearly faltered, Tristan shifted and she got a good look at his face. Seeing the agony in his eyes, she simply reacted.

Her voice catching on a sob, she spoke his name again, then stepped into his arms, his agony becoming hers.

Another sound was wrenched from her as Tristan crushed her in a hard, fierce embrace, his hand roughly tangling in her loose hair as he jammed her head against him.

Immobilized by the onslaught of need, Amber clung to him, certain she would collapse if he let her go. She had never experienced anything like it—the heavy surging of feeling two halves coming together, the awesome power of two universes colliding, the stunning rush of wanting. It had been too long for her, this push-pull with him. And now it was all too much—too much need, too much unsatisfied hunger, too much raw emotion. Yet not nearly enough. Lord, not nearly enough.

Her breathing out of control, she locked her arms around him, pulling herself flush against him, needing him, needing more.

Hoarsely whispering her name, Tristan backed her into the shadows, then spread his hand wide in her hair and turned her head. His heart pounded in tandem with hers, and he brushed his mouth across hers. The surge of raw sexual energy was like being struck by a lightning bolt.

Her breathing ragged, she lifted herself higher and opened her mouth, needing the heat of him. Tristan shuddered, grinding his mouth against hers as he crushed her even tighter. Body to body, heat to heat, he took her mouth, and Amber yielded everything to him, her need fired higher by his.

Everything she had ever believed about herself— about the kind of woman she was, about her moderate level of sexuality—was simply incinerated by that hot, wet plundering kiss. Making a sound of restraint, he tried to tear his mouth away, but she grasped his face, holding him to her, unable to bear a separation. She knew if they didn't finish this, if they didn't take this to the final completion, she would simply crumble into tiny pieces.

His breathing was raw and labored as he ripped his mouth away and fumbled to untie the belt of her robe, roughly pushing her pajama bottoms off her. Another tremor shuddered through him when he touched her nakedness.

Terrified he might stop, that he might do the honorable thing, Amber locked her arms around his neck, her breath catching. But he had not thought of stopping. Yanking back the robe, he hooked one arm under one leg and lifted her up. Pelvis against pelvis, he held her fast as he claimed her mouth again, his thick hardness fused against her.

Amber had never known this fever of need, this raw, urgent hunger, and she gave herself up to the frenzied sensations, knowing Tristan would not let her fall.

Roughly changing the angle of his mouth, Tristan

thrust against her, and the pulsating heaviness in her groin intensified. Desperate for more, Amber sobbed and locked her legs around him, transfixed by the unbelievable sensations he'd set off inside her. He moved again and she clutched him, her senses disintegrating, desperate for more, much more.

Tearing her mouth away, she lifted herself higher, her voice barely coherent. "Please, Tristan. Please," she begged hoarsely, rubbing against him again. The unsatisfied pulse thickened, and she found his mouth, desperate for the taste of him, wanting to center her pulsating need.

On a jagged intake of air, Tristan caught her jaw and dragged his mouth away, then jammed her head under his jaw. His breathing still raw and labored, he tried to gentle his hold. Fighting a lungful of air, he stroked her head, his voice so rough it was as if he was speaking through some unmanageable pain. "Amber," he whispered brokenly, his breath hot against her ear. "Damn, but I can't take that kind of risk with you."

But Amber was too far gone to stop. She was protected by the pill. The hunger centered in her was getting stronger. She rocked her pelvis, her breathing just as labored as his. "It's okay," she pleaded with him, her voice breaking. "It's okay. Please, Tristan."

Desperate to persuade him, she moved against the hard ridge under the soft cotton of his pj pants, and he clutched her and stiffened, his body rigid with tension. She moved again, and he clutched her tighter. Then abruptly he turned, backing her against the counter. Bracing her weight, he fumbled with his pants, and Amber cried out when she felt him free and hard.

Blinded by sensation, she arched, expecting him to thrust into her, but instead he pressed his hard heat against her moistness. He started to move, sensitizing her even more. The sensations began to gather and Amber stiffened, right on the brink. On the very brink. As if aware of what was happening to her, he choked out her name and thrust his hardness into her, his body grinding into hers. And in that instant, Amber lost contact with reality.

Every thrust sent her higher and higher until her whole body focused into one white-hot light; then everything exploded, and pulses of release ripped through her, a million lights going off in her head. And on a tortured groan, Tristan twisted his hips, his own release pumping into her.

Incoherent and shattered, she hung on to him for dear life—on to her lifeline, her rock, her center.

It seemed as if an eternity passed before bits of consciousness sifted down, like remnants of fireworks. Trembling and weak, and feeling as if every bone in her body had been liquefied, she folded around him, aware of how tightly he was holding her, aware of how badly he was trembling.

Her face wet with tears, she wrapped both arms around his head and tightened her legs, an unbearable tenderness welling up in her as she cradled him against her.

She was so shattered, she was incapable of speech. But she was filled to the brim with feelings for him, and she gently combed her fingers through his hair, wishing she could wrap up every inch of him. He was so infinitely special. So infinitely precious.

Tristan turned his face against her neck, his hand moving to cup her jaw. Then as if too spent to move, he tightened his hold. His voice was muffled as he spoke, his tone very gruff. "Are you okay?"

Moved beyond words by his concern for her and overcome with the need to comfort him, she pressed her mouth against his temple. Her own voice was uneven as she whispered, "I'm better than okay." She stroked his head, then hugged him. "I think I'm in heaven."

His chest rose on a deep intake of air. Then he tightened his grip on her face for a moment. He didn't say anything but she felt him smile. And she hugged him again.

As if gathering together what remaining strength he had, Tristan slid his other hand up her back. "Hold on."

She nodded, wrapping herself around him even tighter.

The muscles in his back bunched as he carried her across the kitchen. With a minimum of fuss, he carried her up the stairs into his room.

Amber knew she should let go and stand on her own, but the thought of separating from him was just too much to bear. Instead, she hung on even tighter, her throat cramping. She could not bear to let him go. She just could not. It would be like ripping her own body in half to disconnect from him.

At the edge of the bed and with Amber still wrapped around him, he paused, pushed his pants down and stepped out of them, then slid his hand under her robe. His touch was gentle, caressing. "Let's get rid of this," he said, his tone husky.

Trusting him to hold her, Amber straightened and

let the garment slip off her arms. He maneuvered her pj top off, and then she wrapped herself back around him. She felt him take a deep breath as she kissed him just beneath his ear. Another faint tremor coursed through him, and he tightened his hold on her.

His breath caught and he clutched her. Amber closed her eyes and hung on, his movement bringing on another contraction.

Finally, after what seemed like some aeons, Tristan locked his arm around her hips, turning his face against her neck. He spoke, a tinge of amusement in his voice. "I think we're both going to fall—hope for the best."

Smiling in response, Amber flattened her hand between his shoulders. "Tell you what—I'll leave the how in your skilled hands."

She was rewarded with a husky chuckle. "Well, then, you'd better hang on." He shifted his hold. Then with sheer strength and physical finesse, he got them into his bed, with her flat on her back and him cradled between her upraised knees. The feel of his body on top of hers made her go breathless and just a little bit crazy again.

Bracing his weight on his elbows, he lifted his head and gazed down at her, the moonlight washing his face. Taking her face in his hands, he studied her, a slow smile appearing. His voice was like rough velvet when he spoke. "Ooh-rah, Amber, you are something else."

Holding back a grin, she reached up and caressed his mouth. "You have a few ooh-rah moves yourself, handsome."

His smile deepened. "You're a piece of work, you know that?"

She did grin. "I'm up for the challenge."

He laughed, a low throaty laugh that sent delicious shivers up her spine. "Yes, you are."

Aware that they were both avoiding what had brought them together, Amber raised her head and kissed him along his jaw. It was almost as if they'd silently struck another pact not to open too many doors, and that was okay. This was too special to risk.

Wanting to keep that comfortable easiness between them, she looped her arms around his neck and gave him another grin. She didn't know why, but she wanted to see if she could make him react. Keeping her voice deliberately provocative, she murmured, "You're very, very good, marine."

Chuckling, he gave her head a little shake. "You know how to be a tease. You make me crazy."

Smiling at the ache in his voice, she ran her hand down his muscled back to his buttocks. "I bet I can make you wild and crazy."

His expression altered, and even in the faint moonlight filtering in, she could see his eyes darken, his gaze becoming hot and intimate. Gazing at her, he stroked her cheeks with his thumbs, then lowered his head, brushing his mouth against hers. "Oh, yeah," he breathed, caressing her bottom lip. "That works for me."

With that one light touch, Amber's heart started stammering, and suddenly it was impossible to breathe. Pulling his head down, she brought his mouth into full contact with hers.

The kiss was slow, soft and so unbelievably gentle that it left her absolutely breathless, and her whole body turned to jelly. He flipped her onto her stomach, his hand trailing down her back, followed by his mouth. He made a soft sound at the flag tattoo that went across her lower back. He kissed her skin and murmured, "Sexy." A sudden urgency sizzled through her and she lifted her bottom against the thick erection pressing between her legs from behind to urge him on.

Entering her from behind, he sent his big hand up her rib cage, clasping around her breast as he thrust against her buttocks. Dragging both her arms over her head, he laced his fingers through hers, holding her hands against the bed. "Easy, baby," he whispered, his hot mouth on her neck. "We're going to take our time— slow and easy." He stroked her palms with his thumbs and shifted ever so gently against her. "This time we're going to make it last."

Amber's heart nearly climbed right out of her chest. She didn't think she could stand it. She really didn't. He'd only started and it was too much already.

And Tristan did take his time—goodness, did he take his time. It was just like the kiss, slow, soft, gentle. And painstakingly thorough—inch by inch. Amber had no idea a man could be that dedicated to detail, and he set off reactions she'd never, ever experienced before. She couldn't think of anything, except what he was doing to her. He took it slow and easy. He nearly drove her off the deep end, and she was practically clawing at the bedding before he gave in to her. She was sure she was on the verge of losing her mind when he finally thrust into her, driving her up and over into a soul-shredding release. It was so unbelievable, so explosive, it was as if she came right out of her body. And he was the only thing that held her together.

Like it or not, there was a connection here, stronger than she'd ever experienced with Pete, but she was left with reality. She would go and he would stay in the service.

Like Pete, she would lose him, not to distance, but to duty.

Chapter 10

The first faint hint of dawn had already crept into the room, and Amber awakened, a heavy lethargy swimming through her, the weight of Tristan's arm around her middle anchoring her. She felt as if she didn't have a muscle left in her entire body.

But the pleasant feeling was suddenly dominated by a feeling of enormous responsibility. This was all her doing. All hers. She was not going to let anything detract from what had happened the previous night. She just wasn't. For once in her life, she was not going to assess her actions—or his. And for once in her life, she was not going to be logical and rational. Her much-vaunted sensibleness could just get stuffed. For once, she was going to follow her heart.

It was an easy road to take, snuggled securely in the curve of Tristan's big, beautiful body. Tucking her hands under her face, she basked in the afterglow of finally getting this man to be honest about his needs, his feelings, because there were some. She was quite sure of that. Her heart stumbled as she recalled everything that had happened in that bed. He was amazing, and she had lost count of how many times they'd made love.

Her thoughts stirred up a sexual restlessness in her. She closed her eyes, wanting it to happen all over again. Wanting to turn into his arms, wanting to feel him awaken, wanting him to slip inside her.

Her breathing suddenly uneven, Amber took a hard deep breath and opened her eyes. She had to use the bathroom, but she didn't want to disturb him, especially since his arm was tightly around her as if in his sleep he was afraid of losing her.

She got a bit discombobulated about that. Then he shifted, sighing softly, in a wholly male, totally sexy, deep way, breathing her name on a wisp of sound.

She turned toward him. God, he was so beautiful— and she noticed the scars on his body she was sure were shrapnel. Low on his rib cage, an unmistakable round mark that could only be a healed bullet wound. She reached out and traced the raised tissue. Her hand looked small and delicate against his wide rib cage, pale against his sun-warmed skin.

She let out a heavy sigh, then took a deep breath, maintaining control. She wasn't going to lose it, not here, not now, not with him.

She wasn't a fool, and no matter how connected she was to him, the reality was he was entwined with the corps. His identity was deeply entrenched.

"Amber…" he murmured, "…smell good." He rolled onto his stomach, his breath leaving him on another sleep-filled sigh and warming her shoulder.

Amber realized that having knowledge about what Tristan really did for the Marines gave her an unfair advantage over him. First off, she knew more about him than she'd told him, and second, she'd had time to mesh the man with the file.

He was more than just a sniper and his file held a lot of classified information. Tristan was black ops, a Force Recon marine. He was an elite operator, the kind of man that could use stealth and deliver lethal action from out of thin air.

Knowing that he was legendary in his work and one of the best US Marine Recon operators that had ever served only made her all the more determined not to make him choose between her and the corps. In his file, Dr. Cross had evaluated Tristan's mental state after he'd come off that Force Recon mission in bad shape. It showed the extent of his dedication and his guilt.

He went off the grid, which isn't surprising for a Recon marine. That isn't my worry. It's that he exhibits self-destructive behavior that is too wholly connected to the corps and his identity as a man is connected to what he does as a marine. I feel that Master Sergeant Michaels needs the time to understand himself in terms of who he is outside of being a marine. He would benefit from an assignment that has him training others and getting a mental break from constant field service that could have caused enough stress to alter his thinking.

It's my recommendation that he be forced into another duty assignment and no longer be approved for any missions until he is reassessed after eighteen months. Once that time frame is up and after it's clear that he's had a chance to assimilate the concepts that

I have put forth to him, then he would have the opportunity to go back into the field.

Master Sergeant Tristan Michaels is a very dangerous man, definitely to our enemies, but also to himself. It would be prudent to give him the time that he needs to work out who he is outside of the missions, the danger, the stress, the constant need to rise above his duty and simply rest. He's earned this. He wouldn't admit to me or to his commanding officer that he is fatigued. That would be admitting that he was weak and/or had failed the corps in some way.

To conclude, the consulate tragedy where Master Sergeant Michaels lost his objectivity regarding his own identity and that of the corps was a turning point in his young life. His dedication and courage and sense of duty propelled him into an exemplary field operator who has saved countless lives in the fulfillment of his duty.

Please be advised that Master Sergeant Michaels will not be amenable to the cessation of field operations. He has told me that he feels that the reaction to his disappearance is being overblown and he is more than fit for duty. So he didn't check in and was a bit undernourished and dehydrated. He's fully recovered and ready for duty.

But, of course, as my previous comments indicate, I am not convinced of this, and as his therapist I believe the next time he goes out could be his last. His abilities and skills are not in question. It's his thinking that needs altering. He needs a healthy balance between his dedication and his duty. He needs to discover the value of what he has to offer others against the isolation of completing a mission that puts him in imminent *danger. There must be a balance between these, as well as good, solid judgment as to the best way to carry out his mission.*

He is a very personable young man, and I am sure that with some mental and physical rest, he will see that he jeopardized not only his mission but himself in the process. His judgment must be sound and balanced in making decisions about his welfare, the welfare of his platoon members and the good of this country.

I understand the need for tough, brave, well-trained and disciplined operators. It's imperative, but MS Tristan Michaels needs to be sidelined for his own good and the good of the corps.

He had more medals than she could count, commendations up the wazoo, and all this because he was completely dedicated 100 percent to what he did. It left nothing over for anyone in his life. She knew all this before she slept with him, before she'd got attached. But sometimes some things were worth the heartache and the pain that would follow.

He was worth it.

Because he was gung ho about what and who he was. Until he could separate himself from what he did, there wasn't much of a future for them.

It appeared that Tristan was still caught up in what his therapist stated was his inability to see himself separate from the corps. It wasn't about the fact that he couldn't commit to her, to pursuing a relationship that was something more than physical, because Amber was sure it was. She had no doubt.

She wanted that chance to help Tristan see it and become it, but no one could alter the course of someone else's thinking.

And her own issues were not insignificant, like the one where she needed to prove to everyone she met that she wasn't second-best. That she was worthy got twisted into nothing but a competitive situation that only led to strife.

He'd shown her that regardless of his dedication to the corps, he could feel and react to her on a personal and very intimate level. More so than any man she'd ever met. She wasn't sure if that was because he'd worked so hard to be the man he saw in his mind's eye or if it was because of his own personal experiences, but Amber saw it and reacted to it. She needed to let go of being perfect, being number one, and settle for being the best that she could be in that situation. It took an enormous amount of stress off her and made her feel lighter than air.

She was now exactly where Tristan was worried she'd be. There was no getting around it, and even though it hurt, she wasn't sure she wanted to change anything. He'd wanted her and had in that moment been able to transcend his resistance. Had the courage to give in and let this wonderful thing happen.

She knew what it all meant. He'd been in a terrible fight, and the only kind of fight Tristan was ever in was a firefight—bullets flying, life or death, no quarter asked, none given, everybody out for blood. The one that had almost ended his life on that mission where he'd disappeared.

He was the US government's gunslinger.

But he had to figure out what else he was good at besides gunslinging. That was his dilemma. Not whether to take this job with his friend Rock or not, but about whether or not he could define himself away from the corps.

The fact that she understood didn't help. She would be leaving here probably tomorrow, maybe even today if she could wrap things up and get a flight out of Reno. Get to the vacation she really needed.

Reaching up, she gently ran her fingers back through his thick hair, her fingers caressing a face of high cheekbones and lean angles, a beautifully formed nose. Carefully, softly, she touched her mouth to his, then pushed herself away. She didn't get far.

In an instant, he was awake, his hand coming up and holding her in the bed, his eyes wide open—every muscle and tendon in his body tight and radiating one single message: ready.

Ready for anything was more like it. She was startled by his sudden transition into utter and complete wakefulness. Good Lord, he'd been sound asleep, snoring.

"Don't go," he said, holding her gaze, his voice soft, a sleepy contrast to the alertness pulsing through him like a heartbeat.

"I…I wasn't going." At least not very far. She acknowledged the fact that she should put some space between them, get some air, give herself at least a half a chance to think straight. Something that was impossible to do when she was close enough to breathe him in—and they were close. One of his legs was half over her, his right arm extended and clasped around her waist. With every breath he took she felt his stomach rise against her. "Just need to use the facilities."

"Good." His hot blue gaze slid past her to the door. His face was stark, his expression deadly serious, as he watched the emotions play across her face.

It gave her pause. It unnerved her. She knew what he was doing—searching for threat in her and in his surroundings, which sent a small shiver through her. The thought that she could hurt him wasn't something that sat well with her. Because she had to eventually go.

He looked at her for a second, an unreadable expression on his face, before his gaze slid away again.

"Amber, I…" He started to say something but then didn't, and suddenly she felt a little tongue-tied herself.

Oh, yeah, she thought, they were getting off to a great start. The silence drew out between them. Then it extended until she couldn't quite bear it.

She pulled out of his grasp and ducked into his bathroom, shutting the door and doing what needed to be done.

After taking care of business, she came back out. He was still on his stomach, lying on the pillows and looking sexy and better than any man had a right to look. Seeing him propped up on those pillows—his arms over his head, showcasing the tantalizing curve of his biceps, his torso bare and heavily muscled—made her completely weak in the knees.

Only half of his face was visible as he lay against the linens, his dark hair such a contrast to the white pillowcase. The heavy stubble on his face and his one eye were enough to melt her bones. God, the way the man *looked* at her.

His arm flexed and he reached out his hand. There was no way to resist, no way to tell him that this was going to hurt them both when it was over, no way to avoid the damage that was coming.

She knew he could see it, too.

She stepped closer and slipped her hand into his. The warmth of him shivered over her.

"Are you cold?" His whole demeanor heightened.

She closed her eyes and swallowed. "No."

He drew her against the bed and she folded down. Bringing her hand to his mouth, he pressed a kiss to her palm, his velvet lips brushing up over the heel of her hand to her wrist. Everything just going liquid.

He rose up and pressed his face into the center of her body, his arm sliding around her back. She ran the palm of her hand over his silky hair. "Tristan," she whispered as he kissed her stomach, licking her skin, drawing her nipples into hard, aching knots.

He bit her rib cage, drew his teeth up to the underside of her breast, and she gasped, her fingers tightening in his thick hair. As he turned his body to better feast on her, she saw that he was completely hard, completely erect. He was a well-endowed man, and she covered his smooth, hard erection from the base of his balls all the way to the tip.

With a growl, he thrust into her hand and clamped his mouth over her breast, sucking hard. She cried out, and he dragged her down with a powerful thickening of his biceps until she was beneath him.

Then his mouth was all over her.

Tristan couldn't think. The taste of Amber was in his bloodstream, a powerful pressure in his chest, his dick, his heart.

And, damn, it wasn't supposed to be this way.

She should have been like any other woman he'd bedded. The act was what was good, not the woman he held in his arms. But it was the opposite here and maybe that was why he'd resisted so hard—because he'd known she would blow his mind, blow him out of the water.

She was soft and wet as his fingers slipped over her core, and when she arched, her nipple popped out of his mouth.

"Geezus, Amber." He rocked against her, then lifted her hips and pressed against the heat of her, his dick throbbing. "Wrap your legs around me, babe," he said, watching the way her face absorbed all the sensations he was stirring in her.

Then he was pushing inside her—and everything slowed down, way down.

It was incredible, the sensations intensely sweet, the rush of the emotion overwhelming.

He swore softly. She felt amazingly good. He nuzzled her neck, thrusting into her, and felt himself die a little from the pleasure—and the pain.

There was no way on earth for him to stop.

How was he supposed to let her go?

His hand fisted in her hair and he pulled her head back, exposing the beautiful column of her throat. The whole thing was amazing, the heat, the smell, the softness—Amber taking him again and again. It had been so long. It had been forever since he'd been inside a woman, and this was Amber. All she had to do was breathe to make him hot.

But she did more, sealing her mouth over his and sucking on his tongue and just flat-out filling his whole body with the exquisite tension that only she could seem to evoke in him.

He moved and tucked his arm under her bottom, holding her tighter, lifting her, pushing deeper—and then he came. He felt the warning signals, felt that first sweet edge of release and was helpless to stop it. He didn't have the strength. He didn't have the will. Not this time.

Oh, God. It was soul wrenching, a melting orgasm that started at the back of his skull and the base of his groin and flowed out of him, taking him deep inside himself, deep inside her. It was timeless sensation, and it lasted forever, and all the while she kissed him, holding him, her mouth on his so hot and sweet.

"Amber..." he groaned, pushing himself deeper, his body shuddering. He'd needed her for so long—even before he'd met her—only her.

He buried his face in her throat as the powerful wash of pleasure drowned him in wave after hot wave.

His breathing ragged, his heart pounding, he collapsed on top of her and she wrapped her arms around him. "Tristan," she whispered as the room began to lighten with the dawn. A dawn he didn't want to come. There was more to come in this investigation, but it was winding down and he knew it. She knew it. Looked as though Randall Mayer had killed James in a hunting accident.

She would be able to write her report and the case would be closed and she would head off to Aruba. He would once again have his house back. He'd eat alone and sleep alone. He'd prove he was fieldworthy again and he'd go back out. More black ops and secret missions. More of serving his country and the corps, because that was what he was all about.

He would let Rock know that he couldn't take the job he was offering. He was dedicated, and with dedication came the duty and the oaths he swore to uphold. Getting out left him feeling empty and...scared.

He closed his eyes as her hand went over his head, her caress so…loving. Damn, he didn't want to go there. He didn't want to acknowledge how sweet, how tough, how desirable Amber was to him. It would only make it that much harder to say goodbye.

"Don't, Amber," he whispered, his voice rough and uneven. "Don't."

Turning into his embrace, Amber pressed her face against his neck and took a deep breath. He supported her upper body and he wrapped one arm around her back. "We'll get through this and it will all be okay. Copy that?"

"Solid copy," she said, moving her head and looking him in the eyes. "Can I ask you to hold me? Until the morning? Until whatever happens, happens?"

Stroking her sweet, flushed face, her hair a tousled beautiful mess, he smiled, then dragged her hard against him, squeezing his eyes shut.

It was a long time before he let her go, before he was emptied out enough to regain some control, and it was even longer before he was finally able to let the last of it go in a rough, shuddering sigh. He felt so raw inside, it was as if he had been stripped.

He settled against the mattress, taking her down with him, not even allowing an inch of air between them. She closed her eyes and huddled in the crook of his body, the terrible hollow feeling persisting in his chest.

He fell asleep again with her snuggled close to him. When he woke up, the shower was going and the clock read six.

He got out of bed and entered the steamy room. Pushing back the curtain, he met her eyes and, tough cookie that she was, she smiled. "Good morning, handsome." Reaching out, she pulled him inside.

They washed each other, and he took great pleasure in shampooing her hair, all those thick blond locks soapy and silky against his hands. He massaged her scalp and she leaned into it.

"You've got some magic hands there, marine."

He kissed her neck. "You're damn beautiful for an NCIS agent, sweetheart."

She giggled and he wrapped his arm around her waist and drew her against his body. Then he slapped her soapy, wet butt as she jumped forward and punched him on the arm. "Rinse," he ordered.

She gave him a watch-out look and complied. As soon as she was done, she picked up the shampoo bottle and squeezed out a dab. She pushed him into the spray and said, "Lean your head back."

He dropped his head and she slipped those wonderful fingers of hers into his hair and gently roved over his scalp, giving him as good as she got. He groaned softly and she pressed little kisses against his shoulder blades and to the middle of his back.

She told him to rinse.

Once they were done, they stepped out and he enjoyed helping her to dry off with a big fluffy towel, stealing kisses as he went.

She cupped his face and ran her thumb along his cheekbone. "You're not so tough, Tris."

"Yeah, well, don't go spreading that around."

"Darn those man points." She laughed and wrapped her towel around her. She leaned in and gave him a long, wet, knee-melting kiss. "I'm making pancakes again."

He couldn't speak, only nodded.

Then she was gone. As he ran the water for his shave, he ignored that wayward inside voice telling him to stop being an ass. But he was sure about his course of action. He'd been working for eighteen months to get his field-operator position back. He intended to go into Doc Cross's office and pass his damn test.

He closed his eyes, remembering those three months he'd been off the grid. After Tony, the other marine in the op, died, Tristan had to constantly move. Any other Recon marine would have cut his losses and given up the mission. But Tristan couldn't fail. He'd carried Tony's body back through enemy lines, not once being seen, dropped him at the base, filed his report and gone back out. He'd ignored orders, ignored his common sense. All that he could think about was getting the mission done and done right.

He looked at himself in the mirror, his blue eyes looking haunted. Doc Cross had tried to tell him it was battle fatigue and that he wasn't making rational decisions because of the death of Tony. Tristan wouldn't admit to him that seeing Tony die had brought back all the consulate crap he'd thought he'd put in the past.

"Maybe you were right about that, Doc," Tristan said to his reflection. And if Doc Cross was right about that, maybe he'd been right about other things.

Tristan turned off those thoughts. This kind of thinking wouldn't get him back in the field.

He finished shaving his face and headed down to the delicious aroma of pancakes. As he went to the coffeemaker to set it to brew, Amber's cell phone rang. She answered it in her usual upbeat voice. Then she said, "Where?" After listening for a moment, she looked at Tristan and he knew this was a significant find.

"Please have it tested ASAP." Then she hung up.

"What is it?"

"That was Garza. He found Mayer's rifle. He took a chance, he said, and followed along what he surmised would have been Mayer's trail if he had killed James by mistake. He said he found it buried in the snow. They're going to run ballistics on it now."

He could see it in her face. This was going to be the next-to-last piece of evidence they needed to close this case. The only other piece would be Mayer's autopsy.

It was just one step closer to Amber leaving.

He should be relieved.

He wasn't.

Chapter 11

"Everything is going to plan. That bitch will be out of here probably tomorrow and it'll be business as usual."

"Pure genius in taking care of the situation the way you did. She doesn't seem to have a clue."

"What do you expect? She's a woman, and they're really only good for one thing."

"Ha! My wife knows her place. Too bad you couldn't teach Special Agent Dalton hers. From what I heard, she gave you a good dressing-down."

"Shut up! I don't need the reminder that she had the nerve to take me to task in public."

"Carl came through. I wasn't sure he was going to."

"It took some…persuading. But if he knows what's good for him, he will do as I told him to do and keep his big trap shut. It's a piece of cake. No one will ever know."

"Good to hear." His chair squeaked as he shifted and

then dropped his voice. "We still have those guys coming in for some weekend fun?"

"I don't know. We might want to lie low after this incident for a bit. Mayer really blew it with his need to go against our rules."

"He paid for it and the others will fall in line. We won't have any more problems with anyone."

"Yes, we dodged the bullet…" The man laughed.

"Let's make this one our last for a while, then. To be safe. So, we'll make it a good one. Just have to make sure we have what those boys are looking for."

"Oh, I think we can manage that."

Amber was on the phone again, working out her flight arrangements. The coffee was brewing, and Tristan grabbed a plate and loaded it up with her fluffy pancakes. He tried not to stare at her. It was damn hard, but he managed to pull out his laptop and catch up on some paperwork he had to do before his final class. He'd be ready to go back to Doc Cross in six weeks.

He took a mouthful of pancakes, savored it, chewed and swallowed.

The coffee finished brewing, and just as he was going to rise to get himself some, her call ended and she automatically reached for his bulldog mug and poured him a cup.

She walked over to the table and set it down. His heart did a little flip. Okay, over coffee? It was as if they were…cohabitating, as if she didn't think anything of knowing exactly how he took his coffee.

She huffed as she went back to the stove and dished up her flapjacks.

"What's wrong?"

"They can't get me into the hotel tonight, so I will have to wait until tomorrow."

He intentionally stuffed another mouthful of syrupy goodness into his mouth so he wouldn't say something and prove to her and himself that he was quite stupid. As soon as he finished the bite and washed it down with a mouthful of coffee, he said, "Ready to get out of the snow and ice?"

She regarded him silently for a moment, then raised her brows as if he might be a slight bit slow. "Does Mickey Mouse have ears?" She snorted. "As I've said before, I might have grown up in Vermont, but I'm not a fan of the cold. Except for skiing and snowboarding, ice-skating, too, but then I want a warm lodge and hot chocolate."

"I haven't had a vacation in a long time." He finished the last of the pancakes. She pointed at the stove, silently asking if he wanted more. He shook his head.

"Where was the last place you visited?" Amber took cream in her coffee. A lot. She cut her pancake and he watched as she slipped it in her mouth. He needed to stop looking at her lips.

Snapping out of his ogling, he said, "My parents back in Unalaska, Alaska, a tiny little city two klicks from Dutch Harbor, the busiest international fishing port in the United States."

Her eyes brightened as if his disclosure of where he'd lived during his childhood was a big deal to her. He didn't usually have these kinds of conversations with people, but it felt easier with Amber.

"What's it like to grow up in Alaska?"

"Cold," he deadpanned.

She laughed and pushed his shoulder. "Other than that, Tris."

He smiled. His sisters called him Tris. The only females besides his mother that called him by that nickname. Rock called him a pain in the ass, and his brother usually called him jarhead. He rather liked that she used it. "I mentioned my father's a fisherman and it's damned hard. Gets harder as the fishing gets tougher. The town is pretty small—about 4,300 people—but it has the distinction of being bombed by the Japanese in World War II, insists on having a separate zip code from Dutch, and is an airliner hub."

"Dutch Harbor… Wait, what kind of fishing?"

"All kinds, and yes, crab, too."

Her eyes widened and she set down her fork. "He's one of those fishermen from that Discovery Channel show?"

He shook his head. "He's not on the show, but runs his own boat. He's pretty disappointed that none of us were interested in continuing on with our family tradition."

"That must have been hard for him."

It was the most surprised his father had ever been when first Thane, then Tristan, had opted for the military. "It was. I went into the Marines as soon as I got my high school diploma. Thane had already gone into the navy two years before, and my little sisters had wanted nothing to do with crabs, although Nova did the books for my dad. She's a whiz with numbers. It was the Coast Guard Search and Rescue that was her main interest. She went to the Coast Guard Academy as soon as she graduated, but Neve went directly in. Nova wanted to fly, so she was doing the officer haul."

"That's pretty cool. A swimmer and a flier?"

"She will be great at it. Are you and your sister close?"

She looked away, her eyes going immediately pensive, her mouth pulling down a bit. Oh, there was some tension there. "Sort of, but we have our differences."

He rose, grabbed his plate and set it in the sink, then poured himself another cup of coffee. She twisted around in her chair.

"Why is that?"

Silence. Then she turned back around.

He brought the carafe with him and topped off her mug. She busied herself with adding the right amount of cream. Amber avoided his gaze, something she'd never done. She was always Ms. Direct.

He reached over and lifted her chin. "You don't want to talk about it. I get it. We don't have to. It's your business."

Amber made a face and then folded her arms, huffing out a breath. "She was popular and beautiful, and I was completely not. I was tall, lanky and athletic. Always the girl boys were after…to be on the basketball team."

"They must have been blind and stupid."

She shook her head and wrinkled her nose. "It all sounds so petty when I say it out loud."

"Hey," he said, covering her hand. He tried not to care that she laced her fingers through his. "You feel the way you feel. Can't help that, right?"

She shrugged. "I was so jealous. I had to work twice as hard to get noticed. I guess that made me competitive."

"I kinda like that about you." He squeezed her fingers. "And as for your lanky, athletic body, I'm not seeing any problems there. But, if you want, I could take another look. Might take me some exploration and re-search, though, to make a final decision."

Dancing lights blossomed in her eyes and she nudged him with her knee under the table. "Men, such animals."

"Well, you also have something else going for you."

"Oh, yeah? What is that?"

"You make great pancakes."

She was laughing when her cell rang, but the amuse-ment faded after she answered, listened for a few sec-onds, then said, "Thank you." She hung up the phone. "They have a match on the ballistics. Mayer's rifle killed James. That is pretty conclusive to me and really no way to dispute it that I can see. No evidence to suggest anything else."

"What about the autopsy on Mayer?" Tristan asked.

"Ready in about an hour. Let's head over to the col-onel's office and fill him in. As soon as I get word on the death of Mayer, which I suspect was simply hypo-thermia, I will be briefing my boss and then head out to the Reno airport tomorrow." She scowled.

"What's wrong, Amber?"

She hesitated, then said, "Nothing."

Tristan drove in silence over to headquarters, and they briefed a tight-lipped, unhappy Colonel Jacobs, who was disappointed in the terrible tragedy. Mr. and Mrs. Con-nelly had collected their son's body and were in the pro-cess of getting it shipped to DC.

"Why DC?"

"They're burying him at Arlington. They debated on it but decided that James deserved a full military funeral and to lie with his comrades in arms instead of in their home state of Kentucky."

His eyes stung, and his throat tightened. He rose abruptly. "Sir, may I be excused?"

The colonel looked at him, then away. "Dismissed."

Tristan left the room, and as soon as the door closed behind him, he rubbed at his eyes, feeling both weak and hollow. He walked briskly to the conference room and shut the door. The face of the young marine who had been on guard duty with him the night the consulate had been attacked and overrun flashed in his mind. "Dammit," he swore softly and under his breath.

Arms came around his waist and Amber pressed against his back. He wanted to push her away just as much as he wanted her to hold him tighter.

He was so unaccustomed to being comforted. As alien to him as giving up.

He tipped his head back and clenched his jaw. It was not a good time for memories. Or for remembering. But that didn't stop the emotions piling up in his chest.

Forcing himself to let go of the air jammed in his lungs, Tristan stood there trying to rein in a flood in his chest. It was as if everything just came tumbling at him all at once. Doc Cross warned him about this. He told him there would be a trigger and then he wouldn't be able to contain it all. He also said it wasn't a bad thing, that Tristan had to "deal to heal."

Doc Cross and his corny sayings.

Force Recon had been one hell of a ride, all right. One that took him places he'd never expected to go. He wanted the constant distraction that being a Recon marine would give him. There had been times when his aloneness got so big he felt buried by it. And he had figured he would go to the grave with this awful hole in his chest. Then something happened to change that.

First James had drawn him out against his will. The kid's enthusiasm, their interests and James's skill were infectious. Before Tristan knew it, he had let his guard down and allowed himself one of the few friendships he'd had since Rock bulldozed his way in.

Now there was Amber.

But that wouldn't help now. She was heading to her well-deserved vacation and he would be going back into active combat duty. He was adamant about not keeping a woman on a string while he was serving. It wasn't fair to her.

"I'm sorry, Tristan," she said. "I'm so sorry."

"It's not all about James," he rasped out, and he wanted to bite his tongue.

Her arms tightened. "What is it, Tristan?"

He turned around and faced her, leaning into the table for support. He hadn't opened up to anyone about this. Not his family, not his buddies, not even Doc Cross. The doctor had prodded and he'd pushed, but Tristan had kept saying he was over it and it wasn't affecting him. Now he was realizing that Doc Cross did think this was one of the issues he needed to resolve. Suddenly he'd gone from thinking he could handle it to losing it.

She didn't say anything, just let him have his space. Let him make the decision to share this with her. It was tough to talk about it. Always had been, but with Amber, she just seemed to make everything complicated and easy at the same time.

"That kid got to me." He blinked several times. "It's hard, Amber, to make friends in this type of life."

She nodded, moving her hand from his waist and sliding it up his chest. "I've never been in combat, Tris.

I've seen the ravages of war with the clients I served as a JAG lawyer and as an NCIS agent, but not firsthand."

"It's a singular and a group experience. Everyone else in combat is going through the same thing. The gamut of emotion, fear, sense of duty, fear, determination—then there is the individual experience. Fear is, of course, something you train yourself to handle. You have to. Before I was a sniper or Recon marine, I was a fresh face, a full-of-himself guy who thought I'd make a difference. That was important to me."

"Did something happen to change that?"

He closed his eyes, his throat working, and Amber sidled closer, her presence more of a calming one. "Almost fourteen years ago, after basic, I was assigned to guard the US consulate in Banyan. It's a small, cold town adjacent to Latvia."

He shifted and she settled against his hip, her face turned up to his. Her phone buzzed and he glanced down as she pulled it out and checked it. But when she returned it to her back pocket, he swallowed hard.

He felt as if he had an entire rock pile in his gut. "I was observant. I rarely missed things that other people overlooked. There was increased unrest in a town over from the consulate. Anti-American type of unrest and I wasn't quite sure if it was terrorist or just dislike." He ran his hand through his hair and looked away. "It wasn't my job to make decisions about the security of the ambassador. Contrary to popular belief, marines aren't really stationed at embassies or consulates to protect diplomats. They are there primarily to protect secret information—embassy buildings often process classified information, and many host CIA personnel, as well. Marines are there to protect—and if necessary, destroy—any classified information so it doesn't fall into enemy hands. Foreign officers are told in their initial training not to think of the marines as their personal bodyguards in case of an attack."

She regarded him with a skeptical look on her face. "I see. So you couldn't stop…"

"No. I couldn't. Not at first. It was my mission, Amber. I had to carry it out to the letter before I was free to do anything else."

It had been something he'd learned through training, but it wasn't put to the test until Banyan. Then it had become stark reality. "It's easy in theory. You fulfill your mission. You know what that is and it's in granite. But, in practice, to let people die for documents… Not so clear-cut in the heat of the moment."

"Oh, Tristan. That must have been so hard."

"People died, Amber, including the guy I'd bonded with at basic. He was a good guy and I had to…" He stopped talking, his jaw taut, and she wrapped her arms around his neck.

For a moment he couldn't speak, as he let the heat of her compassion warm that cold, cold part of him. "It was part of my job to protect anyone in the consulate, but when the attack started, I was holding them off so that documents could be destroyed." Damn, but that had rankled. It was his mission there, but he was bothered by the thought that even a split second in getting to the ambassador and the people who had died might have made the difference. "There weren't enough of us. I had suggested to the guy responsible for protecting the ambassador that he should beef up security. He thought I was inexperienced and talking out of turn. He told me to do my job and he would do his."

"That's not on you, Tristan."

She was right there. "No, but I have to reconcile my actions, Amber. My mission required me to ignore my buddy while he died on the other side of the door, a door that I couldn't open."

It warred with *leave no man behind* and *protect your platoon member's back*. He'd had no choice. "When the documents were destroyed, I tried to protect the ambassador. I was alone and wounded at the end and... although the documents were destroyed, I lost the ambassador and three other people. Once help arrived, I was not looked at...kindly by NCIS. They cut me no slack. It was more like I was being interrogated instead of being interviewed. After that, I couldn't continue in the corps as a marine security guard. I applied to and was accepted into sniper training, then into recon."

"You've been through so much and I have so much respect for you. I know it's hard to think that James died tragically, but, Tristan, it's not your fault. Just like the consulate deaths aren't on you. You did your duty during that event. You don't have to keep feeling you need to atone for those deaths."

He gave her a curt nod. She said the same thing Doc Cross said. But eighteen months ago he was a different guy. Stressed-out, combat weary, his barriers all in place. Maybe not so much anymore. James had a hand in breaking them down, and Amber disarmed him like no other person he'd ever met in his life.

Feeling he was stepping across a very dangerous line, and sharply aware of how hard his heart was pounding, he covered the hand on his chest. The feel of her was almost enough. Almost.

His heart lumbering, he tightened his hold, rubbing

the back of her hand. "Thank you, Amber." He didn't want to let her in, but he felt that it was just too late. She was already there and he was only asking for trouble.

"That was Dr. Thompson on the phone. Must be about Randall Mayer's autopsy."

This time when they stepped into the morgue, Amber stopped dead. Dr. Thompson was sporting a huge black eye and favoring one arm.

"What happened?" Amber asked.

He forced a smile and said, "I was clumsy and walked into a door. I'll be fine."

It looked more to her that someone had punched him.

"What do you have for us on Randall?"

"He died two days ago, approximately an hour after he tried to run you down."

"Cause of death?"

"Hypothermia."

"Could you please send the report to my email?"

"Of course. You'll be leaving?" His eyes flicked to Tristan, then back to her.

"Yes, the ballistics on Mayer's rifle matched the bullet fragments you found in Connelly."

"Looks like this is wrapped up. Have a safe trip back home."

"I'm actually heading to Aruba for a vacation."

"Even better."

They left the morgue. "I guess we'll never know what happened on the mountain, although why James was up there in the first place still bothers me. You'll get your house back. You won't have me messing up your kitchen making my pancakes."

He gave her a sidelong glance. "I love your pancakes."

Her cell rang and she looked down at the number, but it abruptly cut off. Must have been a wrong number. She tucked it in her jacket. "I'll leave you the recipe."

"It won't be quite the same," he murmured.

"No…it won't," she replied.

Back at his town house, Amber went upstairs to her room and pulled out her suitcase. She started stuffing everything inside without thinking about it. Everything for her vacation was at the bottom of the bag. She should be happy, grateful, relieved. She was going back to her life. Getting a vacation she richly deserved. But, instead, she felt miserable and a little hollow.

It bugged her that the resolution to Connelly's death seemed so senseless, and it didn't sit well with her not to have answers as to why Connelly had been up the mountain in the first place. Where had he been for forty-eight hours?

Then there was Tristan. They had got close. She wasn't going to deny that. Both emotionally and physically. At first he'd been a closed-off grump, one of his mechanisms to keep people at bay. Now he seemed to be pulling back into himself.

She experienced a rush of hurt, and she closed her eyes, making herself take a deep breath. What had she expected him to do? That was who he was, and it was how he lived his life. And she had gone along with it. Mostly because getting involved with him was simply beyond temptation. She had to acknowledge right here and right now that he hadn't been some kind of rebound guy. Not like she'd thought he was—someone who found her desirable and had soothed the humiliation of getting dumped.

She wasn't sure what she even expected him to do. He was in the service and he intended to remain in the service. He wasn't going to give up anything for her and how could she expect him to. They barely knew each other. It was irrational. Her life was in DC and she was going back to it. NCIS was everything she wanted, and she'd come to that decision later in her life. This was the work she wanted to do, even on the days when it was hard to take.

His life was on the battlefield, a man driven to reconcile past actions in a life-and-death situation that had a gruesome outcome. He had fulfilled his duty then and it had cost him dearly. She wouldn't judge him or his actions.

She knew what she was getting into when she'd slept with Tristan and knew it wasn't going to go anywhere. So, she couldn't feel any regret about it and she didn't. What she regretted was meeting him under these circumstances where the situation felt impossible. It was her own fault for falling for him. She rubbed at her temple. It was okay to admit that because she was aware of how true it was.

Feeling completely drained, she tucked a loose wisp of hair behind her ear, folded the last of her clothes and zipped her case shut.

She checked her phone and saw that her flight was on time. She called the hotel one last time to confirm her reservation and then lay back on her bed.

She heard his bedroom door close. After a few moments, she pulled her report up on her laptop and spent the rest of the evening working on it. She'd email it to Chris in the morning and the case would officially be closed.

Tomorrow she would finally be sitting at that bar in the warm waters of that amazing pool. She was going to bake the chill out of her bones and get some perspective on Tristan Michaels. She would enjoy her vacation as best she could, even through the heartbreak of leaving him forever.

Chapter 12

When she got up in the morning, Tristan was gone. She did some yoga and then ate a light breakfast. She checked once more to make sure her flight was still on time. She'd have to leave here at noon to make it. She had about four hours to kill, so she set herself up at Tristan's kitchen table, made herself a cup of coffee and brought her report up on her laptop to go over it one more time.

She tried not to let Tristan's absence bother her. Even though it felt as if he didn't care, she knew he did. Men didn't withdraw for no reason, and she was well aware that Tristan dealt with people on a regular basis by keeping himself tightly closed off. He wanted distance between them, which meant he felt the need for that distance. Which then meant he cared about her.

Well, it didn't matter one way or the other. She was leaving.

While she was in the process of checking all her contact numbers, Dr. Carl Thompson's number snagged her attention. She stared at it for a moment, then realized why it seemed familiar. She reached over and grabbed her phone and brought up her call log. It was the number from yesterday afternoon that had abruptly cut off.

She hit Redial and there was no answer. She left him a voice-mail message, then hung up. When she got to the section on her report where she indicated she'd requested the roster of the Sportsmen Unlimited list, she discovered after checking her email that she hadn't received it. She picked up her phone and dialed. Ken Marshall answered.

"I'm tying up loose ends, Mr. Marshall, and I see that I haven't received the roster for the members of your group."

"Are you sure?" he said. He sounded...nervous.

"I'm positive. I'm assuming you're not going to make me get a court order for a simple list, Mr. Marshall."

"No, no. Of course not. I'll send it to you immediately." He hung up and, after a few minutes, her email dinged with the list. She pulled it up and perused it. But her mind kept going back to the sound of Ken Marshall's voice. She opened her browser and pulled up the national organization and clicked on the list of members. Her eyes scanned until they snagged on a name that jumped out at her.

Sean Garza.

Her gut twisted and her senses tingled. Garza was in the same hunting group as Mayer. Why wouldn't he have mentioned that? He'd seen the renewal form in her hand and had asked about it.

She picked up her phone and dialed Ken Marshall

back. He answered, and she said, "Why is Sean Garza's name not on your list but he's listed as a member on the national list?"

"Oh, um, must have been a mistake."

"Other than being members of the same group, what was the extent of the relationship between Deputy Garza and Mr. Mayer?"

There was silence for a moment. "They were hunting buddies."

"Friends?"

"Yes, close friends."

"I see. You will want to fix your roster, Mr. Marshall."

"Yes, thank you."

For a minute after Amber disconnected the call, she sat there. So the vibes from Garza weren't unfounded. There was something…underhanded about the man, something that rubbed her the wrong way that had little to do with his ego,

He'd found the rifle and the car. He had been pushing the investigation toward a friendly-fire theory. And he hadn't mentioned that he knew Mayer well and, in fact, had hunted with him.

Her phone rang and she answered. "Amber, it's Colonel Jacobs. Morgan has brought to my attention that you asked him to gather data on our statistics for service members that have gone AWOL. He found an alarming number and checked the numbers against the national statistics and found it to be abnormal. He then checked for disappearances regarding all of our service members and found that to be also alarmingly high. This wasn't caught because there was a command change from last year to this year. I'm going up the chain of command on this and will get to the bottom of it."

"I'm running some leads on this case, and I'm going to postpone my flight and stay here a few more days to run this information down. I'm going to call my boss and clear it with him."

"Please keep me apprised of your progress."

"Please thank Corporal Morgan for being so thorough on this, sir."

"Will do."

When Chris's face popped up on her screen, she took a deep breath.

"Amber, what's up?"

"I just called the airlines to postpone my flight, and Josh and I from hotel reservations are now really best friends."

She heard Vin chuckle in the background. "Why are you postponing your vacation again?"

"Chris got me into this mess. 'One day,' you promised me."

"I know. I know. So, what's going on?"

"There's been a development."

When she told him about the AWOL report she'd requested and the results, along with Garza being buddies with Mayer and showing up on the list of members in the Sportsmen Unlimited group, Chris got that investigator expression on his face. The one that said she was onto something. "Do you have a theory?"

"Not at the moment, but I have a few leads I want to check out."

Chris ran his hands through his hair and sat back. "I want you to be careful."

"Yes, sir."

"Do you want me to send someone else out there?"

Amber stiffened. Was he replacing her because he didn't think she could do the job?

"No, sir. I will finish out this assignment."

"All right. Do you have any more information?"

"Not at this time. I wanted to check in with you and get your permission to keep this case open."

"You have it. I will touch base with the director. If there's nothing there, let me know and get on that plane. Otherwise, check in regularly."

"I will."

"Make sure you do, Amber," he said firmly.

"I will, sir," she said. Then before he could disconnect the call, she said, "I need to ask you a question. Why was an agent from the East Coast assigned to this case? Don't give me some bull that the other qualified agent is on vacation. Mrs. Connelly mentioned her brother Rick, and the field chief for this area just happens to be Richard Barlow."

He sighed. "He's the kid's uncle. He wanted to recuse himself and his personnel from this investigation, and the director deemed it prudent to assign someone from here."

"I see. Why didn't you tell me?"

"I was asked not to by the director, as he wanted a completely unbiased investigation. It was need-to-know."

"I can accept that. His parents deserve to find out what really happened to their son. Right now, Chris, I'm getting the feeling that I don't have all the answers. What happened to James in those two days he was missing is still a mystery. I intend to dig until I find out what happened."

"That tenacity is the first reason I hired you, and

your sense of justice is the second. Check back with me this afternoon."

She agreed, disconnected the call and went to the closet to get her coat. Grabbing her cell from the table, she pulled the keys for the rental out of her pocket and left the house.

She drove over to the sheriff's department and once inside found Deputy Garza at his desk. He looked up, and for a quick second, she could see his dislike of her in his eyes and his expression shuttered.

She settled in the chair beside his desk and let him squirm for a moment. "I thought you'd be gone by now," he said with that phony charm that was now as transparent as tape.

"I bet you did. I want to know why you didn't mention to me that you were good friends with Randall Mayer. Hunting buddies, in fact."

His lips tightened and he leaned back in a deceptively casual manner. The man was as tight as a drum.

"How is that relevant?" he sneered, his eyes narrowing.

"It's relevant because you handled evidence connected to a suspicious death. You should have recused yourself and let someone else handle it."

"What are you saying, *Special* Agent Dalton? I covered up clues or tried to derail this investigation?"

"I didn't say anything about that, Garza, but now that you've brought it up... Did you?"

He smirked and said, "Very funny. I'm a deputy sheriff and I uphold the law. I wouldn't tamper with evidence."

The phone rang and he picked up the receiver. After

listening for a few seconds, he said, "Where? I'll be right there."

He stood. "Carl Thompson's body was just found in a ravine outside the hospital."

"What?" Alarmed, Amber rose. First she found out that Garza knew Mayer, and now this. Her senses went into overload. "How?"

"Gunshot."

He brushed past her, but she followed him out into the parking lot. "Wait a second. I'm not done questioning you."

He kept walking and she moved around in front of him. "A murder takes precedence over your unfounded conspiracy theories about me. Talk to the sheriff if you have a complaint. Now, get out of my way."

He stepped closer, everything about him threatening. "This isn't over," she bit out and turned toward her car.

She pulled out her cell phone as she reached the driver's side of her car. Just as she was going to dial Chris, pain exploded in the back of her head. She fell face-first onto the cold pavement, the impact of the asphalt scraping the skin of her cheek.

Shock crackled through her. Her cell phone tumbled out of her hand, coming to rest just under the driver's-side door. Dazed, dizzy and incapacitated, Amber couldn't move as a wave of nausea rolled through her. When she tried to crawl, pressure landed in the middle of her back, pressing her down. She turned her head, as the pant leg of a khaki uniform and brown boot filled her vision. Her arms were pulled viciously behind her back and the cold feel of steel snicked around her wrists. Her eyes slid shut as another wave of dizziness took hold of her, the sudden, crushing weight of a headache making it hard to think.

She was roughly lifted, and her head lolled back, the harsh breathing of a man heavy in the frosted air, then the sound of a trunk being opened. Then the empty sensation, as if she was floating for a split second.

Her body landed heavily, her shoulder wrenching from the awkward position. He violently shoved a gag between her lips, the taste of oil heavy on her tongue, and she fought to open her eyes. Then a binding was placed over her mouth and tied behind her head, pain sizzling across her scalp as he roughly brushed over the raw abrasion where he'd hit her. Panic clawed at her throat and she tried to move, but dizziness gripped her again. She managed to open her eyes as the trunk lid descended, cutting off the sunlight and latching with an ominous, final click. She felt the car lurch into motion as she lost consciousness.

Tristan pulled up to the house, noting the absence of Amber's car. The emptiness he'd felt this morning when he got up intensified. She was gone. Finally. Off to her much-deserved vacation. The way he'd acted last night was for the best. He wasn't sure he could hold her and then let her go. So a quick, painless goodbye. He winced as he got out of the vehicle and headed up the walk. He couldn't convince himself that something real hadn't happened with her. But the situation hadn't changed.

He was going back into Force Recon. He had six more weeks here and then he'd be out of the US. With his schedule and her going back to DC, clean and quick had been the best course of action.

He opened the door and stopped dead. Her suitcase was at the bottom of the stairs and her laptop was sitting on his kitchen table. He looked down at his watch and, sure enough, it was after noon.

He pulled out his cell phone and put a call through to her. It rang and rang until it went to voice mail. He walked over to the laptop and woke it up. It was on the password screen, so there was no way to know what she'd been working on.

He went into the kitchen and brewed a pot of coffee and poured himself a mug, on edge, waiting for his cell to ring so that he could hear her voice.

After forty-five minutes, he dialed again and it rang and rang. Then it was picked up.

"Hello?"

It was a man's voice and Tristan got a sick feeling in his gut. "Who is this?"

Cautiously the man said, "Deputy McKenzie. Who is this?"

"Master Sergeant Tristan Michaels. Where is Amber?"

"Amber?"

"Special Agent Amber Dalton. This is her phone."

"Then you got a problem, sir. I found this phone under a vehicle."

"Where are you?"

"Mono County Sheriff's Department parking lot, the back one where we keep the cruisers."

"I'll be right there."

He ran back out to his car and drove as quickly as he could to the sheriff's department. Pulling up, he saw a man in a deputy's uniform standing next to... His stomach sank... It was Amber's rental car.

He didn't park, but lurched out of the driver's seat, not even bothering to close his door.

As he approached the man, Tristan's eyes went over

the car. "You McKenzie?" he barked, and the guy nodded, Amber's phone still in his gloved hand. Tristan took it when he lifted his arm and opened his palm. "This is her car. Have you seen her? She's about five-eleven, long blond hair, green eyes."

"Right, drop-dead gorgeous blonde. Yeah, she's hard to miss. I remember seeing her and you, too, before with Garza."

"Yes, that's right. Have you seen her today?"

"Sure did. She was here earlier at about eleven. She spoke with Sean, then left with him. They looked like they were arguing to me, but I could be wrong."

"Is Garza here?"

"Yeah, he just got back from a murder over at the hospital in Bishop."

"What? Who?"

"Dr. Carl Thompson. He's one of our autopsy guys. Damn shame. Gunshot."

Cold dread snaked down Tristan's spine. He took off at a run for the sheriff's department with the guy shouting, "Hey, you can't leave your car here!" Ignoring the woman at reception, he barreled through until he caught sight of Garza. The man saw him coming and the look on his face was defensive and sly. Tristan knew. He just knew. Garza was involved somehow in James's death. He didn't know how, but Amber was onto it. It had to be the reason she hadn't left.

Tristan never slowed. He brought all two hundred and sixty pounds of protective, enraged muscle into his forward momentum as Garza rose from his chair then back-pedaled at the swiftness of Tristan's charge. He slammed into Garza, propelling him rapidly across the short space that separated him from the wall. Tristan shoved him hard, the man trying to pry Tristan's hands loose. Chairs scraped across the floor and shouts sounded out behind him, but his focus was on Garza and it never wavered. "Where is she, you son of a bitch!"

"Who?"

Tristan's face contorted. "Don't play dumb with me!"

He struggled against Tristan's grip, but Tristan slammed him again, holding on tight. "Let go of me!"

"Answer me! I know she was arguing with you. Amber! Where is she?"

"What? I don't know. She was here and she left. I've been at a murder scene for the last two hours."

The sheriff's voice boomed across the office. "What the hell is going on here?"

Hands grabbed Tristan and pulled him off Garza. Tension tightened in the room as he glared at Garza.

"He thinks I know where Amber Dalton is," Garza said, straightening his uniform. "I don't. I told him she was here and she left."

"She couldn't have left! Her car's still parked outside and her cell phone was underneath it. If you've harmed her, you bastard—"

"What are you saying?" the sheriff demanded, cutting him off.

"Special Agent Amber Dalton has been taken. She's missing!"

Tristan stalked to his car. The sheriff had dragged him and Garza into his office. He'd been concerned about Amber but had insisted that Tristan leave the station unless he had proof that Garza was involved in her disappearance. He agreed to impound her car and keep it here under lock and key until Tristan contacted NCIS. Tristan kept her phone.

When he got to his vehicle, her cell phone rang and Tristan wheeled into a parking spot, answering, "Hello."

"Who's this?" a male voice said.

"Who's this?" Tristan demanded.

"Amber's boss, Supervisory Special Agent in Charge Chris Vargas. And you are?"

"Master Sergeant Tristan Michaels. I'm working with Amber."

"Where is she? I'm checking in. Amber was supposed to call me. She's never late."

"I was just about to call you. I can't find her. I have her cell and I found her car here at the Mono County Sheriff's Department. She was here to see a deputy and now she's missing."

Tristan heard a voice in the background. "Hang on. I'm putting you on speaker. I have Amber's coworkers here with me. Special Agents Vincent Fitzgerald and Beau Jerrott."

He heard another man's voice. "This is Fitzgerald. This deputy's last name wouldn't happen to be 'Garza,' would it?"

"I'm afraid so."

"That's bad news. Amber asked me to do some checking for her regarding Sean Garza's last two jobs. Both sheriffs said he was an egotistical jerk. He had altercations with other deputies, suspicion of abuse in both places. One of the deputies in Plato, Colorado, went missing. They questioned Garza, but they found nothing to connect him to the deputy's disappearance. He told me that he suspected Garza, but when he quit, there was nothing he could do to hold him there. That case has gone cold and is still open."

Tristan hit the steering wheel hard with the heel of his hand. Panic was not a normal state for him. Ever. He needed to calm down, think rationally, but the possibility that Garza had already killed Amber made him crazy with gut-clenching pain and rage. "I know he has her, but I can't prove it and I have no authority here to force anything," he said through clenched teeth.

Another man's voice with a hint of a French accent came over the line. Must be the other agent, Jerrott. "That's a bold good-for-nuthin' to take her in broad daylight outside a sheriff's department. Sounds like he thinks he's invincible."

"It gets worse. The doctor that did the autopsies of both Connelly and Mayer was murdered today. When we saw him yesterday, he had a black eye and was favoring his arm. Said he walked into a door, but he could have been worked over. If he covered something up from the autopsies… I don't like this at all."

Chris's voice came back on the line. "Sit tight, Master Sergeant. We're heading out there now."

"Thank God. Hurry."

Tristan went back to his town house, but he couldn't sit still, and finally he couldn't stand this inaction. He had to find her, and the only clue he had was that damn list of members from Sportsmen Unlimited. He brought up the website and went through the list. As he got close to the end, despair settled in until… Dammit. The name jumped out at him like a snake out of a bush.

Scott Werner, MWTC's chief of police.

He called the police department, but Chief Werner wasn't there. Tristan indicated it was an emergency and they patched him through to his wife. She explained he was off the grid, as cell-phone reception up in the mountains was spotty.

That was when Tristan felt a glimmer of hope. "Mountains? What is he doing in the mountains?"

"Hunting this weekend with his friends at my brother-in-law's cabin. It's quite a ways up into the Sierra Nevada."

"Can I get the address, Mrs. Werner? I must speak with him now. It's urgent."

"Oh, dear. Of course."

As she rattled it off, Tristan typed it into his phone and hit the navigation button. He ran upstairs to his room and stripped out of his clothes. He donned long johns then his Gore-Tex mountaineering pants, both items designed to handle moisture, along with a long-johns undershirt, cotton pullover and Gore-Tex shell. Downstairs, he grabbed his heavy parka and stamped his feet into two layers of boots.

Stuffing his heavy-duty gloves into his pockets, he zipped the parka and pulled out his cap. He set it over his head and ears. He pulled out a desk drawer, removed his gun case and opened it. Checking the clip and the safety, he tucked the gun into the waistband of his jeans, grabbed his keys and slipped out the door.

He called Special Agent Vargas, but they must have been on their flight, because there was no answer. He disconnected the call and decided to try him later after he'd had a chance to talk to the chief, who could hopefully shed some light on where Garza might have taken Amber.

He drove way too fast, but it still took him thirty minutes to get to the base of the road that wound up into the mountains. He had to slow down to handle the switchbacks.

As he got close he noticed a lot of tire tracks and, for whatever reason, a sense that he had developed over many combat tours tingled. Not one to ignore his instinctive sense for danger, Tristan drove his car off to the side of the road behind one of the parked vehicles.

He slipped out of the car and closed it as silently as possible. At this time the sun was starting to dip into the horizon, the day spinning into twilight as he crouched and ghosted through the trees. He heard voices and approached, using all his training to stay not only hidden but silent.

He saw the cabin ahead of him. More parked vehicles and two men standing outside smoking. There were lights on in the cabin, casting a yellow glow on the snow. Tristan used trees for cover as he ran from one trunk to another on the hard-packed snow, luckily not leaving any tracks.

He was close to the window when he heard a familiar voice and his blood ran cold. He made it to the window and he crouched, lifting his head just enough to peer inside. Relief rushed through him. He saw Amber, her long blond hair spilling across the floor, her hands cuffed behind her back, her face pale, eyes closed, her cheek scraped, an obvious bruise forming on her delicate skin.

The door opened and Garza strode in with Werner right behind him. He approached Amber and went to one knee, grabbing her by the hair, dragging her up.

Her eyes popped open. He could see that she was hurt, dazed, but her eyes blazed defiance. She was magnificent. Garza said something to her and her face froze in shock and horror. Then she snarled and kicked him hard in the chest with both feet. He flew backward and Werner helped him up.

Garza's face was a red mask of hatred and threat as he shrugged off the chief's hands.

Trying to stay calm, Tristan pulled out his cell but saw immediately that there was no signal. He debated going back down the mountain and getting help, but he was afraid to leave Amber. He had no idea what they had planned for her, but he was damned happy she was still alive. He shoved the phone back into his pocket, blindsided that Chief Werner was involved in whatever had happened to James. There was only one way to save Amber and it meant letting himself get caught. Deciding that he couldn't take the chance on leaving her, he went to the corner of the cabin. There was no one there. He crept forward but froze when he felt the barrel of a gun poke into the center of his back.

"Don't move."

Now all he had to do was survive.

And, hell, he was a master at it.

Chapter 13

As soon as Chris landed, he checked his cell and saw that he'd missed a call from Tristan, but when he tried to reach him the call went right to voice mail. He called Colonel Jacobs's office and talked to Corporal Morgan, who was very concerned. He told Chris as soon as he hit the base to come straight to headquarters. The colonel would be waiting.

Beau was getting the rental while Vin and Chris grabbed the luggage. As soon as Beau got to the entrance, they loaded up the vehicle and started out for Pickel Meadows. Chris had never been more worried about an agent since Vin's fiancée, Skylar Baang, had been hunted by her Russian kidnappers and Vin had gone off the grid, and when Beau and his now fiancée, Coast Guard Investigative Service Agent Kinley Cooper, had their harrowing mission go terribly wrong in Cuba.

Now Amber was missing and Chris blamed himself for sending her here. But the case was tailor-made for her with her sharp mind and her attention to detail. True to form, she had rooted out what appeared to be a conspiracy.

Vin fidgeted in the backseat. "Can you stop driving like an old lady, Jerrott?"

Beau swore softly in Cajun French and glanced at his coworker in the rearview mirror. "I'm not driving like an old lady. I'm going seventy-five. It just feels slow because we're worried about Amber." He swore again, his voice seriously lethal when he said, "If *anything* happens to her…"

"That dirtbag's life is *over*," Vin said, just as deadly.

Silently, Chris agreed as they sped down the highway toward MWTC. "Beau, push it to ninety. I'll take care of the highway patrol," he said as he pulled out his cell.

When the door burst open and someone shoved a man through, Amber was disoriented from being hit on the head and thrown into that sick animal Garza's trunk and left in there while he'd handled Dr. Thompson's murder. One she was sure he'd committed. She was still reeling from what Garza had told her they planned to do to her. She was trying to manage her fear.

Then she recognized the man and suddenly, against all the despair of her predicament, she had hope. "Tristan!"

He looked up at her before Garza kicked him in the ribs. "Michaels! Nice of you to join us." Garza pulled a handgun out of the small of his back and pointed it at Tristan's head.

"No," she screamed at the same time as the chief.

"I want him alive. I've always wanted to know what

it would be like to pit myself against a bona fide Special Forces Recon marine."

Tristan pushed himself up on his hands until he was in a sitting position. Garza scowled and waved the gun to indicate that Tristan was supposed to move closer to her. He complied. His jaw was unshaven and grimly set, and she recognized that kind of tension in a man. Deadly.

"Give me your cuffs," Garza said, and the chief handed them over. Garza smiled as he jerked Tristan's arms behind his back and cuffed him.

"Pit yourself against me?" Tristan said, his eyes narrowing. "How?"

The chief smiled and Amber still couldn't reconcile the short, balding milquetoast chief as the ringleader of these men. She was sure it was Garza pulling the strings, but he followed the chief's orders to the letter.

The chief walked over and crouched down. "You don't understand, Sergeant."

His voice was scary calm. "Why don't you enlighten me?" There was a coiled energy in him—as if he was locked and loaded and all he needed was the pull of the trigger.

His features looked as though they had been hacked out of granite, but there was something dark and intense in his eyes, something so *dangerous* it made even her swallow hard.

"They're going to hunt us, Tristan," she said, unable to keep the horror out of her voice.

His head whipped around to her, then back to the chief. "You hunted James? I'm going to kill you with my bare hands," Tristan said, and she marveled at how his voice only got quieter.

Even the chief pulled back as if Tristan was going to rip him to shreds. "James was an unsanctioned hunt," the chief said, as if he was talking about a wily fox instead of a wonderful human being. "Randall was never very good with patience. He kidnapped James and released him much too close to where you were conducting your class. He almost got away. He was a worthy opponent, one of the best I've heard of so far, and Garza and I have hunted our share of military and law-enforcement prey."

"You are all sick and twisted animals. James was only twenty-five years old. He'd been through two tours serving his country, protecting you and your rights. How dare you hunt him like an animal!"

The chief nodded. "I agree. Randall squandered what would have been a satisfying kill. He was dealt with. No one in my operation steps out of line and lives."

Tristan's face was a mass of pain and rage. He was so tense next to her that Amber could feel the heat coming off him. "You've been hunting people on base!"

"I got bored with game hunting a long time ago. Then we joined Sportsmen Unlimited—where the *unlimited* really stands for something."

"Geezus," Tristan said.

"I suggest you conserve your energy. You're going to need it tomorrow."

He rose, heading for the door. Tristan said, "I'd suggest if you want to live, you should let us go right now."

The chief turned and there was deep gratification in his face. "Oh, this is going to be a great hunt."

"Are we going to be paired up?" Tristan said.

"No," the chief said. "We're going to split you up. It'll be more fun for us."

Garza approached Tristan and crouched down. "Aren't you cocky? I bet Amber knows all about that." He waggled his eyebrows at her. "Wouldn't hurt to have a real man to compare you to. Too bad the chief is going to take you. But then…" He looked at Amber. "She's no consolation prize. I got a feeling she's going to give me a good time and when I run her to ground, an even better time. I'm going to see how feisty she really is."

"Last chance, Garza. Let us go." Tristan's voice was a flat, dead calm.

Garza laughed.

"You'll never see me coming and you'll be dead before you hit the ground."

Garza punched Tristan, knocking his head to the side. "Well, tomorrow I'm going to have your girlfriend and then I'm going to kill her. Sweet dreams."

They left the cabin and slammed the door shut behind them. Amber heard the lock turn.

Tristan's gaze locked on her. He spoke, his voice low and ragged. "Are you all right?" He shimmied his arms under his butt so that his cuffed hands were in front. Amber did the same. He draped his arms over her head and dragged her against him.

Locking her jaw to stop the weakness from taking hold, Amber grasped the back of his head, molding herself to him. Her throat was so tight she could barely get the words out.

Hauling in a deep, ragged breath, he tightened his embrace, his face still buried against her neck. "God, I thought I'd lost you," he whispered roughly, holding her as if he couldn't let her go. "I almost went crazy."

Tears burning her eyes, Amber clasped his head even tighter. "I can't believe this is happening. That Mayer hunted him, Tristan. It's heinous. That's why there were so many service members AWOL. They've been doing this for two years. They started with hikers and snow-mobilers, then started on military targets because they were deemed more challenging."

He swore viciously under his breath. "Did they explain to you how this was going to work tomorrow? Any advanced information I have will be helpful."

"Garza told me that there was no escape, but to be a jerk, he said if I was smart, fast and resourceful it was possible I could get away. It was obvious he didn't believe I was any of those things. He made that quite clear. But he told me I would get a fifteen-minute head start. Then he and three other hunters would chase me." She took a breath.

"Garza's an overconfident, egotistical asshole and that's going to be his downfall. So, you're doing great. I know this is terrifying, but tell me everything."

"I'm so glad you're here." Trapped by the intensity of his gaze, Amber stared at him, all her feelings for him swelling up inside her.

"I would never leave you alone or abandon you, Amber. I'm in this until my last breath."

Tears stung her eyes. "Oh, God, Tristan." This could be it. It could really be over. Really over. Her life was down to a matter of days.

"Come on, sweetheart. Tell me the rest."

Her voice wobbled, but she cleared her throat and her voice got stronger. "If I make it to nightfall, they have agreed not to hunt me but let me rest. In the morning as soon as the sun rises, they will be coming after me again."

"Sporting of them," he said through clenched teeth.

"All right. I'm going to explain to you how to survive the night, then about moisture and dehydration. Then, Amber, I'll need to give you tips on how to avoid hypothermia. I need you to listen to everything and ask any questions you have. It's crucial you do everything I say until I can get to you."

"Tristan, you're going to have four armed men after you."

"I know. They're all going to die. I swear to you that I will get to you as soon as I can."

It was as if he gave her a shot of electricity. Experiencing a sharp hot-and-cold rush, she curled her fingers into his shirt to steady herself. She just stared at him, thinking about what he'd just said, then realizing that he was a Force Recon marine. He was not going to hesitate. He was not going to hold back. He was going all out tomorrow and unleashing the weapon the Marines made him into. A lethal, thinking, hard-muscled warrior. She could see it in his eyes, feel it in every line of his body, knew it in her heart. If anyone could save her tomorrow, it would be him. It was her job to stay alive.

"Do you trust me?"

He had thrown open a door to possibility—a door she desperately needed, a door that let in a whole new set of options. She cupped his face with her bound hands. "Yes. I trust you with my life."

"I won't let you down." He pulled her close and whispered, "Are you still afraid?"

"A little less now."

He kissed her mouth. "Good. We're going to get out of this. So, listen to me. Do exactly what I say. I'm going to tell you where you can get a weapon. When Garza catches you, instead of a mouse, he's going to find he has a tiger by the tail." He smiled.

She closed her eyes and took a breath.

"But first, you run."

"Tristan."

"No, Amber. Run and keep running. Don't stop, don't fight, don't think until you can act. You'll have them right in your crosshairs. I'll show you where you can get a weapon." He grinned.

She grinned back at him and more of that fear diminished.

"I will find you. I promise. Stay alive. Keep moving. Survive until I get to you. I know this mountain like I'm the wind and the snow. I have the best training in the world and they just bought more trouble than they can handle. We may be miles apart, but we're going to do this as a team. They'd be smart to put a bullet in my head right now."

"Tristan. Please don't say that."

"So, run. I will find you. Stay alive, baby. That's all. We are not going to die tomorrow. They are."

She nodded. Hit with a giddy weakness, Amber closed her eyes and pressed her forehead to Tristan's, held on to him, forcing air into her lungs. And something hard and tight let go in her chest. There was a chance for them. If she didn't blow it. There was a chance. Gathering her strength, feeding off his confidence, her heart fluttering like crazy, she opened her eyes and stared at him. Leaning forward with her eyes still open, she kissed his mouth. He stared right back, his eyes as open, intense and focused, and he kissed her back.

"Repeat after me."

Managing as tough a smile as she could, she tightened her hold on his shirt.

They said it in tandem. "We are not going to die tomorrow. They are."

Later they were fed. Tristan was sure it was to keep them up to their exacting standards. Weak prey wasn't very much fun to hunt.

As soon as they left the room, he turned to her. "Okay, let's get started. There are two types of weather—wet cold and dry cold. Wet cold is where it can get to 50 degrees during the day and freezing conditions at night, like in the valley. Then it warms up again during the day. Dry cold means the temperature doesn't get above 14 degrees. In dry-cold conditions, there is no thaw. That's what we have here in the mountains. There will be no thaw, and the possibility of warming when the sun comes up won't happen. Factor in windchill, which is how cold it *feels*, and it's going to get damned cold."

She walked to the window and gazed out. He knew the scene before her. Nothing but a white vista of snow. A wilderness devoid of any shelter, warmth or help.

"That's the first thing you need to manage. Put as much distance as you can between Garza and yourself. Then slow and allow the heat you're generating to warm you."

She kept her back to him and remained silent. He had no idea if she was truly seeing what she was facing tomorrow or was entirely inward at the moment.

"There are going to be two main cold-weather problems that you have to guard against," he continued. "Frostbite and hypothermia. Frostbite means that your skin has fallen below the freezing point, and ice crystals are forming within your skin cells, killing them. Tuck your hands under your armpits when you stop to rest. Make the rest periods brief."

She'd had to accept and process a great deal today and, despite her few brief lapses into panic, she'd maintained extremely well. He didn't know her well enough to know her breaking point. Maybe she didn't know, either. But from the steady set of her shoulders, he didn't think she was teetering on the brink. Yet.

"Amber?"

"Yes, warm them under my armpits. Got it." She turned around then. "Explain hypothermia, including the symptoms, so that I can be aware of them." She moved her manacled hands to push back a wisp of her hair.

For some time now he'd been juggling the need to protect her and take charge of the situation so she wouldn't suffer any more than necessary. But Amber wouldn't expect any quarter. "Hypothermia is when your body loses more heat than it produces and your core body temperature drops. Some of the symptoms of hypothermia are slurred speech, stiff joints, loss of coordination, slow pulse, uncontrollable shivering and mental confusion. Many times, getting wet in addition to the cold leads to hypothermia, and the result can be as severe as a coma or death."

Her face went a little white there, but she pressed her lips together. He watched her tighten her spine, set her jaw, and he couldn't be more proud. He rose and joined her at the window. "To fight hypothermia, try as best you can to not get sweaty. This will be hard if you're running, but do your best. Most heat is lost through your head, so when you're running, take off your hat and as you cool put it back on. Otherwise, always keep it covered."

He knew imagination was often far worse than even the harshest reality. She'd already seen a lot. He respected her enough to not pull any punches or sugarcoat a thing. "This isn't going to be easy and I'm not going to minimize the danger here. But the worst thing you can do is panic. Remember, you are going to have an advantage. I'll get to that last."

She nodded and took a deep breath. "You know I was supposed to be in Aruba. Hot, white-sand beaches, warm, surf and a lot of alcohol."

He laughed. "You planning to be drunk the whole time?"

"That hadn't been my plan, but if I make it there—when I make it there—they better keep the mai tais flowing."

His mouth kicked up. "Would you send me a selfie of you in your bikini?"

That got the laugh out of her that he'd hoped for.

"Are you sure you can handle that, marine?"

"Ooh-rah. I'll do my best, ma'am. Use all my training in keeping my tongue in my mouth."

She laughed again, grabbing his shirt. Then her smile faded. "Tell me what to do about shelter."

Something so powerful welled up in his chest. He tugged her against him until she was in his arms, her cheek tucked against the steady beat of his heart. "I'm sorry," he said, pressing his face against her face. "Sorry any of this is necessary."

"I'm sorry, too. I should have been more aware that Garza was bad news. I miscalculated and he took the advantage. I'm not going to let that happen again. I promise."

"It was broad daylight at the sheriff's department. Who would have thought he would be that demented?"

She nodded. "Point taken. Shelter?"

He didn't let her go and that was all him and nothing to do with her needs. "If I don't get to you by nightfall, make a shelter. Make sure you're not in an avalanche spot. Check for accumulated debris and broken tree stumps at the base of the clearing. If you find both, chances are you're in an avalanche chute. The side of the clearing is a much better shelter location. You should also avoid areas near overlooks and cliffs. Start looking for an ideal spot as soon as the sun touches the horizon. You don't need to get too fancy—your goal is to make it through the night.

"Dig a snow trench deep enough to provide a wind-break. Pile and pack additional snow on the windy side for further protection. Gather as much pine boughs, leaves, anything soft to line the bottom for insulation. Once you climb in, cover yourself with copious amounts of pine or any other leaves you can get. Snow is a better insulator than your average tent, so your emergency shelter should get you through the night. Hillsides provide good wind shelter, but low-lying areas are colder and damper, so avoid them.

"Make your shelter as small as possible to help retain heat. Stack up tree branches to the entrance to block the cold and retain heat."

"I suppose I should manage my sweat while I dig and gather—moisture is my enemy in the freezing cold."

"Bingo, babe. Once you've built your shelter, you should focus on water and warmth. The human body can survive for about a week or less without water, depending on conditions. Dehydration can set in within a few hours. It's important to remember that water is just as important in cold-weather survival as it is in hot weather. A minimum of two quarts of water is needed for survival, and in cold conditions, you should drink even more. Eating snow may seem like a great idea, but it will lower your core temperature and actually bring on dehydration. Wrap it in cloth and suck the water out as it melts. Try to find open water—rivers, streams, lakes and springs. It's best to get your water from a fast-moving body and strain it with some cloth to remove large bits of sediment.

"Use the COLD acronym to help you remember these important tips. *C* for clean. Try to minimize dirt and sweat. *O* for overheating, because sweating causes moistness, which causes you to chill faster. *L* for loose. Keep your clothes loose to allow blood flow. And *D* for dry. Wet clothing is your enemy in the cold. Keep your neck area loose to allow moisture to escape."

She stood there for a moment assimilating everything he'd told her. He thought about tomorrow and what they would face apart and together. He would gladly lay his life down for Amber. No hesitation, no fear.

"You're going to be amazing, Amber. I know it."

"You do? I'm going to take that at face value."

He cupped her jaw, smoothing his thumb along the edge of the bruise. He could only hope he'd get the chance to bruise Garza tomorrow. The man was worse than an animal. Softly he said, "Why did you leave the JAG Corps?"

"You checked up on me?"

"I like to know who I'm dealing with. But, actually, you told me, remember."

She bit her lip. "I checked up on you, too. I already knew about the consulate, the mandated break from combat and your therapist, Dr. Cross."

"I don't think it's a secret that it messed me up."

"Tristan."

"You can't fix everything, Amber. I learned that a long time ago, but we're not talking about me. JAG?"

She looked away, then back at him. "I was prosecuting this guy. Exemplary soldier, decorated, and something didn't feel right to me. It was…off. So I did some investigation on my own and I discovered that his girlfriend framed him for the murder of her parents. I resigned my commission and left. I put in an application for NCIS the next day. I get more satisfaction in bringing bad guys to justice than I ever did prosecuting them."

He tucked her hair behind her ear. "You are something else, aren't you?"

"What is that supposed to mean?"

He cupped her face and slipped his arms over her head, to drop to the small of her back. She gasped. "Yeah, you feel that, too. Don't you? It's like an electric shock under the skin."

"A buzz."

He nodded. "I wish things could be different, but, Amber, I can't make any promises. I can't. My life… the corps—"

"It comes first." She looked in his eyes for the longest time, then gathered herself and said, "Thank you for being honest about that. It's just that I really hate coming in second."

"That's not it, Amber."

"It feels that way, but I trust you. I looked at the man you are, with the deep convictions you have. I've seen the respect in your students' faces. I've seen what lengths you would go to protect them. And what you are willing to do for me, because you thought it was the right thing. That's the only measure I need."

"Amber…" He didn't have the words to express himself.

"That's how I know if I ask you for a promise you'll keep it, no matter what."

He pressed his forehead to hers. "What promise do you need from me?"

"If for some reason I don't make it—"

"Amber, no—"

She shook him. "Please, Tristan."

He sighed and nodded.

"If I don't make it, would you go see my parents? Would you tell them how brave I was even if I wasn't? How hard I fought to live? So it will give them some measure of peace. And this is very important. My boss, Chris, he is amazing and this is going to kill him. Tell him this isn't his fault, that I was proud to work for him and to be part of NCIS. Tell Beau and Vin that I love them like brothers and serving with them was a privilege even if they made me do all the grunt work because I was the probie. Could you do that for me?"

His answer was to take her mouth. Right then. No preamble, no slow lowering of his lips to hers, no choice given. Just a choice made.

He was going to make damn sure she could deliver all those messages herself.

The surprise of it kept her still, but for only a second. He mentally braced himself against the sheer softness, the warmth, the welcome she gave him. He respected her. He knew then how well and truly entangled he'd become. It had never been like this for him. Almost irrational. He relied on instinct, on rational thought. Not on emotion and his dick. Or his heart. Life wasn't set up to be fair about those things, and he'd had enough of the unfair part of life.

Then she moaned, just a little guttural sound in the back of her throat. And her bound hands came up to slip over his head, her hands fisting in his hair as she pulled his mouth down even harder on hers. And kissed him back with every ounce of intensity she had in her.

And he knew there was no way to protect himself from this. Or from her.

He never even tried.

Chapter 14

Amber was so tempted to sink into that blissful oblivion only Tristan could provide. Escape the overwhelming worry and fear, even if for only a few moments. But in the end, even Tristan couldn't transport her. Their kiss eased from the powerful need she was already coming to crave to something quieter and yet perhaps even more compelling in the way it nurtured something else inside her. And that something was hope.

When he lifted his head and looked into her eyes, she said, "We're going to live."

He nodded.

"I'm going to be drinking mai tais in that pool bar in Aruba with the cold of these mountains as nothing but a memory."

He nodded again, then took her hand and drew her with him as he walked across the main room and through the bedroom door. The cabin was beautifully decorated with a woman's touch. It might be rustic, but it was rustic chic. The bed looked hand carved with a detailed motif of all different types of animals, and the comfortable-looking pillows and bedding were in rust and brown tones. They were here to get a good night's sleep, both of them aware that being as rested as possible would give them the best advantage tomorrow.

She clutched at him. The odds almost overwhelmed her again—eight armed men.

"Ah, babe. It's going to be all right."

"Are you just saying that? We won't even be together to fight."

"No, not at first, but we will be together, Amber. There is no doubt that if they don't let us go, there won't be any quarter given on my part. Splitting us up is their first tactical mistake because I won't be distracted. Their second is underestimating you."

He drew her toward the bed and they sat down on it together. "I'm going to maneuver you toward the north."

"But that's deeper into the mountains."

"It's part of my plan. Also, about two miles to the north is a stream. That's where you can head to get rehydrated. Drink as much as you can. Then walk along the stream. The ground will be frozen, but near the water, there will be less snow. It'll throw them off. We're lucky it hasn't snowed in a couple of days and a lot of it is hard packed. Fewer footprints. This is going to be tricky, but there's going to be a cave. You'll see it getting rockier as you head north. The cave mouth is hidden behind heavy brush, but there are three rocks piled next to it. I put those there so I could find it easily. There's a propane heater, food, MREs—meals ready to eat—so don't get too excited, and water. The water will be frozen, but should thaw fast once you get the heater going. I have these hidey-hole stashes all over this mountain to teach my guys how important it is to be prepared and if we ever got caught in a bad situation and needed shelter quickly we could survive for a couple of days."

"A radio?"

"No, most radios are limited in their range, so I didn't store any of those." He took her hands in his. "Amber, there's a handgun in that cave. A Colt M45A1. It's hidden under a shelf of rock in the back in a Pelican storm case, along with a knife, a Ka-Bar."

That made her breathe a little easier.

He smiled. "Yeah, they won't know what hit them. It's comparable to your Glock. Point and shoot. It's highly accurate with a hair trigger."

"I think I can handle it. I'm very good with a gun."

"I'm trying not to get off on that. With your training at Quantico, I'm assuming you know how to incapacitate and how to kill in hand to hand."

"Yes. Explosive movement to the C2."

"Neck break. Most effective. There's no incapacitating here. You are straight-out going for the kill. I know you've heard all this. But because you're a woman, a man may overpower you. It's a fact. They are out to kill you. Bottom line. You kill them first. Ooh-rah."

"Ooh-rah."

"There's a difference between what you do and what I do. I'm not in situations where I am trying to take people in for crimes or am under any obligation to hold fire when I'm engaging the enemy. You are. You operate under certain conditions as a law-enforcement officer. Throw all that out. No hesitation. Two in the chest, one in the head are the best combinations and to make doubly sure that guy is out of the game permanently."

"I'm comfortable with that."

"Amber, where have you been all my life?"

"The fact that we're sitting here discussing the best way to kill someone, I can honestly say, is not the worst first date I've ever been on."

He chuckled and dragged her hard against him. "Survive tomorrow," he said fiercely. "Kill without hesitation. Stay alive until I get to you. Then we'll be an unbeatable team."

She already knew they were an unbeatable team and she wished that there was a future for them, but she had to accept the decisions that Tristan made. His choices.

"You haven't even brought up the idea of escaping now, tonight."

"That's because there are armed men behind the door, and if we try to run now, they'll be shooting to kill us, whereas in the morning, we split their party and we have an advantage of a fifteen-minute head start. We won't be bound like we are now. Not that I can't take them on bound. I just like our odds better than running blindly into the night."

"If you're worried about me keeping up..."

He smiled but his eyes remained serious. "I'm not. But if I'm being honest, I'm worried about you. I don't want anything to happen to you, so I'm suggesting we go this route. There are pros and cons, but I think waiting is better."

"I trust your judgment, Tristan. I trust you." She was completely exhausted, wrenched by her feelings for Tristan, scared for both of them. She couldn't handle much more, even if it was something to make her feel good. Her emotions were barely restrained beneath the surface as it was.

She couldn't imagine getting through this without him.

He pulled her gently toward him, caught her and held her tight. "We need to get some sleep. We'll need the energy for tomorrow."

She nodded, not trusting herself to say anything lest she break down completely. She didn't want to feel hopeless, but she was still scared.

Tristan, as if sensing her turmoil, wrapped his arms around her and held her for a moment, hugging her and accepting her arms snaking around his waist with a deep sigh and a kiss to her temple. "Let's go to bed."

Any other time those words would have filled her with anticipation. But it wasn't just about getting physical with Tristan. There was so much more to the man than his rocking body. Now all she could think about was getting some rest and praying to God she could sleep without nightmares.

They folded down to the bed, still holding on to each other. She remembered quite easily being with this man. The first two times had been about heat, sweat and ferocious need. Then poignant and sad when he'd come to her before she had been ready to leave.

Her thoughts drifted there and clung to those moments like a lifeline, helping her to block out the reality of the moment and spend some time away from the negative emotions of fear and disgust. Away from the place where men actually thought it was sport to hunt human beings.

Beyond the bone-deep fatigue, beyond the sheer terror and almost debilitating fear…there was a wealth of desire. A need to discover him, bit by bit, until she knew everything about him—every curve of muscle, what turned him on, every gasp he made and what it meant, every breath he took and every need explored.

Now she understood how life-threatening situations could bring on the need for life-reaffirming ones. Her sudden voracious hunger for him was limited by their terrible circumstances.

"I wish…"

"I know," he said firmly. "Believe me. I know."

He slipped his bound hands over her head, burying them into her hair. He cupped the back of her head with both hands and slowly drew her mouth to his, his eyes on hers as their lips met.

She took his kiss, letting her eyes drift shut as sensation after sensation poured through her. He rolled on top of her, and it was such sweet seductive torture to want to go all the way with him and be unable to. But the warmth of him and the comfort of his body offset the harsh reality of what they'd been through and would have to endure tomorrow.

And with their future uncertain, the moment they were sharing took on so much more meaning. She willed herself just to feel, to truly live in the moment and this moment only.

Her body aligned with his effortlessly, as if they had been sleeping together forever, falling into place as easily as she'd fallen for him. Her eyes were already drifting shut as she shifted enough to press a soft kiss over his heart, before tucking her arm across his body. Then she draped her leg across his, wanting to feel him as close as possible.

Tristan woke early, before dawn. His internal clock was hard to ignore. He also didn't want to be roused by their captors. He lay in the dark room for a moment, almost able to pretend that this was just another day. Another day that would include Amber in his arms, in his bed, in his life.

He shied away from those thoughts. He had promised himself he wouldn't go there. His plans were set. He needed to go back into combat. It was an internal goad as strong as his need for her. He didn't want to analyze why.

He didn't want to delve too deep, even though that was exactly what Doc Cross had told him he needed to do. He also had told him that it wouldn't matter if it was eighteen months or ten years. Tristan would have to decide to make that journey and he would have to not only need to have the courage but determine when the time was right.

He resented that Dr. Cross insinuated that Tristan was hiding out in combat. That he was using it as a crutch. Damn the doc for bringing all this up in the first place. The time he'd gone off the deep end and lost himself to that mission had been his lowest point since… Banyan.

Amber shifted in her sleep, making soft sleep-filled snuffling noises, and he made an oath to the rising day that by the end of it, those men would be dead and they would be home free. He would make it his mission.

His plan was easy. He called it his weakest-link strategy. He'd set a punishing pace. He didn't care who these guys were. They couldn't keep up with a battle-hardened marine, one who was acclimated to this altitude, knew the mountain intimately and could disappear. Hunting animals was nothing compared to hunting a Recon marine, and they were foolish to think that they weren't in danger from him. He might be unarmed, but he didn't need a gun or a knife to kill them.

It would only speed up the process.

Tristan's weapon was and always had been his mind.

He shook Amber and she rose immediately. Only seconds later the cabin door opened, and Garza and Werner came inside. Removing her cuffs, they threw appropriate clothing at Amber and told her to change.

Tristan left the room, crowding them out and shutting the door, daring them to even test him. Garza smirked and both of them backed off.

As soon as Amber came out of the room, they shoved both of them outside into the frigid day. The sun was climbing into the sky. They took off his cuffs and he reached for her and entwined his fingers with hers.

"Amber," he said, his voice nothing more than a rough whisper. "Stay alive."

"Tristan," she said, making his name a vow.

"You have fifteen minutes starting now," Garza sneered.

It took every ounce of willpower in him to break away from her and take off. He never even looked behind him. He had to compartmentalize his fear and concern for Amber. He had to trust that he'd given her the knowledge and the means to make it.

He loosened his collar and took off his hat and gloves, stuffing them in his parka pockets. He zipped the pockets closed, and as he warmed his muscles, he got into the rhythm of his running. They were lucky the snow was hard packed and there had been no snowfall for a couple of days. He ran full out and was only getting warmed up. He veered toward the trees and it was easier going where the snow was sparser.

Operation Weakest Link had begun.

An hour later he hadn't even seen them in the distance. It was sufficient time to double back and take them out one by one.

He'd covered a lot of ground and would have to double-time it back to Amber, but he didn't want her subjected to Garza. His breathing was steady as he started to move back the way he'd come. He hid when he saw the chief was in front of the other three. They were straggling now. As soon as they passed him following his trail, he swung out of his hiding place and, like a dark ghost against the white backdrop, he took the last man from behind. The guy never had a chance to call out or get a shot off.

One down, three to go, then Amber. *Hold on, sweetheart. I'm coming.*

The next man was thoroughly out of shape. He was lagging quite a bit behind the chief and the other two men. Tristan caught him while he was leaning against a tree.

Tristan ejected the bullets and broke down the rifle, throwing the parts along the trail as he went.

The next guy was definitely more aware. He kept his eyes moving and, after the disappearance of his buddies, was on alert.

Tristan trailed him through the trees, realizing that the chief would be getting to the end of Tristan's trail soon and would know that Tristan had doubled back. That was okay—he'd be ready for him. The guy's vigilance cost Tristan more time. But as soon as he was out of sight and around a bend, he rushed up and hauled ass. A rifle at close range was a difficult shot to make. It wasn't like a handgun. Rifles were better and more accurate at a distance. As long as he got beyond the barrel, he could disarm him.

The guy turned and the rifle discharged, but the bullet whizzed past as Tristan used the snow to slide right under the barrel. With a scissoring move, he knocked the man off his feet. The man then pulled a knife and sliced at Tristan, catching his cheek as Tristan jerked back.

They stared grimly at each other as blood trickled down Tristan's face and into the collar of his jacket.

"What do they call that? First blood, marine?"

Tristan grinned. "Yeah, that's what they call it. But I guess it only matters who gets the last blood," he said, low and menacing. The guy was scared, his eyes wild. Tristan couldn't be calmer. Tristan wrapped his arm around his upper body, hunching to protect his neck. "It's your move, asshole. You want to hunt me? Come get me."

The guy lunged, and as the hunter's arm came around to slash him, Tristan sidestepped away from the slash and scissor blocked. He clasped his attacker's wrist, pulling the man toward him and dragging his arm underneath Tristan's armpit. With his free hand, he went for the knife hand hard, breaking the guy's wrist so he dropped the knife. Tristan stepped on it and shoved the guy away. He bent down and picked up the knife. The guy scrambled backward, then turned and started to run. Tristan bent down, picked up the rifle and sighted through the scope. Taking a breath and letting it out slowly, he pulled the trigger. The guy dropped to the ground. Tristan walked the short distance and peeled off the guy's cap and stripped off his coat, then put a bullet in his head. He dressed the guy in his cap and coat and shrugged into the dead hunter's jacket. He took the knife scabbard off the guy, tucked the knife back into it and hooked it securely to his belt. Then he slipped the rifle strap over his shoulder and looked down the trail, his eyes narrowing.

Using the back of his sleeve, he swiped at the stinging cut on his face. Still heated from the tussle with the dead hunter, Tristan loped off toward a good hiding spot.

One to go. For just a moment his worry about Amber broke through, but he pushed it back. *Focus, Michaels.*

"Hey, Werner!" Tristan yelled at the top of his lungs. "I got him!"

The chief was going to be on alert after those gunshots. He had no idea that his buddies were already gone. Tristan waited until he heard the sound of someone approaching.

"Where are you?" the chief yelled out.

Tristan waited as Werner got closer. He sighted through the scope, waiting for his shot.

As soon as the chief stepped from the clearing, Tristan pulled the trigger. The bullet knocked the man off his feet and down he went.

Tristan never hesitated as he made a beeline for Werner's prone body. As he approached, the chief raised his rifle and aimed it awkwardly. He got a shot off and Tristan dived away. The bullet cut through his sleeve and he felt the sting and burn of it as it bit into his skin.

He was up and running the minute he hit the ground, but so was the chief. He ran through a copse of trees and Tristan increased his speed. The bastard had been wearing a vest! He was prepared. Tristan caught him at the end of the tree line and the chief threw a punch, but Tristan ducked it. He hit the man in the gut and then flipped him onto his back. They rolled in the snow and the chief elbowed him in the face and scrambled away. He went for the rifle, but Tristan grabbed the barrel and the shot went wild.

The chief, his face contorted, lunged, but Tristan sidestepped. They were right at the edge of a cliff and the chief's arms windmilled. At the last minute, he grabbed Tristan's jacket and Tristan was falling.

He hit something hard and was dazed and reeling. The sound of the chief's death cry cut off abruptly.

His vision went gray and anguish clutched at him. *Amber!*

Amber had been running for so long she'd lost track of time. She'd followed Tristan's instructions to the letter. She'd run full out for an hour, nothing new to a runner like her. Then she'd doubled back, giving the hunters trailing her a wide berth. As soon as she got halfway back down the trail, she veered north and headed for the stream. She wasn't sure she could make it by nightfall, but she was hoping that Tristan got to her before the sun went down. She didn't relish spending the night out here by herself.

She tried to minimize her sweat, but her exertions were extensive. Tristan's strategy so far had worked like a charm. They didn't expect her to double back, rather to run like a scared animal, something she wasn't. She had to stay focused and calm or there was going to be no way out of this.

She kept moving, feeling that any moment a bullet could rip into her back. As the afternoon wore on, Amber started to flag. She stopped, taking a brief rest.

She needed water. She remembered what Tristan had said about eating the snow. She thought for a moment, not wanting to sacrifice her gloves or her hat to use as a container.

Then it occurred to her. Her bra! It would be perfect. She could pack the snow into one of the cups.

She made quick work of getting it off and getting the snow inside. Her fingers were numb when she finished. Tucking them back into her gloves, she warmed them under her armpits. The wind whipped at her and she gritted her teeth as it froze the exposed skin of her face. As soon as most of the numbness had gone, she grabbed up the bra water sling and pressed it to her lips. She sucked, and the warmth of her mouth melted the snow. She drank for several seconds. Then she was up and running again.

When the day slipped into afternoon, she realized that something had to have happened to Tristan. He should have been here by now. She closed her eyes against the worry and the anguish, hoping against all hope that he was all right. The thought of this world without him in it was too bleak for her to handle.

By the time late afternoon rolled around, Amber was exhausted, sweaty and starving. Her energy was lagging and she worried Garza and his buddies were catching up to her. If she was cold, then he was, too.

But the cold, the fear, the constant movement were taking their toll. She wasn't going to make the cave by nightfall, and it looked as if Tristan wasn't going to make it to her. She stopped and leaned against a tree, laboring.

A shot rang out and hit the tree near her resting hand. She took off, slipping down the other side of the hill, her heart pounding. She looked toward the sky. Dusk was falling, but the sun hadn't touched the horizon yet. She scrambled along the ravine, going sideways instead of trying to labor up the other side. Spying a copse of trees, she headed for the shelter and ducked inside. The ravine was now covered in shadow, and it would be much harder for them to pick up her tracks. She ran through the woods, using the trees as natural barriers, her breath sobbing out of her. As she broke out the other side, the sun had touched the horizon and she was safe for the night.

She bent over double, her lungs feeling compressed, her heart racing. *Oh, God. Where are you, Tristan?*

She took a much-needed breather, but as soon as the sun went down, it was going to get much colder. Her feet were numb, but not painfully so. It was time to make shelter, but she wondered fleetingly if she should take the chance and try to make it to the stream and the cave.

She figured she had to be close. But navigating this terrain at night…she wasn't sure. Cold prickled along her skin, and the sweat from her body had dampened her clothes. There was nothing else for her to do. She had to press on. Even with a snow shelter, she didn't think she would survive the night. Already, she was feeling lethargic and a bit muddled.

She did some jumping jacks to get her blood flowing, decision made. She was pressing on, taking no chances Garza would be true to his word.

She dropped to a brisk walk, winded and exhausted. As it darkened, she had to slow to a crawl. Once the moon rose, the almost fullness of it lent her the light she needed to see.

Everything was cold by the time she stumbled into

the stream, water splashing, reviving her. She stopped and just swayed there. Beyond empty, her body throbbed with a stiffness that seemed to reach down to the very marrow of her bones. She looked around, almost confused as to where she was, why she was out here. The only thing her mind could grasp on to was that if she kept moving, she would be warm. She crossed the stream, the water icy against her waterproof boots, chilling her already-aching feet.

Walk along the river until you get to a rocky outcropping. There will be three stones at the entrance.

Whose voice was that? It was important and very sexy.

She stumbled along and fell down and lay there. She knew she shouldn't, that it wasn't a good idea, but she couldn't seem to muster the energy it took to even lift her head.

The cold enveloped her until she felt she was burning with it. It was consuming her.

Amber! Stay alive!

With her last ounce of strength, she pushed herself up, and that was when she saw the rocks. She headed toward them. Opening. She needed to find the opening. Finally she discovered a depression in the rock, then an opening covered by heavy brush. She looked back over her shoulder and saw that there were no footprints to cover on the rock.

She slipped inside and pulled the brush over the opening. Heading to the back of the cave, she breathed a sigh of relief. She fell to her knees and pushed the little red button on the heater. There was a whirring noise and then blessed heat started to pour out of the wide face.

Huddling as close as she could get to it, she sat there for a long time.

Slowly she came back to herself. She realized that the water and the food were gone and there were two empty propane tubes. Someone had been here and cleared out most of the stores. She rose, stumbling to the back of the cave and the overhang of rock. She reached beneath… into empty air.

Her breath hissed out and she felt something snap inside her. Despair and fear overwhelmed her. Exhausted, she rolled into a ball. The heater sputtered and shut off. The dark inside the cave was absolute. Tears trickled down her face as she squeezed her eyes closed.

Tristan.

Tristan jerked awake just as the sun was sinking into the horizon. He moved gingerly, realizing that, surprisingly, he was okay. His elbow hurt and his back felt bruised as hell, but he was intact. He was on a small ledge just above where he and the chief had gone over. He got to his knees, completely chilled and shivering. Looking up, he assessed the cliff. Climbable. It didn't matter. He was going to attempt it. If need be, he'd freaking sprout wings and fly out of here. Nothing was going to keep him from Amber.

"Hang on, baby," he whispered as he fit his boot into a crag in the rock and hauled himself up. Bit by bit, hand over hand, he traversed the rock wall until he reached the top. He hauled himself over, then inch by inch pulled himself up. As soon as he got to his feet, he headed for the cabin.

He got there just after dark. Breaking in, he closed the door behind him. He searched frantically for a phone, but no landline. Garza had smashed both of their cells. When he tried the computer, he noticed the router was gone. No internet. He had to get warm before he went out again. He would be no good to Amber if he died from exposure. He paced and downed warm water straight out of the tap rather than the cold in the fridge. He grabbed several energy bars and stuffed them in his pockets. He ate a few and drank some more water. When he was sufficiently warm, he headed for the door.

The whole time he debated with himself. If he could get his car going, he could go down the mountain and get help, but they'd taken his keys. By now there was sure to be a full-out search and rescue, but there would be no way Colonel Jacobs or Amber's boss could know where they were.

He decided against it. If he went down the mountain and Amber died from exposure or Garza, he would never be able to live with himself.

Decision made. Committed. He ran off, heading directly to the cave.

Amber woke in the dark. The cave was holding some of the heat from the heater, but she couldn't stay here and had no idea how long she'd been sleeping. Either Garza would find her or she'd die from the cold. She had to move, and her best bet was heading back toward the cabin and the road down the mountain. She rose but was hit with indecision. Something had happened to Tristan, and it could be just a delay or he could be... *No!* She wouldn't think that. He was alive. She was sure she would know if he'd died. She'd feel it.

She looked out of the cave and discovered that it was getting close to sunrise. She slipped out and headed for the stream. After drinking her fill, she started back the way she had come. She could smell wood smoke in the air, which meant that Garza and his friends were near.

As the smell got thicker, she became more cautious. All she had to do was get past them and run as fast as she could back to the cabin.

She trembled, but she wasn't sure if it was from the cold or from fear.

"Lookee here. I found a little rabbit in the woods."

Garza lunged at her from the shadows and clamped his hand around her ponytail. She cried out as he dragged her back against him. "She's a pretty little rabbit with a big mouth."

She elbowed him in the gut and got satisfaction from the *oomph* he made. As soon as she was free, she ran. He caught the back of her parka hood and dragged her around, punching her in the face. The shock of the pain rammed into her temple and down her neck. Her lip split and she tasted blood. Amber flew backward and landed heavily on her back, hitting her head hard against the packed snow.

He kicked her in the ribs, and agony exploded across her chest and abdomen. Then he walked around her. "It wouldn't be as satisfying to put a bullet in you right now. Because you like to shoot your mouth off."

"Screw you, Garza!" she managed to say around the pain.

He straddled her, clutched her parka in his hand and dragged her face up to his. "Let me show you what a real man can do." He reached for her pants and started to tug on them. Amber went crazy, punching and kicking. He backhanded her across her cheek and snapped her head to the side. Then he leaned on her windpipe.

She clawed at him, struggling to breathe as he got her pants just over her hips. "You'll forget all about that marine. Looks like the chief bagged himself a trophy."

"Not quite."

Garza reached for the rifle, but Tristan kicked him in the face and he fell, half on, half off Amber. She was dazed, sucking in air now that she could breathe.

The weight of him disappeared and she could hear a struggle, the smacking sounds of fists hitting flesh. When she regained her senses, she saw Tristan and Garza facing off not far from her. Garza's nose was bleeding and his lip was cut. Tristan's face was set and there was murder in his eyes.

Garza lunged, and Tristan ducked and came up with a sharp jab to Garza's ribs, doubling him over. Then Tristan punched him in the face, sending him reeling. Dogging him, Tristan punched him again, and Garza fell to his knees. Tristan grabbed his head, brought his knee up and drove it into his jaw. Garza went down.

Tristan kicked Garza in the face when he groaned. Then he lay still.

Dizziness swamped her as her eyes closed. Moments later she heard him dropping to his knees in the snow.

"Amber," he said, his voice broken. "Talk to me, babe."

Her head lolled and she worked hard to focus on his voice. Then her eyes fluttered open and he filled her vision. "Tristan. I knew you would come. Are you all right?"

"Yes. Come on. We can't stay here. We've got to go." She saw the cut on his face, the dried blood on his coat sleeve. He'd been hurt.

"Tristan, your face, your arm."

"Scratches. They're nothing."

Amber's blood ran cold as she heard the three others with Garza calling for him.

"Stay here," he whispered and disappeared into the dawn's pale light.

A man materialized through the trees. He saw her, raised his rifle and sighted down the scope, but then Tristan stepped out of the trees with a deadly-looking knife in his hand. He grabbed the guy, sliced the knife across his throat, and then Tristan was running for her.

Chapter 15

He grabbed her hand, but she could barely feel his grip or her feet, and she stumbled when he pulled her up. He jerked up her pants and she realized what Garza would have done if Tristan hadn't been there to rescue her, the horror of it adding to her slow movement.

It was as if her body wouldn't work. Tristan dragged her along and she stumbled again. "Tristan, I can't." Her speech was slow, as if she was drunk. He stopped and bent down, set his shoulder in her middle and scooped her right over it.

She was sure they were headed right toward the cabin. She tried to muddle through it, hanging upside down as Tristan moved so fast through the snow. "Are we going in the wrong direction?"

"No, babe. Hang on."

"I'm so cold." A shiver racked her body, her breathing shallow as if she couldn't catch her breath. She'd lost track of how long she'd been outside. It had been all about nonstop running, heat and cold, then heat again. Being shot at. Sick of the running.

But Garza had been slowly stalking her and she'd been out straight. He'd overpowered her and he'd… Her brain shied away from that. She shivered some more, starting to get sleepy. She knew it wasn't good, but she was so tired.

"Stay with me, baby. You okay?"

"So tired, Tristan."

Before she knew what was happening, he was climbing; she could feel the elevation by the position of his body. Then she was off his shoulders and he laid her out, settling down with her. "Be quiet," he whispered in her ear. She shivered and felt the last bits of her endurance trickle out of her body. She heard his voice and started awake, but Tristan's hand on her chest kept her down. Her only thought was to run.

The voices passed under them, and it was clear Garza was pissed. Good. She hoped Tristan had kicked his ass but good.

Some time elapsed after the voices faded into the distance, and Tristan stood, the snow creaking beneath his feet. He picked her up in his arms and walked to the edge of the roof.

"We're back at the cabin?"

"There are so many tracks around here because of the number of people who traipsed around here before they let us go. We can lose our tracks by walking in theirs."

"That's very clever."

"Hang in there, sweetheart. We're almost there," he said, either a few minutes or an hour later. She had lost total track of time and her shivering was now uncontrollable.

Then she felt him descend. A grayness filled her vision, and before she knew it, he was laying her across his lap. She could feel his jerky movements as if he was trying to go fast and the sound of metal clanging and the crackle of something. Her eyes were just too heavy to lift.

He stripped her of every stitch of clothing. She felt the heat on her face, and then Tristan was covering her and enveloping her in the warmth of his body.

The darkness surrounded her and she dropped down into it like a stone into a cold pool without so much as a ripple.

It had been harrowing there, touch and go when he'd stripped down to warm her core. Garza had hurt her, more than physically. He could see that. Clamping his jaw shut, he forced himself to concentrate on other things, like how they were going to get out of this. He really didn't have a whole lot of options. Amber was tough. He didn't discount that, but she'd been through quite a bit of trauma already, least of all getting knocked around by Garza. The only way the man thought he could alpha her was to force himself on her.

His expression set, he went back into the cave. For his own peace of mind, he checked on her, crouched down—she had been in bad shape by the time they had got here. She was curled up on the makeshift bed, very soundly asleep, her hands tucked under her face. He rested his hands on his thighs so he wouldn't touch her, his expression fixed as he watched her sleep.

What bothered him the most was her dull look. Her

special effervescence—that rare kind of energy that could light up the whole room—was gone. It was as if her bright spirit had been extinguished, and she just looked so fragile. For that alone he was going to kill Garza. Her face and torso were beginning to discolor where the man had punched and kicked her.

Aw, God, if Amber could only be his. He closed his eyes. He'd give anything if he had the right to hold her, to wrap her up and keep her safe.

Ever since she'd appeared in his life, she had been his still center, filling the emptiness in his life. He wasn't sure what he was going to do without her in it, but just knowing she was alive fortified him somehow.

And it would have to be enough.

Amber stirred, curling tighter, and Tristan suspected she was cold as the thermal blanket slipped off one bare shoulder and he pulled it up and over her. Some of her hair had come loose from the ponytail, and he very gently lifted the strands away from her face and tucked them behind her ear. His throat cramping up, he let his hand linger a moment—a brief, perfect moment before he tucked the cover under her chin. Feeling as if he'd just got punched in the gut, he turned and moved away from her.

Closing his eyes, he took a deep, uneven breath. He had let himself get too close. Too damn close and yet it wasn't close enough.

Careful to make as minimal sound as possible, he brewed some coffee on the small stove he'd stashed there and waited for her to wake up. Glancing at her clothes, he guessed they would be dry when they were ready to get out of here tomorrow. He was sure Colonel Jacobs wasn't sitting on his hands. That man was all about action.

He would take the shortest route down the mountain, but it was a more treacherous descent. He would have to take the risk. Garza and his hunting buddies would be searching for them, and although Tristan had the one rifle he'd managed to grab, they were unarmed and outgunned.

Amber came awake with a soft cry and he rushed across the room. "It's okay, babe," he soothed as she looked around, dazed and afraid. She reached for him and he wrapped her in his arms. His insides bunching up, Tristan realized that she was in far worse shape than he'd originally thought. She was running on empty.

"Where are we?" she murmured. "What happened?" Her eyes centered on his cut and she reached up, gently touched his face. "Your arm."

"Took care of it. I'm fine." He pulled her tighter. "We're in one of my caves. We're safe, sweetheart. Remember, we were kidnapped, forced to run." He lifted one of the thawed water bottles to her lips. "Drink." She obeyed, then took the bottle away from him and drank it all.

She gasped and nodded. "I was so cold." She looked up at him, her face still too dazed for his comfort. "You saved me." Seeing Amber reduced to this made him clench his jaw. For the first time in his life, he felt a murderous rage.

"You're safe. We're going to get out of this just like I told you at the cabin. Chief Werner is dead and so are the three men that were with him. I killed another one with the knife I managed to take off one of the guys with Werner. That leaves Garza and his other two flunkies."

At the sound of his name, she shuddered. As though there was an enormous energy built up in her, she met his gaze, her shoulders square, her chin up. And when she spoke, her voice was shaky with emotion. "I thought he was going to kill me and I was so winded and so cold," she said, as if trying to hold everything in. "I can't believe you were there. For me. Thank you. Thank you so much."

Her whole body seemed to radiate energy waves as she swallowed and spoke again. "You saved my life."

His throat suddenly tightened. Unable to tear his gaze from her face, he spoke, his voice gruff. "You did great. I was proud of you for eluding him so long and for the fight you put up. You were so damn tough."

Her expression transfixed, she stared up at him. Then suddenly she covered her face with one hand and started crying. "Tris…"

Feeling torn apart, he said, "Hey, come on." He softened. She continued to cry without responding. "Amber, you're killing me here, sweetheart."

But he was sure she never heard a word he said. And in spite of all his rules concerning her, he just couldn't stand to watch her fall apart like this.

His face contorted, he reached for her, pulling her into a tight, secure embrace. As if under enormous pressure, his heart felt suddenly too big for his chest. Closing his eyes, he swallowed hard and tightened his hold, years of rigidly suppressed feelings boiling up inside him. Having her in his arms—with her entire body pressed against his—was almost more than he could handle, and he clutched her closer, grimacing as he pressed his head against hers. A dam had broken loose in him, and every single feeling he'd ever had for her came raging out.

He knew that giving in to this impulse was the worst mistake he'd ever made and he also knew he was going to pay dearly for it. Because there was no way, not after experiencing the feel of her body molded against his, that he would ever be able to beat down all those long-denied feelings. Never in a million years.

He eased in a painful breath and pressed his face against her hair, saturating himself in every unbelievable sensation. Ooh-rah, but she was a miracle. And he loved her. With absolutely everything in him. He knew he had no business feeling that way, but he did. And nothing—nothing—was ever going to change that.

His throat tight and his eyes burning, he held her head against him, clenching his jaw. If he could, he'd take her right inside him and keep her there forever. She was everything to him. Absolutely everything.

As if unloading some terrible stored-up pain, Amber finally cried herself out and she turned her head against his shoulder. She pressed her hand against his shirt and whispered, "I got your shirt all wet. That's bad for the cold."

He couldn't resist the urge to hug her, and he gave her a reassuring squeeze. His voice was low and rough when he answered. "I'll give you a pass this time, baby."

Loosening his hold, he swallowed hard and rocked her gently against him. He wanted her to get that spunk back, but he understood how it felt to be devastated. Amber never did what he expected. Instead, she nearly knocked his feet right out from under him when she slipped her arms around his waist, rested her head on

his shoulder and stayed exactly where she was. She released a long sigh, as if expelling the last of her tears.

With her warm and soft against him, Tristan locked
his jaw and made himself take a deep, slow breath, the
heat from her body making his blood thicken. Ah, but
it felt so good to hold her—so damned good.

He tried to move away from her as he felt her body
slackening in sleep, but she tightened her hold on him.
"Tristan," she murmured softly. "Don't leave me."

He melted. All barriers down, he was raw to the bone.
He couldn't refuse her.

Amber didn't awaken—she was torn from sleep. In
the middle of a dark, disturbing dream, cold, frantic
hands had reached into her psyche and pulled her out
of slumber. She emerged with a terrible sickening sensation only to find Tristan wrapped around her. She
was disoriented and weak. Her body ached in several
places. Her face throbbed, her ribs protesting and her
hip aching. But the feel of Tristan's strong, hard body
was all she needed, the anchor in her storm.

She looked up to find hard, dark rock above her, the
smell musty. Her eyes roamed over the walls, with a
cache of supplies tucked up against a far wall. The ceiling was high, the space almost as wide as the length
of Tristan's living room and dining room combined.

She was reclining on a sleeping bag, with several
thermal blankets over the top, keeping in all that delicious body heat that was not only being generated by
her naked body but Tristan's, as well.

The air around them was warm and moist, coming
from a portable heater that was running on what looked

like a small propane tank. Memory surfaced. It was just like the one she had used to warm up and save her life.

Everything was still, a stillness that held something other than simple quiet. Heart bumping hard against her breastbone, she tangled her hand in his hair, reveling in the feel of him. His soft, even breathing soothed her. She hadn't been sure she'd ever see him again.

Memories came flooding back like a cascade of terrorizing nightmare images. Garza... Oh, God. Tristan had come out of nowhere. Simply nowhere. He'd killed another man with a knife.

He'd rammed into Garza, who had been... Amber closed her eyes, thinking about what he had been about to do. He couldn't cow her, couldn't get her to back down, and she'd fought like a madwoman. Used every ounce of training she'd possessed, but she'd been running for so many hours on fear and adrenaline, cold, hungry, parched. He'd had all the advantage.

Her hand tightened in Tristan's hair and she made a soft sound. His eyes popped open and he had that *ready* look on his face again. "Amber, are you all right?"

"Tristan, please make love to me."

He rose up on his elbow, his face caught between tenderness and desire. "Amber, you've been through so much... Maybe that's not..."

She tightened her hand in his shirt. "I need you, please. I need to get the memory of his hands on me out of my head. I need you, Tris," she pleaded.

"Amber—"

She cut him off with her mouth settling over his. He made a soft sound as if he could find no way to resist her. Already the memory of Garza was fading, fading away with the heat of Tristan's mouth. "Kiss me, Tris," she commanded on a phantom breath.

His deep midnight eyes locked on hers, his gaze lethally intense, her body so aware of his. For a moment they just breathed, their lips barely touching. Every time he caressed her, she felt cleansed, pieces mending and returning back to being whole, the shattered part of her healing. She shivered at what she saw there in the depths of that ocean of blue. Then he lowered his mouth a fraction of an inch and kissed her softly, gently. His lips, firm and smooth and oh-so-clever, moved against hers, rubbed over hers, seduced her as she softened and responded.

"Yes, Tristan, like that," she whispered. "Just like that."

He slid his body closer, pushing her onto her back with the force of his kiss. As he deepened it, he groaned at her surrender, his hand sliding along her face. She winced and whimpered at the pain. "Sorry, baby," he murmured, gentling his hand, caressing her temple as his fingers delved into her semi-bound hair.

She wanted him. It was a litany that played over in her head. The terror, the uncertainty of whether he was dead or not, the agony of not knowing all dropped away at the heat of his mouth.

She slipped her hands under his layers of shirts and he reached back and grabbed the neck, wrenching everything over his head and off. Then his mouth was back to hers.

She sent her hands over his wide chest, the muscles flexing as he kissed her, exploring the smooth planes and ridges of his body, marveling at the strength there, drowning at her response to his fever-hot skin. She saw the white bandage stark against his arm, brushed her fingers over it, so thankful it was a minor wound.

She couldn't get enough of touching him, feeling his solid strength under her hands when she had thought maybe she'd lost him. Her own life hanging by a thread.

She needed the life that pulsed in him, rubbing over his heart, feeling the hard, rapid thud, his erratic response to her, her heart matching his beat for beat. She pressed against him, needing that power and warmth against the length of her body, to absorb him through her pores. He trailed fire down her throat and over her breasts as she arched her back, his mouth burning her nipple, sucking on her until everything in her twisted with the pleasure of it, what was left of her breath vaporizing.

Tristan growled low in his throat as he sucked powerfully on her, tracing his hands down her back, exploring every graceful curve, every plane and hollow. He pressed and arched her more as she cried out when he used his teeth.

Then both his hands were on her butt and he lifted her into him, pressing her hips to his, showing her how badly, how urgently, he wanted her. She wrapped her arms around his neck and hung on, mirroring his actions over the smooth material of his alpine pants.

"Too many clothes," Amber groused, making a soft protest when he pulled back from her. But her gaze fastened on his, and she watched, breathless and intent, as he discarded his boots. Everything in her focused on the man as he shimmied out of his protective layers.

He was a work of art, the way a man should look. Everywhere on his body were ripped muscles, cutting into his abdomen, his chest, his thighs and his arms.

He'd carried her for miles when she could no longer walk. Had sheltered and protected her with everything he had, every ounce in him.

Because of him, she'd survived. Because he was a master at knowing what to do, a master of the cold, a master at being prepared—her master defender all the way to his core.

She was in love with him. In love for the very first time in her life. A feeling that she couldn't encompass because it was too large, too full, too overwhelming.

It was amazing and it hurt, but she was going to take what he could give because love was about giving, not receiving. If she had to leave here after feeling all that she was feeling, it would be enough.

She had to make it enough.

"Tristan, omigod, I thought I had lost you," she said between heavy kisses, lingering kisses, rapid kisses.

He was broad shoulders and lean hips. Taut muscle on graceful limbs. He was the man who had against all the odds come back for her. Risked his life to save her. A man who was completely and beautifully aroused, his thick erection jutting out from his body.

He had given her a good fight and she had wrestled with her own feelings for him, but not anymore. She was done in by hot blue eyes, integrity as tough as granite, a heart both strong and tender, and a character that was rare and special.

He held her at bay because he didn't want to hurt her. Was sure that going back to the corps and active combat was what was right for him. All these years, he'd been fighting that consulate battle, was still fighting it, and until he realized that, he wouldn't…couldn't let go and make a commitment to her.

She still offered him everything she was, everything her heart could hold. Without words. Without strings.

Her gasp was audible when he moved and covered her. His eyes locked on hers as he kneed her legs apart with a raw, aching need, settled himself between her thighs with a very gruff, sexy male sound of his own.

Amber's breath fluttered in her throat in anticipation. He was all hot, hard male above her, his dark expression a mask of need. She offered herself totally, opened herself, wound her legs around his hips.

And he filled her. Slowly. Inch by inch. His eyes never left her, taking in every expression on her face, sliding all that hard thickness into her. Pressing deeper, deeper until she gasped his name. When the joining was complete, he pulled out and plunged into her again and again until they were moving in tandem, fused and hot and desperate.

He rocked into her, pumping deep, and everything released on a hot, tight ball of pleasure that made her hips undulate, and she cried out as Tristan took his own pleasure, riding the crest of hers.

He braced himself, his head back, his body bowed. Then he collapsed and rolled to his side, pulling her against him.

Imperceptibly, he tightened his hold, committing every single sensation to memory. Sensations to call up and remember after she was gone.

The wind whipped through the mouth of the cave but barely touched him as the heater kept them warm. Amber stirred at the sound, her head looking to the cave mouth, her body tensing. "It's okay, babe, just the wind."

Releasing a long sigh, she flattened her hand against his back and shifted her head. And just as imperceptibly, she tightened her hold. "You feel so safe," she whispered unevenly. "It feels good to have someone to hold on to for just a little while."

Her honesty made his heart roll over and his chest clog up. Feeling as if he might turn inside out at any minute, Tristan closed his eyes and rubbed her back. His throat was so tight he couldn't have spoken if he'd wanted to. He had never expected this to happen, this chance to simply hold her like that. And he had never let himself even think about it because it had always been so far out of his reach. Until now.

Aware of every curve and hollow of her body, he continued to hold her, wishing this moment could last forever.

After a long silence, Amber sighed and pulled away, then looked up at him. With so much gratitude in her eyes that it nearly broke his heart, she met his gaze. Her expression remained very sober, and she continued to stare at him. She had the same quiet tone in her voice when she spoke. "You are an amazing man, Tristan. Smart, tough, decisive and brave. So, so brave."

His gut knotted and he found it suddenly hard to breathe. It was as if she had just reached inside his chest and grabbed his heart, and he had a hard time keeping it together. Everything he'd done up until now, all his medals, all his service, everything paled in comparison to having this woman think that he was all those things. He forced a half smile. His voice was so gruff it didn't even sound like his own when he answered. "Are you kidding me?" he said. "You held your own. You were a *beast*."

She huffed a little laugh. "Great, that's the way I want you to think about me," she said, her tone very husky.

He thought of all the reasons he'd fallen in love with

her, but that directness of hers, that honesty, which was a fundamental part of her, was one of the things he admired most.

And it made his chest tighten even more.

He ran the backs of his fingers over her soft cheek and she pressed into him. Then he worked his throat and locked his gaze on hers. "I think you're beautiful. So damn beautiful." He almost said he'd do anything for her, but he held back. This all was so different, so new and strange, and he felt the need to take the time to think. He couldn't offer her anything until he was sure he knew what he wanted.

Feeling suddenly very exposed and needing something to do, he rose and stood, then dressed. He grabbed up several MREs, power bars and some water. "Eat and drink all this." Then he went to the mouth of the cave. There was a funny ringing in his ears, and his voice seemed to come from a long way off. "Get some sleep, sweetheart," he said, his tone strained. "I'll take the watch."

Then he went out into the cold and it hit him like a wall of frost, his heart thundering like a freight train in his chest.

He hadn't been prepared for her, for her to be so open and honest.

And the act had stripped away a defense system that had been in place ever since that long-ago consulate takeover where he had lost himself.

Chris accepted the mug of steaming coffee Colonel Jacobs shoved into his hands. They were in the conference room at headquarters and had been here all night trying to work out how to find Amber and Tristan Michaels. It was as if they'd disappeared off the face of the earth.

Corporal Morgan poked his head into the office and said, "There's an Officer Mendez on the phone for you, sir. He says it's urgent."

"Patch him through."

When the conference-room phone rang, the colonel put it on speaker.

"Colonel Jacobs."

"Sir, this is Officer Mendez over at PD."

"Yes, what is it?"

"Chief Werner's wife just called. She said her brother-in-law went up early this morning to join a hunting party and it seems that the cabin has been broken into and everyone is missing. Her brother-in-law is concerned. He found blood in the snow. He also noticed a car with military plates. She gave me the numbers and I ran them, sir, and they are registered to Master Sergeant Tristan Michaels. I saw that he's been missing since yesterday."

"Where is this cabin?" the colonel said as Chris pushed off the wall and Beau and Vin both came awake. "Morgan!" he shouted as Mendez started to rattle off the address.

Vin was already entering it into his phone.

When Corporal Morgan came to the door, the colonel said, "Get me a bird on the double! No need for that, Fitzgerald. We won't be driving."

Amber squeezed Tristan's hand as they slipped out of the cave. When he checked the rifle it had only one bullet in it.

"Stay hidden here. I'm going to scout ahead. We can descend. It's going to be a trek and hard going, but it's the shortest way down. Garza knows that. It's our only chance. I'll be right back."

Amber stayed out of sight as she watched Tristan head across the expanse of snow. Then she saw Garza. He was moving parallel to Tristan. Without caring that she would expose herself, she shouted, "Tristan!"

He hit the deck and the bullet from Garza's gun missed him. Two men broke from cover and pelted toward her. She headed for Tristan, then noticed the broken trees and the debris at the bottom of this hill.

Suddenly, in the distance, she heard the sound of chopper blades at the same time she heard an audible crack. The snow beneath her feet started to slide. The two men who were after her stopped dead. Tristan rose and Garza fired again, forcing him to take cover behind a rock. Amber looked down. The snow was breaking away right beneath her feet.

Tristan yelled for her to move, and there was only one hope, the low-hanging tree branch that was just out of her reach.

She began to run, but the snow really started to slide as if there was a conveyor belt beneath her feet. At the last possible moment, she leaped for the branch and caught hold of it just as she lost her footing.

Tristan watched as the two men who had been after Amber weren't so lucky. They went down under hundreds of pounds of snow and then got lost in the great tumble of snow as it poured over the edge of the cliff. Garza was down the mountain, clear of the slide. He turned to look at Amber and raised the rifle to his shoulder, sighting down the scope.

A helicopter buzzed up over a hill, distracting Garza

as Amber held on to the branch. A shot rang out and Garza dropped.

Tristan had guessed that, like Werner, Garza was wearing a vest and he put the round in his head.

One shot. One kill. A perfect cold zero.

Chapter 16

Back at his town house, with her boss and coworkers taking up the couch downstairs and two sleeping bags, Amber lay in the bed, her bruises still tender, her body exhausted and her mind unable to shut down.

Chief Werner was dead, along with the three men who had planned to hunt Tristan. Tristan had killed one of the men who had been chasing her with Garza. The other two had perished with the avalanche, and Garza had died with Tristan's bullet through his forehead.

Lance Corporal James Connelly had died because Randall Mayer had wanted to prove to his "hunting" buddies that he could bag himself a highly trained marine. Randall had kidnapped and murdered James in cold blood. According to Garza, James had proved to be more than Mayer had anticipated, which made Amber say a silent prayer for James. He'd almost made it to

Tristan, almost had outrun his killer. Mayer got what was coming to him, but it had been Police Chief Werner who had been the ringleader, with Garza as his muscle.

Their hunting ring was exposed, along with the death of Dr. Carl Thompson, making them accessory to not only Dr. Thompson's murder but also the military personnel they'd killed. After a search of Chief Werner's home, a kill book had been found with the names of all the victims. The others involved in the ring were in custody, including Ken Marshall, the chapter leader of Sportsmen Unlimited. Amber was finally free to head to Aruba. But where once she had been excited, she now only felt leaden and resigned to spend a week in paradise alone when all she wanted to do was wrap herself around Tristan…forever.

It was the squeak of a floorboard that dragged her out of sleep, but before she was fully alert, she felt a hand rest against her bruised jaw with infinite gentleness.

She opened her eyes, her heart contracting when she realized Tristan was leaning on the mattress with one knee, naked except for his blue cotton pajama pants. His hair was damp, as if he'd just had a shower. Not sure if it was a dream, Amber wet her lips and spoke, her voice husky with sleep. "Tristan?"

He gave no response, his face obscured by shadows, but even in the faint starlight, she could see the rigid angle of his jaw. But what she couldn't see, she could feel in him—and it was terrible tension, as if he was clamping down on some awful emotion.

She heard him try to clear his throat as he dragged his thumb across her cheek. His voice was rough and very uneven. "How are you doing, sweetheart?"

He shifted his position, sliding his arms around her,

gathering her against him. Overwhelmed by a mixture of sharp relief and unbearable sadness, Amber wrenched her arms free of the blanket and wrapped them around his neck, hanging on to him for dear life. Locking her jaw to keep her own emotions contained, she pressed her face against his neck, a sob trapped in her chest. He clutched her head against him, his rib cage rising sharply; then he made a ragged sound and slid deeper into the mattress, pulling her underneath him as a violent shudder coursed through him.

A feeling of deliverance pouring through her, Amber dragged one leg free, holding on to him with every ounce of strength she had as she twisted under him, clutching him even tighter as his full weight settled between her thighs. It was as if every feeling she'd ever had for him had been magnified a hundredfold, and she turned her face against him, tears slipping down her temples. He was everything to her. Everything. And she was grateful for this reprise. So grateful. She wanted to tell him what was in her heart, but she knew it would only make things that much worse.

They had already said their piece. Tristan had made his decision and it was final. He wouldn't allow her to wait around for him when he wasn't sure he would ever be available to her either physically or emotionally. He wasn't going to let her even have hope that down the road he might change his mind.

He was going back into combat, and it terrified her that she would never know how he was doing.

He said he had to get it all straight, assimilate all that he had learned, all that Amber had made him think about.

Amber caught the back of his head, her fingers tangling in his damp hair, emotion upon emotion piling up in her. It was as if they were fused together by desperation, by their individual sorrow, by all the things they couldn't say, had already said, and it was too much.

Far too much. And it got worse when she realized his face was wet against hers.

Not this warrior. Not her hero, her anchor. Not that kind of anguish. Clenching her jaw to contain the awful pressure in her chest, Amber shifted her hold, trying to completely enfold him, trying to tell him without words that she would do anything to keep him safe.

"It's okay, baby," she said softly, wiping at his cheeks with her thumbs. "It's okay."

Shifting his hold, Tristan caught her by the face, then softly—so very softly—kissed her, his mouth warm and moist and unbearably gentle. Amber was blindsided by his gentleness, this man who had been all kinds of grumpy when she'd first met him. So closed down.

As he deepened the kiss, tightening his hold on her, they needed no more words. Just actions. They moved together, against each other, taking and giving, holding and letting go.

In the morning when she woke, he was gone, the scent of him lingering on the linens as she buried her nose into the pillow next to her head.

Heartsick, she got up, dressed and took her luggage downstairs. It was over. She knew it was over. The shower was going when she passed the bathroom.

Chris was in the kitchen with Vin and they were discussing sports.

Tristan was at the table, looking disreputable with his unshaven jaw and his disheveled coal-black hair. So it was Beau who was in the shower. For a moment,

Tristan drank her in. Then Vin said, "Morning! Tristan was telling us you make some mean pancakes. Think you could whip us up a batch?" He gave her the disarming Vin smile that had won him his fiancée, Sky.

Chris leaned back into the counter and eyed her. "Sia makes mean pancakes, too. Rafael loves them. I'll have to see how they measure up."

"Rafael is his adorable little boy," Amber said, giving Tristan a soft look, one he returned.

"There's soon to be another little adorable in the house. Sia's pregnant again."

"Chris, that's great." Amber hugged him and he tightened his hold on her. Vin encompassed them both.

"Group hug!" he said, making her laugh. God, she loved these guys.

Tristan smiled and said, "Ah, Agent Vargas, now you've done it. Amber loves a challenge."

She sure did, but she'd somehow fallen short with Tristan and she couldn't help it. It rankled and created a tiny bit of heat in her. Lifting her chin and rolling up her sleeves, she headed for the stove.

"No one beats me at pancakes," Amber said. Her cell rang and Tristan reached for it. Then his eyes narrowed. He picked it up and answered it.

"Listen, pal, stop calling Amber." She could hear Pete's puzzled voice on the other end of the line. "Who am I? I'm the guy that thinks Amber is the most beautiful, toughest goddamned woman on this planet. You. Blew. It. Don't call her again. She is so not interested." He calmly disconnected the call and set the phone down on the table.

Beau started to clap, Vin grinned like a fool, and Chris laughed outright.

Afterward, full from one of her best batches, even Chris had to agree they were better than Sia's, but he swore them all to secrecy.

As they rose, Amber reached out and tucked a folded piece of paper into Tristan's camo shirt pocket. He gave her a meaningful look and she smiled.

Then it was time to head to the airport where Chris, Vin and Beau would go back to DC and she'd get on her flight for Aruba. Tristan picked up her bag before she could reach for it and preceded her out. It had started to snow. Again. That would mean more shoveling for Tristan. Chris popped the trunk and Tristan set her bag inside and moved back onto the curb as her coworkers deposited their own carry-on bags inside.

Chris slammed the trunk and moved around to the driver's side of the car. Amber gave Tristan a brave smile, tilting up her chin. She wanted to hug him, kiss him, but her coworkers were standing right there.

Snow floated down slowly like feathers, settling on his shoulders and in his dark hair and lashes. The bleak sky mirrored the feeling deep in her gut.

Expelling his breath in a violent shudder, Tristan took the two strides that separated them. In front of her boss and her two coworkers, he pulled her roughly against him, nearly crushing her. With tears stinging her eyes, Amber cradled his head, absolutely torn apart, so fresh from their ordeal, from his heroic effort to save her life. She knew in her heart that he had never intended this to happen. But she also knew this was his final goodbye.

And it nearly killed her.

Tightly closing her eyes to try to dam the tears, she continued to hold him with all her strength, afraid if she loosened her hold just a little, he would disappear like smoke. She had no idea how long they stood like that, clinging to each other, afraid what would happen if they let go. His chest rose sharply, pressing against her as he took a deep, uneven breath, his mouth sliding along her cheek to her lips. He kissed her deeply, and then he said, "Take care of yourself, sweetheart."

She gripped the back of his neck. "You, too, marine. You stay safe," she said fiercely.

Tristan turned and went back into his town house, and Amber turned and headed toward the rental car. Chris was behind the wheel and Vin in the front seat. She met Vin's eyes through the glass and his compassion was almost too much to bear. She slid into the backseat, where Beau was sitting. "We all set?" Chris said, starting up the car. She met his gaze in the rearview mirror, his look telling her he was happy and relieved to have her safe.

Amber held it for a moment, thankful to have such a great boss and two solid, caring coworkers. "Good to go," she said more brightly than she felt. "Time for my much-postponed vacation. I know you're all jealous."

They grumbled, pretending they were totally envious and good-naturedly wishing her a good time as Chris pulled away from the curb. She couldn't help one more glance back. In the picture window, Tristan watched her drive away, his hand flat against the glass. She pressed her hand against the car window and kept her eyes on his through the thick, white drifting snow until they went around the bend and his town house and the sight of his stoic, handsome face disappeared from view.

She turned back and, without a word, Beau reached

over and snagged her hand with his. He squeezed it once and held it all the way to the airport.

Tristan stood up in front of the new class of scout snipers who had just arrived and were settling in. They had a week before the class would officially start, and Tristan was taking some leave to recover from the harrowing two days in the mountains.

His imposed exile from Force Recon would be over in six weeks. He reached into his pocket and felt the paper that Amber had tucked in there. He pulled it out and saw it was her pancake recipe.

Suddenly, with that goal so close, Tristan found that it had somehow lost its importance. He caught himself thinking about Rock's offer, urging him to get out and work with him in something that he knew Tristan would love. Going into business with Rock would be amazing, and he acknowledged to himself, finally, that Rock was his best friend. He'd given the man enough crap over the time they'd known each other, but like the moniker he carried, he'd been a rock.

Tristan had thought his decision was clear. Another tour with Force Recon. But as the day wore on, his thinking began to change. He had options. He could stay here at MWTC. Colonel Jacobs had already voiced his decision that he wanted Tristan permanently.

He could retire early and go into business with Rock.

Or he could get back into combat.

Hide in combat.

Not as important as it once was to him. Before James died…before Amber.

There was something to be said for getting close to

her. And he had. He'd got as close to a woman as a man could. He was in love with her. Deeply in love.

Something he'd never experienced. In the past, he'd found no-strings women to take care of his physical needs. Ever since Banyan. Had always been that way, and for the first time he questioned why that was. Why he had been treating women this way and never letting them get close to him.

Now he was connecting more to that Banyan incident. Remembering and accepting what Doc Cross had tried to bring out through their sessions when Tristan had stubbornly insisted that Banyan had nothing to do with why he was a loner. That perhaps experiencing that anguish had made him gun-shy of *any* relationship. All he'd known was the corps, since he was eighteen. They had made a man out of him, and there was always a price to pay. That cost had been high, and he had closed himself down to do the job he'd been trained to do, pushed his unresolved feelings of guilt deep inside and closed it off so he could perform the duty he'd sworn to perform.

Semper Fidelis.

Semper Fi.

Maybe that had led him to believe that not dealing with it would make it go away, quietly. But now he knew that it had only sent him into special-ops training that would allow him to be part of a team but completely on his own.

Then it rocked him. The realization that made him pause and suck in a breath. All his choices had stemmed from that incident and shaped him into the man he'd become. Some for good, some not so good.

All relationships had suffered, not only with the op-

posite sex, but with his family, with his personal relationships. Every single one. He'd unconsciously isolated
himself from the possibility of adding to the guilt that
stemmed from his actions at the consulate. People he'd
cared about had died because he had to carry out his
duty. Now this was being dredged up because of James
and how close he'd got to the boy without really meaning to. How much closer he wanted to get to Amber.

Everything about her enticed him. Her strength of
character was in tune with his own. She cared about
people, about this case and its outcome. If she was a
good person—and she was—he would have to acknowledge that, and then these other feelings for her would
have to be examined.

Damn, the lengths he'd gone to protect himself were
just becoming clear to him, and it shook him and his
foundations down to the core.

The bottom line was that Amber had made him feel
again, made him examine all the excuses he'd put forth
about his own hang-ups. And now she was gone and his
life felt emptier than it had before.

He closed his eyes and stood there for a moment,
just absorbing the ramifications of everything she was
to him. He couldn't let her go. He'd be a fool to let her
slip out of his life.

He picked up the phone and the call connected.

"Dr. David Cross."

"Doc, it's Tristan Michaels." Then he started talking.

One more endless, sunny, beautiful day in freaking
gorgeous Aruba.

Why did she wish she was back in the frigid Sierra
Nevada? In a cozy cave making love to a man who was

a marvel in not only the field of battle but also in bed. She'd brave the cold for Tristan. From the swim-up bar, located in the pool, she swiveled around on the underwater stool and let her eyes wander over all the happy, smiling people. She scowled. Maybe she should book that windjammer cruise and go swim with the freaking dolphins. Oh, man, she really needed to go soak her head.

Okay, she acknowledged, *it hurt! Okay!* It hurt way worse than her sham of a long-term relationship with Pete. After Tristan had told him off, he hadn't called again. She was glad, because she missed Tristan. Losing him hurt more than anything had ever hurt in her life. She sipped a mai tai, but even the sight of the colorful little umbrella couldn't lift her spirits.

What did that say about her judgment?

Nothing good, she knew that much, but that wasn't the worst. The worst was the pining. She longed for Tristan, for his touch, for the sound of his voice, in a way she wouldn't have thought possible. It was unbearably needy of her to want a practical stranger so much, all the time. She wanted to kiss him, breathe him in, be with him, and in her own twisted way, she managed it as best she could—and it had killed her to walk away.

Life, love and heartache had derailed her on a case that was supposed to take her no time at all. Emotionally she was a mess.

And she could lay that right at the feet of Master Sergeant Tristan Michaels, her master defender. She had only just begun to poke and prod at her pain. She needed another mai tai. She signaled the bartender and he set another one on the bar. A very hunky, almost naked— well, except for his blue-and-yellow swim trunks—

gorgeous hottie gave her a hopeful smile. She barely acknowledged him. She switched out the glasses and went back to her wallowing.

He'd walked into her life a total stranger, and a week later, he'd walked back out entrenched deep in her heart. That alone should be enough to fuel some serious soul-searching, but the rest of it was even worse. She hadn't just fallen in bed with the man—she'd fallen in love.

But he'd been crystal clear. He belonged to the corps and there was no room in his life for a relationship. He didn't want that. She closed her eyes, unable to handle coming in second again, even though he'd been adamant that she hadn't. It felt too much as though he hadn't been willing to sacrifice for her, put her first.

Who was she kidding? He was one of those silent warriors, and *stealth* was his middle name. It was God, country, and then everything else came after that in varying degrees.

She sipped the mai tai and looked around again, deciding that she was sufficiently waterlogged. A dark head of flattop hair caught her attention, but it disappeared behind a large umbrella.

She'd been doing that all day. Every time she saw a military cut. "Oh, hell," she muttered under her breath. Here she was, thinking about him, and now she thought she saw him. This was a habit she had to break. Every thought she had turned to him, and she didn't have a clue as to where he was or what he was doing or what had happened to make him decide they couldn't be together.

That dark hair caught her attention again. It was thick and black for a flattop. Her heart caught, and then she saw those broad shoulders encased in white camo and combat boots. It had to be 90 degrees out and Tristan stood before her as if he'd morphed from the base of the Sierra Nevada to the sunny, sandy, beautiful beach in Aruba.

She'd been taking a sip and it went down the wrong way. She coughed and his eyes found her. Without missing a step, he walked right into the pool, combat boots and all, and waded to her.

Dazed and devoid of a coherent thought in her head, she coughed hard and he patted her back. Her knees wobbled and his arm slipped around her waist as he took the mai tai and downed the drink in one swallow, then set it on the bar.

"Wait... I need that."

He took the little umbrella out and tucked it behind her ear. "Later," he said.

Her heart pounding and her pulse thundering in her ears, she rested her head weakly on his wide, beautiful, solid, lovely chest.

She felt as if she suddenly had too much blood in her body. Too much heat. Too heavy a response. Closing her eyes, she slipped her hands against his chest, closing over the material of his shirt, trying to bring her body under control. This wasn't supposed to happen—not all these primitive feelings, not this fever of need. She had always considered herself fairly low-key sexually, never given to excesses. But she had excesses now—hot, pumping excesses that made her whole body throb.

God, everything had got so short-circuited. This had started out as a simple case of friendly fire and had turned into a rescue mission—Tristan rescuing her. But all of a sudden it had gone way beyond that. Never had she wanted anything the way she wanted to rescue Tristan.

"You need to breathe, Amber, before you pass out."

She raised her head and she saw that his eyes were clear, confident and full of sass. That made her straighten. She pushed him and he went down on his ass in the water. People were already staring and some of them made a soft hissing sound at her pushing a service member down. A big man. She glared at them until they all turned away. "You deserved that."

He sat in the water, soaked and grinning up at her. "Yeah, a delicate woman in a string bikini knows how to knock me on my ass and there is no physical assault required, sweetheart. Ooh-rah."

"Don't call me 'sweetheart.' I'm more like 51 percent bitch today."

He bit his bottom lip as though he was holding back his need to laugh.

Her eyes narrowed and he smoothed his face out, his eyes still so full of joy as he stared at her.

She acknowledged that with her 49 percent sweetheart. "You're losing percentage points, marine."

He held up both hands, water cascading from his sleeves. Unbuttoning his uniform shirt, he pulled it off and tossed it to the side of the pool, which left him in the T-shirt that stretched across his wide chest, outlining hard muscles that she remembered so well, hot and heavy beneath her hands. She stared at him a moment longer, then stepped forward, water sloshing. She set her hands on her hips, intently assessing him. Her tone was blunt. "You're laughing at me, aren't you?"

He set a bland expression, his tone pacifying. "I wouldn't laugh at you, Amber."

She held his gaze for a long moment. Then the corner of her mouth lifted just a little. "The hell you wouldn't."

He tilted his head, looking way too boyish, way too cute, even with that healing cut on his face. And all the love she felt for him rushed into her chest and clogged her throat.

She took an exasperated breath, and then she felt the tears burn her eyes. The laughter disappeared from his face and he scrambled up from the water and rushed to her, dragging her against him.

"What took you so long, Tris?"

"I had to get my head screwed on right. I'm a complete idiot and you should kick my ass all up and down this gorgeous beach."

"I just might do that."

"I'll let you."

She sputtered, "You won't have to let me."

"Okay."

"I assume you're here for a reason."

He gave her that boyish look again, his midnight-blue eyes going serious. The cut on his face was healing, now a thin line, and suddenly she couldn't breathe again.

"Since the consulate tragedy, I've worked hard to make myself emotionally bulletproof." His voice caught. "I never got involved with people. Not like before I'd had to handle the guilt and the responsibility of doing my duty with people dying as a result.

"I hadn't wanted to like James. See that James wanted and openly competed for my approval and attention. I hadn't wanted to see the young man in the uniform so open and gung ho, so downright optimistic. Mostly because it reminded me of myself. Before I lost my innocence in a blood-soaked day that had transformed me from a boy into a man.

"Those NCIS agents stripped me of my identity that

day—how I defined myself—and I've been spending every day since closing myself off. I didn't realize I was doing it. Not until you came into my life and rescued me. Showed me what living was about. I'm so thankful for you, Amber."

Now the tears fell, trailed down her cheeks, and he cupped her face and kissed her. Moved his mouth over her, and she didn't think she would ever get enough of this wonderful man. He broke the kiss and met her eyes. He took a deep breath and let it out.

"I love you, Amber. With everything I have."

Her voice caught on a soft sob. "Tristan, oh, God." She threw herself against his chest, her heart too full.

"I want you to know that you're first in my life, first in my heart. I'm sorry if I ever made you feel second-best."

"That's my issue, Tris. I understand everything you've been through and I was willing to let you go, because I understood that your need for the corps was so strong."

"But it was skewed. Wacked. I was afraid of the pain that came with opening myself to people. Finding it easier to keep closed and relationships at arm's length."

"But you're not anymore."

"No. I'll even overlook the fact that you're an NCIS agent." He leaned in and whispered roughly in her ear. "I'm so gone. For you, Amber."

She wrapped her arms around his neck and sank against him and was soon quite aware that he loved her with every part of his body. He had quite a wonderful hard-on as he pressed himself against her.

"You want to get some of this?" he whispered, hot and raspy against her ear.

"Yes," she murmured breathlessly back, not able to contain how much she wanted this man's body.

"I assume you have a room because I…ah…just got here."

"Oh, right." She giggled. "I have a room with a really nice bed."

"That'll do," he said. "But if we don't hurry up, any flat surface will do."

It was nothing—just his hand against the small of her back—but it had such a dizzying effect it nearly paralyzed her. It was the kind of touch a man gave a woman—a familiar, intimate, protective touch—and it was all she could do not to close her eyes and lean into that light pressure.

She wasn't sure how she made it up to her room and how she opened the door. She concentrated on breathing in, breathing out. And it took every ounce of concentration she had to do that. The only thing she was aware of was Tristan's strong, masculine hand clamped around her waist.

As soon as the door closed behind them, he was dragging her against him, clammy with the air-conditioning. He was shivering. "Let's get you out of these clothes," she said softly.

He hung on to her and said softly, "I'm sorry if I hurt you, baby."

Amber's vision blurred. Her chest filled with feeling for him, and she ripped the T-shirt off him. Emitting a choked sound, Tristan swept her up in a crushing embrace, and Amber molded herself against him, holding the back of his head as he buried his face against her neck. She could feel it—the need vibrating in him, the

energy that just kept building and building. He was literally trembling with it.

Unable to do anything else, Amber hung on to him,
a thousand sensations raging through her. It was as if
they were welded together—locked together by need. It
helped having his arms around her to take the edge off,
ease the desperateness that held them both.

He turned his head and shifted his hold, a shudder
coursing through him. It was as if they were both paralyzed, unable to move, unable to separate.

Amber could feel him gather his control, his whole
body tensing; then he gripped her arm and pulled it
from around his neck, clasping her by the wrist. His face
hardening into stone, he ripped his belt loose, then tore
open the clasp to his pants. She bent down and untied
his boots, fumbling with the wet laces. He toed them
off. With the unbearable tension radiating like a force
field around them, he reached for her and hauled her
into his arms. And their common desperation took over.

This time it was like a storm breaking over them.
There was no restraint. There was no gentleness. It was
desperation all the way. It was as if they were trapped
in this frenzy, and there was only one way out.

It was a night Amber knew she would never forget.
The night her man came back to her and they made a
pledge to each other in a hot, wild and urgent and then
sweet, tender and slow way. With absolutely everything
in between. She had never realized a man could have so
many sensual layers—so many facets—so much stam-
ina. It was as if he was trying to make up for an entire
lifetime in a single night.

When their passion cooled, he held her against him.
She sent her hand over his chest, then up into his hair,

then over his stubbled face. "I'm so in love with you, Tristan."

He breathed a sigh of relief.

"Then I'm set," he said softly, her body curled so intimately against him. It was everything he wanted. She was everything he wanted.

He ran his hand over her torso, his lips tightening even more.

He'd been ready to just don his gear, leave her in the cave in safety and warmth and go out there to track down Garza and kill him with his bare hands. Then, in the glow of the heater, he had seen where the man's hands had hurt her body, the bruises turning black-and-blue.

Now they were nothing but fading bruises.

In this beautiful hotel room on this beautiful island, the cold, fear, danger and death were nothing but a memory.

His love for Amber transcended everything. All his isolation, all the pain and uncertainty, all torment were now healed scars that he would carry always, but were now no longer causing him pain. Like her bruises, they would fade and disappear. So would his strong hold on his fear and doubts, released to stay in the past as he rushed forward to his future with this remarkable woman in his arms.

She had come into his life and shown him there was something as amazing as giving himself over to the corps, to the men and women who stood by him, ever faithful, ever ready to protect his back. He'd made the decision to leave, right then and there, but he would always and forever be a marine.

She reached up and smoothed her hand over his jaw.

"I love you, Tristan. Whatever it takes, whatever you decide to do, wherever you decide to go, I will go with you. I don't want to be away from you. Distance is non-negotiable."

"I'm putting in my papers, Amber. I'm going to retire and accept that job with my friend Rock."

"That job in San Diego?"

"Yes."

She thought for a moment. "Well, there just happens to be an NCIS field office in San Diego. And I've just gotten the word from Special Agent in Charge Richard Barlow, who happens to be Lance Corporal James Connelly's uncle, that if there is anything he can ever do for me, I shouldn't hesitate to ask. I think I can manage a transfer from DC to San Diego."

He closed his eyes, his chest full, his heart so full of this woman.

"Thank you for getting me. For understanding who I am. Especially when I didn't even know myself." He didn't know how else to say what he felt, this utter thankfulness to be in this quiet, wild place with her, to be finding his way back.

"*Semper Fi*, Tristan."

Tristan held her direct and open, beautiful, green-eyed gaze, and he had never felt the meaning of the words more strongly. *Semper Fidelis.* Always faithful.

Always.

Epilogue

Amber cheered as Vin kicked her boss's ass at darts. Sky, exotic eyes aglow, kissed Vin and clinked glasses with him as Chris received a consolation kiss from his wife, Sia. Beau sat next to her with his arm draped over the shoulders of his beautiful fiancée, Kinley, her auburn hair glinting in the overhead light.

"I'm going to miss you, Amber," Beau said as Vin and Chris started up another set.

Amber turned to him. "I'm going to miss you, too."

"I think we got what we were looking for, *mais yeah.* You're not going to miss our wedding, *oui*?"

"Oh, God, Beau! Not for anything."

He smiled. "Can't believe this is happening. I can't wait to see her walk down that aisle."

Kinley nudged him and laughed. "Beau, it's coming up soon. Still time for you to change your mind."

Amber reached out and squeezed Kinley's hand. "Oh, honey. He ain't goin' nowhere."

Kinley looked at Beau, and Amber was sure that was the exact same besotted look that was in her eyes when she looked at Tristan.

"Look at him," Kinley said. "Who could keep their hands off him?"

"And, on that note, we're out of here." Beau rose with Kinley, and Amber stood. Beau embraced her. "Keep in touch, *chère*, and make sure we're all invited to the wedding."

"He hasn't asked me."

Beau kissed her on the cheek. "He will. Take care, and if you ever need us, call."

The going-away party was winding down. Vin sat down beside Amber and clasped her hand. "When you first walked in the office, I thought, *Holy cow, it's Barbie. I wonder how she'll do.*"

"And how did I do?"

"Let's put it this way. I'm going to miss the hell out of you, lady, and not just because you did all the grunt work."

Amber laughed and squeezed his hand. "Thank you, Vin. I'm glad to see you happy."

He rose and Sky sidled over. "Good luck, Amber," she said. "I brought this for you. It's one of my new CDs for stress relief."

Amber accepted it and kissed both Sky and Vin on the cheek.

Vin leaned over and said, "But really, make sure we get an invitation to the wedding."

"Again, he hasn't asked me," she said, rolling her eyes. "He will."

Sia had already said her goodbye and headed out to their car. Amber and Chris were left. "I broke you in, and you're going to take all that expertise and all those smart brains and observant eyes to the West Coast."

"I thought you gave me that friendly-fire case because I was convenient."

"No. I talked the director into giving you that case because I knew you could handle it. We just had to be hush-hush about it. I'm sorry for what you went through. If something had happened…"

"No, Chris, it wouldn't have been your fault. I did my job because I wanted to do it. So don't go there, and besides, it all turned out for the best."

He nodded, kissed her on the cheek and hugged her hard. "So, make sure we get a wedding invitation."

As he walked out, she laughed and shouted, "He hasn't asked me!"

Chris turned back and said with a smile, "Oh, he will."

Amber had already settled into Tristan's new home and given her opinion on the decorating. But her first on-the-job alarm hadn't gone off on time. She burned her breakfast, navigated a traffic jam. By the time she got out of the elevator, she was forty-five minutes late and mortified.

As she came around the corner, two men and a woman were huddled around a small table in the middle of the office. Two wide-screen monitors were situated on the wall straight ahead.

The woman turned her head and gave Amber the once-over. She was Hawaiian with a cascade of long black hair and straight bangs. The woman smiled and walked over.

"Oh, God, I'm so sorry I'm late."

"Supervisory Special Agent in Charge Kai Talbot. Traffic?" Her delicate mouth lifted at the corner in a wry smile.

"Yes, I'll get used to it. I worked in DC."

She turned to one of the men. His hair was a shaggy sandy blond, the poster boy for a California surfer dude, accentuating his really gorgeous whiskey-colored eyes. He had a tight, compact athletic body, and she made a wild guess he was the resident geek. He wore a plain white T-shirt with a black hoodie, black jeans and deck shoes. "This is Special Agent Austin Beck."

He nodded and smiled. "Welcome to the team."

The second man sat back on the table. He looked as lethal as Tristan. He had very dark hair that he wore short and brushed off his forehead. With intense gray eyes and an elegantly trimmed goatee, he was taller than Austin with broader shoulders. He wore a stylish suit and gorgeous silk tie that said he didn't buy either on an agent's salary. Looked like expensive Italian shoes, too. He wore a thick, silver band on each thumb. He resembled the actor who had portrayed the raspy-voiced dark knight, but younger. "And this is Special Agent Derrick Gunn."

Where Austin had been friendly and open, this man was anything but.

"Heard you took out a human hunting ring in the Sierra Nevada," he said, his voice deep and smooth.

"Unarmed," she said.

Austin laughed and nudged Derrick. Austin looked at Kai and said, "She'll fit right in."

* * *

Russell "Rock" Kaczewski pulled off seven successive rounds into the target. Tristan raised his pistol and bam-bammed his way through seven, as well. Then Rock's brother, Dexter Kaczewski, peered at the target. He let out a little laugh, raised his weapon and shot bull's-eyes every round.

"Dammit, Dex, you are an A-hole," Rock said.

"I'll take that as a compliment," he said, nudging Tristan. "See what I have to put up with. Are you sure you want to go into business with this guy?"

The Kaczewski brothers resembled each other from their piercing blue eyes to their big, hard-muscled bodies. Rock didn't have an ounce of flab on him, still in marine fighting shape, his biceps huge. Dex wasn't as imposing as his big brother, but as a navy SEAL he was battle-tested, tough and the kind of guy you wanted covering your six.

"Shut up with that brother bullcrap. Tris and I will take Rockface to the next level."

"I have no doubt," Dex said, loading his weapon with quick ease.

Lieutenant Dexter Kaczewski was currently serving as a US Navy SEAL stationed out of Coronado. He was on leave, but they expected him to be deployed any day.

"How is your little hottie NCIS agent settling in?"

Rock cuffed Dex, who gave him a scowl. "Hey, what was that for?"

"You don't talk about a brother's woman like that, man. Have some respect."

"Sorry, Tristan." He gave his brother a sly look and said, "What about one of those fine twin sisters of yours. Which one is here again?"

Dex knew exactly which sister was stationed in San Diego. "Neve. Nova has actually just finished Coast Guard flight school. Guess where they're sending her?"

Dex grinned. "US Coast Guard Air Station Kodiak?"

Tristan laughed. "Yeah, can you believe that? Back to Dutch Harbor and Unalaska. She's going to be pulling fishermen out of the sea."

"She's not a fan?"

"No."

"She can throw back the ones she doesn't like," Rock said, deadpan.

Tristan and Dex burst out laughing. "She thinks fisherman captains are arrogant asses. Fishermen think the Coast Guard is dumb."

"Wait. Isn't your dad a captain? That will make good dinner conversation." Dex laughed.

"Yeah," Tristan chuckled, remembering how irritated and downright pissed she'd been when she called him from Mobile. "Right in our backyard. My parents are thrilled."

"How is Neve doing?" Rock asked, trying to keep his voice casual and failing. It was clear to Tristan that Rock had a definite thing for his beautiful younger sister Neve. But the guy would never act on it. She was Tristan's sister and therefore off-limits. "I heard she had an accident during a rough rescue at sea."

"She's going to be out of the hospital at the end of the week. Broke her collarbone and she's not being very cooperative, but she needs assistance. She's not too happy about it."

"I bet," Rock said, looking away.

"Funny how both your sisters went into the Coast Guard."

"Yeah, we feel the same way about you, you traitor."

"Hey, I was originally a marine. That still makes me a marine, big brother."

"Ooh-rah."

"Ah, go play in the surf."

Dex's phone rang and he answered, the smile fading from his face. "Yes, sir. I'm on my way."

"You getting deployed?"

"Gotta head out."

"Take care of yourself," Tristan said, and Rock, who had given his brother only insults from the moment he walked into the range, said, "Come back in one piece. You hear me, Dex?"

Dex went to full attention and threw his brother a sharp salute.

"Get outta here," he said with a laugh.

"Are you sure you're ready for this? My parents can be a bit overwhelming and they're big huggers," Amber said.

Tristan turned to give her a wide-eyed, I'm-running-for the hills look. She nudged him and laughed. "Don't even jest about it." She looked at him. "I'm going to knock now."

"This is a dire situation, but I'm going to have to ask you to trust me on this. When I was in special ops we were trained extensively for badass hugging. I'm *armed* and dangerous."

She rolled her eyes, giggling in spite of herself, loving this man more every second. But he really didn't understand because he had never met her parents. "Tristan, you are not taking this seriously." She really tried to keep a straight face.

"Oh, I'm as serious as a heart attack."

"No, you're not, and I refuse to engage in any tomfoolery with you."

"Tomfoolery? Marines don't engage in nonsense. We bring the hurt or the hug. That's just the kind of guys we are."

She shook her head and took a deep breath. Tristan was the first man she'd ever brought home to her parents. She'd moved to a different coast. Transferring and leaving Chris, Beau and Vin had been so very hard, but after meeting her new boss and coworkers, she was sure the agents in the San Diego office would be great, too.

Chris had given her an amazing recommendation, but James's uncle, Special Agent Barlow, was already happy to have her on board. Tristan had finished out his MWTC teaching and turned in his retirement papers. He already loved working with Rock in San Diego.

Her life had changed dramatically because she'd been given what had seemed like an open-and-shut case. But she and Tristan had rooted out an evil, heinous group of men who thought nothing of using people for their own sport. Dozens of murders in several states. It would take some time to work out the tangle. Her only regret was that the chief and Garza wouldn't stand trial for their crimes.

Tristan had been true to his word when she had been desperately scared in the small cabin in the woods. They hadn't died, because Tristan's smart thinking, valor, courage and skill had carried them through. For that she would always be thankful and faithful to this one man who was now her life. And his motto was now hers.

Semper Fi.

"Should I get into my badass hugging stance now?"

He smirked. "I might need to limber up my hugging muscles." He danced around her like a boxer with his arms out, thumbing his nose.

She shoved his shoulder, but that gave her no satisfaction because that rock of a man didn't budge.

"You're forewarned. Oh, and my mom's a bridge hugger. She'll go from one person, right to the next without missing a beat."

"Damn, do you think she'd teach me how to do that?"

"You laugh now, but she's a master at it."

"Okay, I'll watch out for her right cross."

Amber broke into laughter. "My sister is beautiful, by the way, so don't go falling in love with her. She's married anyway."

He cupped her face and kissed her mouth, murmuring, "Amber, I can't see anyone but you."

"Flattery will get you everywhere."

He wrapped his arms around her and squeezed her tight. "I'm just limbering up my hugging muscles," he whispered against her ear.

"Sure you are. You are so transparent," she replied, pulling him close.

The door flung open and her father was there. Without a word, he dragged her into the house and wrapped his arms around her.

"Oh, God, Amber. My baby. I'm so glad to see you." His gruff voice made her press her face against his chest and breathe in his familiar dad scent.

Over his shoulder she could see her mother come out of the kitchen and make a beeline for her. Her sister jumped up from the couch, and before she knew it, her whole family was holding her tight.

Tears stung her eyes.

Then her mother did it. She reached out and bridge hugged Tristan right into the group.

For a moment they all stood there. Then her mother and sister released her, but her dad held on just a tad longer.

After he let her go, he said softly, "When Beau called to tell us you were missing, I swear I lost years off my life. I'm so proud of you."

"You should be, sir. She was brave, strong, and she survived."

"Daddy, this is the man who saved my life, the man I'm in love with."

"The man who wants to spend the rest of his life with your daughter, sir. If I have your permission."

Her dad stuck out his hand. "Thank you, for what you did for my little girl. And if you make her happy, and it's what she wants—you have our blessing."

Amber's breath caught in her throat when Tristan pulled out a ring box. She looked into his beautiful blue eyes and she clasped both hands around the nape of his neck, pressing her forehead to his.

"Are you asking me to marry you, marine?"

"What if I am?" he said, opening the box, the diamond inside sparking off the light, dazzling her. "I hope you like it. Rock helped me to pick it out. He kept joking about how the Rock knows about rocks. He, uh, wanted to get you this huge ring, but I knew that's not what you would want. It's a decent size, but shouldn't get in your way. So, I'm babbling because I'm nervous as hell. I'm going to stop talking now."

God, he was so cute. "I think you have a pretty good chance of getting the outcome you want."

"Is that so?" He smiled and kissed her. Taking the

ring out of the box, he slipped it on her finger and the words of her coworkers came back to her. *He will.* He had.

"I love the ring. It's beautiful."

"I love you, Amber. I know this is quick, but why wait when I know this is what I want? It seems like it took me forever to get here, but I haven't met anyone like you in my life and I can't imagine spending the rest of my life with anyone else. Will you marry me?"

She met his hopeful, intense gaze. She kissed him oh-so-softly and whispered "Ooh-rah" against his lips.

He laughed and pulled her close and, without being able to stop it, there was another round of serious hugging. But like the battle-hardened marine he was, he took it all in stride.

Afterward, after dinner was served, remarked over and eaten, Tristan was dragged into the garage to look at her dad's ships in a bottle.

Her sister, Sammy, looked radiant, rested and beautiful.

"My God, Amber. I'm so jealous of you," she said, leaning into the counter.

"What?"

"I always have been. You were so athletic, all the guys loved hanging out with you and you were so cool about it. Then you became a lawyer, then this kick-ass agent. Then, to top it off, you bring home that hunk of gorgeous man. Congratulations, sis. You've got it all."

Her sister slipped out of the kitchen and Amber walked over to the connecting door to the garage. She watched Tristan listening to every word her dad said, nodding and smiling.

He was so different from the grump that had given her nothing but a hard time.

Her dad turned away and Tristan met her eyes.

She blew him a kiss and he caught it and brought it to his mouth.

Faith was a strange thing. It was believing when there wasn't any proof. Steadfast and sure.

She mouthed *I love you*, and he smiled, mouthing it right back at her. Yeah, her sister was right. She did have it all.

Semper Fi, *my Tristan, my marine, my soon-to-be husband.*

My master defender.

* * * * *

If you loved this novel, don't miss other suspenseful titles by Karen Anders:

JOINT ENGAGEMENT
DESIGNATED TARGET
SPECIAL OPS RENDEZVOUS
AT HIS COMMAND
FIVE-ALARM ENCOUNTER

Available now from Harlequin Romantic Suspense!

COMING NEXT MONTH FROM

⬡ HARLEQUIN®

ROMANTIC suspense

Available November 3, 2015

#1871 THE COLTON BODYGUARD

The Coltons of Oklahoma • by Carla Cassidy

When Greta Colton is wrongfully arrested for murder,
Tyler Stanton unhesitatingly provides an alibi—she was
in his arms all night! But more than false accusations
endanger the beautiful horse trainer...and Tyler might be
the only one who can save her from the oncoming danger.

#1872 COWBOY CHRISTMAS RESCUE

by Beth Cornelison and Colleen Thompson

When shots interrupt a Christmas ranch wedding, two
couples must track down a wannabe killer to stay alive.
Former bull rider Nate Wheeler protects his wife-to-be,
who's carrying the most precious gift of all—their child.
At the same time, sheriff Brady McCall puts his life on
the line for his former love, who witnessed the crime.

#1873 HER CHRISTMAS PROTECTOR

Silver Valley P.D. • by Geri Krotow

Undercover for a government shadow agency, Zora Krasny
has to keep her eye on the prize: bringing down a serial killer.
But she's distracted when she teams up with her childhood
crush, Detective Bryce Campbell, who looks oh-so-good
while bringing down bad guys. Can Zora and Bryce catch a
criminal *and* write their own happily-ever-after?

#1874 KILLER SEASON • by Lara Lacombe

When grad student Fiona Sanders is rescued from a
gunpoint robbery, she can't help but feel gratitude—and
maybe a little more—for handsome cop Nate Gallagher. But
before the two can explore their attraction, Fiona becomes
a criminal's target! It's up to this Texas twosome to solve the
crime—and find the keys to each others' hearts.

SPECIAL EXCERPT FROM

HARLEQUIN®

ROMANTIC suspense

*When horse trainer Greta Colton is wrongfully
imprisoned, oilman Tyler Stanton gives her an alibi—and
provides protection. But Tyler aims to safeguard more
than Greta's body. He'll also have to lasso her heart...*

Read on for a sneak preview of
THE COLTON BODYGUARD,
the thrilling conclusion to the 2015
COLTONS OF OKLAHOMA continuity.

"If all this hadn't happened, then you wouldn't have known
that you were about to marry the wrong man," Tyler countered. "Not that I'm suggesting I'm the right man."

She tilted her head slightly and looked at him
curiously. "Why haven't you married? You're handsome
and successful and I'm sure plenty of women would be
happy to become Mrs. Tyler Stanton."

"The women who want to be my wife aren't the kind
of woman I'd want for a wife. They want it for all the
wrong reasons," he replied. "I got close to marrying once,
but it didn't work out and since then I haven't found the
right woman. Besides, I work long hours and don't have
a lot of time to do the whole dating thing."

"So you just invite emotionally vulnerable women to
share your bed for the night and then move on to the next
woman." She stared at him boldly.

A small laugh escaped him. "You don't appear to me
to be an emotionally vulnerable woman and no, I don't

make a habit of inviting women into my bed. In fact, you're the first who has gotten an official invitation."

She eyed him dubiously.

He leaned closer to her, so close that if he wanted to, he could wrap her in his arms and take full possession of her lush lips with his. It was tempting. It was oh so tempting.

"It's true, Greta," he said and watched her eyes spark with gold and green hues. "I don't invite women into my bed. I wait for them to invite me into theirs. But you're different and the desire, the passion, I have for you is stronger than anything I've ever felt for any other woman."

Her mouth trembled slightly and he continued, "In all of my life I've never been jealous of Mark, but when he hooked up with you, I was jealous of him for the first time. He had what I wanted…what I still want."

Don't miss
THE COLTON BODYGUARD
by New York Times *bestselling author Carla Cassidy,*
available November 2015 wherever
Harlequin® Romantic Suspense
books and ebooks are sold.

www.Harlequin.com

Turn your love of reading into rewards you'll love with
Harlequin My Rewards

**Join for FREE today at
www.HarlequinMyRewards.com**

Earn **FREE BOOKS** of your choice.

Experience **EXCLUSIVE OFFERS** and contests.

Enjoy **BOOK RECOMMENDATIONS**
selected just for you.

PLUS! Sign up now
and get **500** points
right away!

Earn **FREE** REWARDS
HarlequinMyRewards.com
Join Today!

MYR16R

THE WORLD IS BETTER WITH

Romance

Harlequin has everything from contemporary, passionate and heartwarming to suspenseful and inspirational stories.

Whatever your mood, we have a romance just for you!

Connect with us to find your next great read, special offers and more.

 /HarlequinBooks

@HarlequinBooks

www.HarlequinBlog.com

www.Harlequin.com/Newsletters

HARLEQUIN®

A *Romance* FOR EVERY MOOD™

www.Harlequin.com